A Mystery on Tyneside

A Mystery on Tyneside

Agnes Lockwood Mysteries Book Four

Eileen Thornton

Chapter One

Agnes was enjoying a carefree spending spree in the city centre. It had been quite a while since she last visited the Eldon Square shopping mall. With the weather being so warm during the summer months, she had never felt like wandering too far away from the quayside. The gentle breeze from the River Tyne, as it calmly flowed towards the open sea, had acted rather like a fan, keeping her cool while she had sat outside her favourite café near the Millennium Bridge. Even so, there had still been the odd day or two when the heat had been too much for her.

However, that morning there was a slight drizzle when they awoke and Agnes had decided it was the perfect excuse for her to catch up with some shopping. Not that she ever needed an excuse to go to the shopping mall. There was nothing she liked better than to wander around the shops. Besides, Alan, a Detective Chief Inspector with the Newcastle Police, wouldn't miss her as he was on duty. But then wasn't he always? It certainly appeared that way. She couldn't begin to count the number of times they had planned to go somewhere, only to have something come up and spoil it.

On the other hand, Alan didn't like wandering around the shops. If he had accompanied her, she would never have been able to spend so much time browsing through so many wonderful outfits. He hated lingering around women's clothing departments and would huff and puff and ask why she was taking so long. But then, even her late husband, Jim hadn't liked waiting outside the changing room while she was trying on outfits.

In a way, Alan was a bit like Jim, when it came to buying new clothes for himself. He would walk into his favourite shop, flick through the rail of suits until something caught his eye. If he found it suitable, he would pay for the item and leave – job done. Yet, at the same time, Agnes had to admit that the method appeared to work, as Alan always looked so well turned out. It had been one of the first things she had noticed about him.

Agnes glanced at her watch. It was time to make her way to the restaurant, where she and Alan had arranged to meet up for lunch. She had booked a table before setting out that morning; afraid it might be busy when they arrived. Therefore, the only other problem was whether something had suddenly cropped up at the police station during the morning to prevent Alan from joining her.

It didn't take Agnes long to reach the restaurant. Thankfully the rain had eased by the time she left the mall, meaning she was able to make her way across Northumberland Street and along the road to the restaurant, without needing to unfold her umbrella. It was handy to have it tucked away in her bag, but there was always the problem of what to do with it once she arrived at her destination and it was dripping wet.

Leo, the manager, was standing by the door. He helped her off with her coat, before showing her across to the table. However, finding that Alan hadn't yet arrived, Agnes decided to pop into the ladies' room to re-freshen her make-up. Once inside, she hurried across to one of the mirrors above the line of washbasins opposite the door; the last thing she wanted to do was to keep Alan waiting. While she had the whole day to herself, he was limited to his short lunch break.

Agnes swiftly pulled her lipstick from her bag and leaned over the washbasin to get closer to the mirror. However, she had only applied the lipstick to half of her upper lip when, out of the corner of her eye, she saw the reflection of a foot poking out from one of the cubicles. Shocked, the lipstick fell from her fingers and rattled around in the basin as she swung around. Now leaning back against the washbasin for support, she saw that the door to the cubicle was open.

"Are you okay?" Agnes called out, her heart beginning to thud with alarm.

When there was no reply, she slowly made her way across to the cubicle, again asking if the woman needed help. But, yet again, there was no reply. By now, Agnes had reached a point where she could see the woman's foot more closely; she was wearing trainers. Perhaps she had been out jogging and had found it all too much. These things happened all the time. However, as Agnes drew closer, she was stunned to find it wasn't a woman after all, it was a man who was lying on his side. She was about to ask him what he was doing in the ladies' room, thinking that perhaps he was mending something, when, to her utter horror, she saw a bullet hole in his forehead. Blood, still oozing from the wound, was trickling down his brow before dripping to the floor.

Clasping her hands over her mouth, Agnes took a few steps away from the body.

"Oh no," she murmured. "Surely this can't be happening to me all over again?"

* * *

It had been a relatively quiet morning at the station for Detective Inspector Alan Johnson and his sergeant. A disturbance in Northumberland Street had been reported. However, when a couple of uniformed officers arrived on the scene they found it had all blown over.

"It's possible that those involved in the brawl got wind that a street vendor had called the police, so they scarpered," the desk sergeant told Alan. "Everything appeared to be back to normal when the officers got there."

Alan had been relieved to hear the news. If the fracas in the city centre had turned out to be something more serious, he and his sergeant could have been summoned to the scene, meaning lunch with Agnes would have been cancelled.

Agnes was already somewhere in the city buying new clothes for the autumn months. She had suggested waiting until he had a day off so he could accompany her. However, he had been more than happy for her to go on her own. A few weeks ago, he had gone with her to choose a new three-piece suite for the apartment they now shared. But shopping for furniture was a different matter altogether. He had quite enjoyed helping to choose the style and colour of the sofa and chairs for their new home.

When Agnes had first brought up the subject of buying the penthouse apartment, he had been a little hesitant. But that was mainly because he knew the price would be well beyond anything he could afford. The sale of his house in Heaton would never fetch that sort of money and he didn't really want to take out a mortgage; not at his age. However, when he finally voiced his thoughts to Agnes while on their way to view the property, she had assured him that buying the apartment would be a joint venture.

"I'm not expecting you to buy it on your own, Alan. If we agree to buy the apartment, we'll share the cost. The sale of my house in Essex and the sale of your house should cover the price," she had told him.

"Yet, there's the possibility that it won't match the price," Alan had persisted. "Though house prices have fallen over the last year or so, prices for apartments are still rising."

However, Agnes had simply shrugged it off, saying how could the vendors refuse an offer when it was cash in hand? "I could pay for the apartment until our properties are sold," she reassured him.

Alan looked at his watch. It was almost time to leave the police station to meet up with Agnes.

"I'll be off in a few minutes, Andrews. But give me a call if you need me."

His sergeant nodded. He was about to say something, but Alan's mobile rang, beating him to it.

"It's Agnes," Alan said, looking at the screen. "I bet she thinks I've forgotten about our lunch arrangement."

"No, Agnes, I haven't forgotten. I was just about to leave..." he began.

"Alan, you must come now," she interrupted.

"I've just said..."

"No! You don't understand – I've found a body..."

"What? Where are you?"

Alan glanced at Andrews and raised his eyes to the ceiling as Agnes went on to reveal her location.

"Get uniformed officers to the restaurant, ASAP, Andrews!" Alan called out. "Agnes has found someone she says has been shot."

"I called an ambulance before calling you," Agnes continued. "Thankfully, no one has needed to use the ladies' room, so far. Yet someone could walk in here at any moment," she added, glancing at the door. "I haven't even informed the manager. But perhaps I should have said something to him..."

"No! You did the right thing. Leave everything as it is. Keep everyone out. We'll be there in a few minutes."

By the time Alan had finished speaking, his sergeant had already called for officers to attend the scene.

"Also, get Jones and Smithers to..." Alan began.

"I can't," Andrews replied. "They're at some meeting with the superintendent – remember?"

By now, Alan had already grabbed his coat and was heading for the door. "Yes," he replied, swinging around to face his sergeant. "Why did Blake need to take my best detectives with him? Jimmy and Martin are looking into something else, so who are we left with?"

"What about Morris?" Andrews suggested. "He's here – somewhere. He could help us out."

"*Morris?*" Alan almost spat out the detective constable's name as he swung around to face his sergeant.

"Yes, Morris," Andrews replied. "If you aren't going to use him, why keep him on the team?" The sergeant was aware that Detective Constable Morris was not at the top of the DCI's detective list, since he had let the team down a few months ago by admitting to passing on police information for money.

Alan was so angry back then that his first instinct had been to speak to the superintendent about having him removed from the force. However, he had held back and even now, a few months later, he was still reserving his judgement. Maybe Morris's performance today would help him make up his mind.

"Okay, get hold of Morris and tell him to meet us outside," Alan said. "But if he messes up this time…" He broke off and shook his head. "He's out!"

Chapter Two

The DCI found a couple of police cars already parked outside the restaurant when he pulled up. Obviously they had been in the vicinity when the word went out. One officer was standing at the front of the building to stop anyone entering or leaving the restaurant until they had been cleared to do so. Alan guessed another would be somewhere around the back, in case someone tried to sneak out that way. The other two patrol car officers were probably inside.

The three detectives stepped out of the car and hurried into the restaurant. Alan found Agnes waiting near the ladies' room. Though she looked rather strained, she smiled when she saw him hurrying across to her.

"It's okay. I'm here now," he said, as he wrapped his arms around her.

"I'll be alright," she replied, pressing her arms into his back. "You'd better get on with your job."

Alan would like to have asked an officer to drive her back to the apartment, but he was aware from past experience that she would refuse to leave the scene of the crime – especially as it was she who had found the body. He turned and looked around. The two officers had done a good job at keeping the customers away from the crime scene. One was standing guard outside the ladies' room, while the other was questioning Leo Galdi, the manager.

Until today, Alan had never seen the manager look even remotely flustered. Always without a single hair out of place and wearing an immaculate smart suit, with the tip of a pristine white handkerchief peeping out from the top pocket of his jacket, he would miraculously appear at the entrance of the restaurant the moment a customer entered, to greet them with a warm welcome. Even when a patron, who had had too much to drink, behaved in the most irritating way simply to gain attention, he always remained calm while smoothing down the situation.

Today, however, Alan was seeing Leo in a whole new light. His hair was ruffled, probably from him constantly running his fingers through it. Also, his usually untouched handkerchief was clasped firmly in one hand as he repeatedly mopped his forehead. The poor man was obviously in a state of disbelief at what had happened in his restaurant. But then, who could blame him?

Alan walked across to the ladies' room and the officer opened the door in readiness for him to enter. However, the officer raised his eyebrows when he saw Agnes following closely behind.

"It's okay," Alan assured the officer. "This is Mrs Lockwood. You'll recall that it was she who found the body. I need to know exactly what she saw when she first entered the room."

As he spoke, he pulled out some covers for their shoes.

Now inside the ladies' room, Alan stared down at the body on the floor.

"This is exactly how you found the body?" Alan asked, taking a quick glance around the room.

Agnes nodded. "No one has entered the room since I called you. I stood outside the door until the officers arrived. I was here," she added, moving to where she had been standing when she first spotted the body. "I saw the reflection in the mirror."

By now, Alan had stepped inside the cubicle and was busy peering around for any clues.

Meanwhile, Agnes glanced in the mirror to relive the scene. Maybe there was something she had missed. Oops, yes there was; though it had nothing to do with the case. It appeared that in her haste to call Alan, she had only applied lipstick to one half of her top lip. Swiftly scooping up the lipstick from the basin, where it had landed earlier, she re-painted her lips.

Alan backed out of the cubicle and looked around the room. There didn't appear to be any blood anywhere else, other than the small pool by the victim's head. Everything else seemed to be in order. But then, how would he know? The ladies' room was not usually his port-of-call.

"Agnes, when you came in earlier, did anything strike you as being different to how it usually looks?"

"I honestly didn't take much notice, Alan. I only popped in here to check my make-up." Agnes glanced across to the cubicle as she spoke. "But, getting back to your question, everything in here looks to be the same as usual. What on earth could be different in the ladies' loo?" It was then that her eyes rested on the window high on the outside wall. "Well, except for that window."

"What about that window?" Alan asked, his eyes following her gaze to the rather small metal-framed, frosted glass window.

"It's wide open," Agnes replied. Her eyes were still focused on the window. "I have never seen that window fully open before. There was something on the inside to stop it from being opened too wide." She looked at Alan. "You know what I mean – the sort of thing on the windows at the hotel to stop someone leaning out too far and falling to the ground. But here, it's more likely it was to stop people from trying to get in here."

Alan stared up at the window. Even though both he and Agnes had covered their shoes before entering the ladies' room, he still didn't really want to move any closer until the pathologist and his forensic team had scoured the whole area. Nevertheless, even from where he was standing, he could see a metal chain dangling from a hook on the wall. But, was that because someone had broken into or out of here?

Alan didn't get a chance to voice his thoughts, as Dr Nichols suddenly walked through the door. He was wearing his coveralls; ready to get to work on the body.

"Your sergeant said I'd find you in here." He smiled at Agnes, before turning back to the DCI. "If you're done for the moment, we'll make a start." He nodded towards the door, as his forensic team entered the room.

"Yes, I've finished for the time being, Keith," Alan replied. He began to escort Agnes towards the door, but then suddenly stopped and turned back to face the pathologist. "Can you make sure someone checks out that window? It seems to have been tampered with. I'll be somewhere in the restaurant when you have any information."

Back in the corridor, Alan spoke to one of the police officers as he removed the covers from his shoes. "Check the window in the gents. Let me know whether the chain that holds it in position has been broken. You'll find me in the restaurant. I need to speak to the manager."

"Alan, why didn't you tell me that my lipstick wasn't on properly?" Agnes whispered.

"Wasn't it? I didn't notice." Alan looked surprised.

"And you call yourself a detective!"

Chapter Three

Once the manager had finally pulled himself together, Alan was able to enquire whether he had noticed anyone leaving their table during the half-hour before Mrs Lockwood arrived.

"You must understand, Chief Inspector, I do not spy on our diners."

"Of course you don't, Leo," Alan replied. "But I also believe that nothing gets past you."

The manager coughed. "Well, now that you come to mention it, I did see two gentlemen head out towards the men's room."

"Are both men still here?" Alan asked.

"I can see one of them," Leo said, after a swift glance around the room. "He's sitting over there – the man in the grey suit." The manager gestured towards a group of twelve people sitting around a table. "They are here for a celebratory lunch. I only hope all this hasn't spoiled their day – they might…"

"And the other man…?" Alan interrupted, before Leo began a lengthy explanation about how the diners might demand a refund.

"Oh yes, sorry, the other man," Leo said, glancing around the room. "No. I am afraid he isn't here. He must have left before the commotion began."

"What can you tell us about him?" Agnes asked.

The manager stared at her and threw out his arms. "Like what? I don't know our diners personally."

"For instance, had he booked a table in advance? In which case, you would have his name. Or had he just walked in on the off-chance you would have a table free? Was he alone, or was someone accompanying him?"

While Agnes was reeling off her questions, Alan moved towards Andrews. Pointing to the man Leo had mentioned, he told his sergeant to have a few words with him.

"Ask him if he recalls seeing anyone else in the men's room. It seems he went out there at about the same time as our victim." Alan then glanced across at the detective constable, who was talking to a couple sitting at a table near the door. "Also, try to keep an eye on Morris. I'm still not sure about him."

Andrews nodded, before moving away.

Alan re-joined Agnes in time to hear the manager's reply.

"Oh, I see what you mean, madam," Leo said, clasping his hands together. "No, no, no, the gentleman had not booked a table. He just happened to rush through the door and, before I had a chance to welcome him properly, as is my custom you understand, he asked whether we had a table free."

"So, I take it you had a table free," Alan said.

"No! I did not." He screwed up his eyes. "Well, not really…"

"Well then, how did he end up in here?" Alan sounded frustrated.

"If you will let me finish, Chief Inspector," said Leo, wringing his hands together. "The gentleman said that he had heard such good reports about our restaurant that he wanted to try it for himself – with a full a la carte menu. Therefore, Chief Inspector, how could I possibly say no? Head Office insists that we, the managers, should be instrumental in bringing new customers into the restaurants."

"But, if you didn't have a table free, how could you possibly say yes?" Alan shook his head. "Don't bother to answer. My guess is that you always keep a table free – just in case."

"Yes. But, you must understand, all restaurants do this."

"Okay. So this man had the full a la carte menu, then what? He disappeared into the gents? Maybe he just didn't want to pay."

"No, no, no! Let me tell you what happened." Leo sounded agitated again. "Yes, the gentleman ordered the full meal. But immediately after he placed the order, I saw him walking towards the men's room. That is not unusual, it often happens. I thought he would return in in a few minutes. However, as it turns out, I have not seen him since." Leo raised his hand and brushed a tiny speck of hair from his jacket as he spoke. "Once the first course was served and he hadn't arrived back at the table, I cancelled the rest of his meal. I merely thought he had sneaked out when I wasn't looking."

"You didn't think to go out to the men's room and check whether he was still in there?"

"No! Why would I?" Leo replied. He blew a sigh. "Chief Inspector, as manager of this restaurant, I am expected to do a great number of things to make sure that everything runs smoothly. However, I am relieved to say that having to check who is, or who is not, in the gentlemen's facilities is not one of them."

Alan glanced towards the ladies' room, where Dr Nichols and his team were still working. Was it possible that the body lying on the floor in there was the same man who had entered the restaurant without having booked a table?

"Did you notice what this man looked like, or even what he was wearing?" Alan asked. "You know what I mean, anything that would help us identify the man."

Leo shrugged. "Well, as you know, I do not scrutinize our guests. But yes, maybe I can help a little. Let me see," he said, as he rested his elbow in one hand and tapped his head. "The man was clean shaven. He had brown hair, neatly cut and parted on the right. He was wearing a navy blue suit, a white shirt and a dark blue tie. His shoes were…" Leo shuddered, "he was wearing those trainer things. Not what you would see in a high-class restaurant. Also, he was wearing a watch on his right wrist."

"That's great, thank you, Leo. I think you should attend to your customers. They seem to be becoming a little edgy." But then, as Leo moved away, another thought popped into Alan's mind. "Before you go, Leo – did anyone else arrive at the restaurant shortly after the man in question?"

Leo placed his hand on his chin while he thought for a moment. "Yes."

Alan perked up and looked at the people seated at the tables. "Is that person still here and, if so, can you point them out to me?"

Leo chuckled. "It was a woman and, yes, she is still here. She is standing right beside you."

"Okay, thanks, Leo, you can go now."

Alan looked at Agnes, as the manager hurried off to speak to his customers. She was wearing a large grin and shaking her head.

"What?" He raised his shoulders as he spoke. "It was a fair question – the killer might have watched him enter the restaurant and then decided to follow him."

"Yes, you're right. And, who knows, I could be the killer."

"Don't say that – not even in fun. Someone could get the wrong impression." Alan glanced behind him as he spoke, hoping no one was listening. "But, getting back to Leo, I was right, he certainly doesn't miss anything. If only all our witnesses were so observant." He sighed and gestured towards the ladies' room. "His description fits the man lying in there – right down to the watch on his right wrist."

Agnes nodded. "Yes, it does. It sounds to me as though the victim knew he was being followed and rushed into the restaurant hoping to lose them. But, as it turns out, it didn't work. The killer must have rounded the corner in time to see him disappear through the door."

Alan glanced around the restaurant, seeking out his two detectives. Hopefully, they were picking up information which would help solve the case. Morris was first to come into view. He was chatting quite intensely to an attractive, blonde-haired young waitress; only pausing for one brief moment to write something in his notebook. The DCI blew a sigh. He hoped that Morris was noting what the waitress had seen in the last hour, rather than taking details of how to contact her for a date. But, knowing Morris the way he did, Alan felt it was most probably the latter.

Shaking his head, in an effort to dismiss Morris from his thoughts, the DCI turned away and sought out Andrews. At least he could rely on his sergeant. Though, only a few months ago, he thought he was going to lose him.

Sandra, Andrews's fiancée, had been troubled at the number of hours he spent at work. So alarmed at the thought he might lose her, Andrews had considered leaving the force to seek a job with more normal working hours. However, after Alan had given him a few words of advice, Andrews had talked it over with Sandra and it seemed to have worked. The young couple were still together and planning their wedding and Andrews was still his detective sergeant.

To this day, Alan still didn't understand why he had even considered advising his sergeant on his relationship with Sandra. His own love life certainly wasn't anything to crow about. He and his wife had divorced shortly after they were married. Everything they had going for each other had fallen apart after the wedding. Since then, he'd had a few other relationships. Yet none had lasted very long.

Now he was with Agnes, the woman he met at school all those years ago and who he had never forgotten. Yet, even so, they'd had a few problems over the last eighteen months which, he would be the first to admit, were mainly his fault. Nevertheless, they were still together and that was all that mattered.

Sergeant Andrews was still speaking to the large group of people who had gathered at the restaurant for a celebratory lunch. Alan clicked his tongue at that last thought – celebratory lunch. This was certainly going to be a day that none of them would forget.

"I'll be back in a minute," Alan said to Agnes, before heading off to join his sergeant.

Chapter Four

While she was waiting for Alan to return, Agnes looked towards the door and retraced her steps from when she first entered the restaurant. She hoped she might recall seeing something unusual. But everything had looked normal. Turning back to face the corridor which led to the restrooms, she looked up at the small, brilliantly lit glass notice above the archway. The words *Ladies* and *Gents* were written in bold lettering, but there was no mention of an emergency exit.

Until now, she had always believed that an emergency exit would be down that corridor. Maybe the murdered man had assumed much the same thing. Agnes began to move towards the corridor to take a look for herself. However, she hadn't got very far before one of the uniformed officers held up his hand to stop her from going any further.

"Sorry," she said, taking a step back. "But can you just tell me whether there are any other doors leading off from that corridor, other than the two leading to the ladies' and gents' rooms?"

The officer stared at her for a long moment, before taking a couple of steps backwards into the corridor. He glanced up and down, hardly taking his eyes off her for more than a second, before shuffling back into position.

"No, there are no other doors," he said. "Only the two you mentioned."

"Thank you," Agnes replied.

"Is it important?"

"It might be," she replied.

She turned away and looked around the restaurant. There had to be another exit somewhere in the restaurant; if for no other reason than as a means of escape should there ever be a fire. All buildings had to have a fire escape these days. Health and Safety had seen to that.

It was then that her eyes were drawn towards another, much narrower archway behind the counter. It was partly hidden due to the large desk, which held the restaurant's computer, only a few feet in front of it. As there was nearly always someone using the computer at the desk, or diners paying for their meals, it meant that the corridor was blocked from sight most of the time. However, above the arch was a small sign showing the figure of a running man. Two words were printed underneath, *Emergency Exit,* again in bold lettering, but the lettering was smaller.

This was the first time Agnes had noticed that particular corridor. But then, why would she? It was so narrow, it could almost have been a tunnel dug out as an afterthought. Thankfully, both she and Alan had never needed to look for another way out of the building. But, getting back to the victim, if he had rushed into the restaurant to escape from someone and had ordered a meal before finding another exit, it was little wonder he had taken the wrong corridor. Maybe, finding himself with nowhere to go, he assumed hiding in the ladies' room would put his assailant off the scent? If so, his ploy hadn't worked.

But the solution to the problem regarding the emergency exit only left Agnes with another puzzle to solve.

As the killer clearly hadn't followed the victim into the restaurant, how could they possibly have known where to find him? Perhaps they were watching through the restaurant window as the victim headed off down the corridor and the assailant was already aware there was no exit down there?

But, even so, how on earth could they have known that their victim, a male, had entered the ladies' room?

Chapter Five

The DCI and his two detectives were now on their way back to the station. Alan was silent as he drove down John Dobson Street towards the quayside. He was mulling over the events of the afternoon. He would have liked to have had a few words with the pathologist before he left but, as the body had been carried through the restaurant and out of the main entrance, Alan hadn't wanted to hold up the proceedings any longer than necessary.

Seeing a body being lifted past the diners during their meal was bad enough, without him holding up the van's departure while he spoke to Dr Nichols. Therefore, as the forensic team were still at the crime scene, he had made a point of speaking to Derek, the man in charge. Alan requested that fingerprints of everyone in the restaurant, staff and diners alike, should be taken and checked against those found in the ladies' room, though it appeared Dr Nichols had left the same instructions. However, Derek warned the DCI that, as there were so many prints in the ladies' room, it might be impossible to trace them. "Some of the prints on the doors are on top of others – they could be days old."

Agnes had left the restaurant some time earlier. But, she had relayed her thoughts to him before leaving and he had spoken to the diners seated nearest to the windows. His first question, as to whether anyone had noticed the man who was the last to arrive, had resulted in everyone shaking their heads. However, when he asked whether anyone recalled seeing someone peering through the window, a young couple told him that they had seen a man holding his hands against the glass as he looked inside.

Though the man hadn't taken much notice, the woman was able to tell him that the man outside the window was in his late twenties and was wearing what looked like a black T-shirt, with a large picture of a skull on the front. He was also wearing a denim jacket and a pair of faded blue jeans, torn around the knees. However, the reason her attention had been drawn to him was because he had a ring through his nose.

"You know what I mean? The sort of thing you see on a bull," she had said, pointing towards the septum in the centre of her nose. "It was so large, it made my eyes water."

On its own, the information really wasn't much to go on – apart from the nose ring, which could prove to be useful. However, the rest of her description, a T-shirt, a skull and torn jeans, fitted a great number of young men in Newcastle these days. Nevertheless, knowing that someone had peered through the window certainly supported Agnes's theory that the victim had been watched while entering the restaurant. Then, whoever it was had taken a closer look once the victim had headed towards the corridor. But, like Agnes, he was puzzled as to how the killer had known exactly where to find his victim, especially as the officer had reported that the window in the gent's had not been tampered with.

After taking a look at the photograph on Alan's mobile, the restaurant manager had confirmed that the victim was the same man who had swept into the restaurant without a booking. Even so, the DCI and his team still needed to learn the identity of the man. At his request, Keith had checked the victim's jacket and trouser pockets, but had found nothing to identify him. Though there were a few coins stuffed into a pocket, there was no driving licence, or wallet holding bank notes and credit cards; something Alan had found very strange. How had he intended to pay for the meal he had ordered?

By now, they had reached the station and Alan swiftly pulled up in his parking spot near the entrance.

"Morris, I would like you to join us in the office. We'll go through what we've all learned during our time at the restaurant, before we head off to the incident room and bring everyone up to speed," he said, as he pressed the button on his car key to lock the doors. Maybe Morris had learned something useful from the waitress, after spending so much time with her.

"So, what can you tell us, Morris?" Alan asked, once they were all seated in the office. "Did you learn anything useful during your inquiries?"

"No, I'm afraid the customers I spoke to weren't very helpful. No one had heard or seen anything – most of them hadn't even spotted the man walking in."

He paused, while he pulled his notebook from his pocket and flicked through the pages.

"However," Morris continued, glancing up from his pad, "one of the waitresses, who had only signed in about thirty or forty minutes before the man hurried into the restaurant, told me that she had seen a disturbance in Northumberland Street. Apparently, a couple of men were arguing about something, but then it suddenly turned into a fight. She also said that, even though she had hurried past the gathering crowds, not wanting to get involved in a brawl, she felt certain that one of the men in the fight was the same man who had arrived at the restaurant without having previously booked a table."

Morris closed his notebook with a snap and gave a huge smile as he looked up at the DCI, almost as though he was expecting a medal.

However, Alan was not at all impressed.

"Why the hell didn't you tell me this while were at the restaurant?" Alan thumped his fist on his desk so hard that his mug fell to the floor, spilling the remainder of his morning coffee over the thin grey carpet. "I could have had a word with her. With the right questions, she might have been able to tell us more."

"I... I don't think she knew any more, sir," Morris faltered. "I asked her whether she might have seen the man in the restaurant anywhere else at some other time, but she said she didn't think so."

"She didn't *think* so?" Alan stormed. "And you left it there! For heaven's sake, that doesn't mean she *definitely* hadn't seen him before. A few more questions about what pubs or discos she used might have jolted her memory. Also, if she had seen the men arguing before it developed into a fight, surely that must mean she had been watching the disturbance for quite a while before 'hurrying past'!" Alan made quotation marks in the air as he spoke. "There is also the possibility that she had made a note of the time, especially if she didn't want to be late on duty at the restaurant. If so, it might have fitted in with the timing of the call to the station, informing the police of a commotion in the city centre. Furthermore, she might also have been able to tell us a little about the other man involved in the incident. Did you think to ask her for a description of the other man? If it were ever to come to a line-up, maybe she would be able to identify him."

"No. I didn't want to push her too hard. Women get upset at that sort of thing."

Alan held his breath for a moment to stop himself from exploding.

"Did she say anything about how the man looked when he entered the restaurant?" Alan continued. "I mean, wouldn't he have looked a little dishevelled, if he had been in a fight? Did you even think to ask her?"

"No." Morris looked down at the floor and shuffled his feet. "Is it important?"

Alan glanced at Andrews and rolled his eyes, before staring back at Morris. "Is it important? Let me explain – Leo, the manager who greeted the man when he first entered the restaurant looking for a table, never misses a thing. Therefore, I'm pretty sure that if the man had walked in looking like someone who had just been in a fight, he would have mentioned it to me. Come to think of it, I doubt he would even have allowed him in, especially as he didn't have a table booked. So, if it was the same man the waitress saw fighting in Northumberland Street, it means he must have found somewhere to clean himself up, before walking into the restaurant. The time difference could be important!"

Alan swung his chair around to face his sergeant. "Get on the phone to the restaurant and find out whether the waitress is still there." He paused and glanced back at Morris. "Did you by any chance get her name?"

"Rose Arrowsmith," Morris quickly replied, without needing to open his notebook. "But she told me that people call her Rosie, because of her rosy cheeks."

"Yes, I was certain you would have taken note of that. I suppose you have her home address and phone number, too."

Morris looked down towards the floor. "Yes," he mumbled.

"Check with Leo," Alan said, looking across at Andrews. "Ask whether she is still on duty. If so, tell him to ask her to wait until one of our detectives arrives, as we need to have a few more words with her." He paused for a moment. "No, wait. Get him on the phone and I'll speak to him."

Alan shook his head as he turned back to Morris. "I saw you talking to the waitress for quite a while. I had hoped that you were gathering information regarding the case. But I was wrong. I think it best if you go to the incident room and join your colleagues."

Morris rose to his feet. "What will happen to me now?"

"At this moment, I honestly don't know," Alan replied, slowly. He sat back in his chair and studied the young detective standing in front of him. "You know, after your undercover work at the hotel a few months ago, I really thought you had the makings of a good detective. You appeared to have changed from your high-school attitude and become one of the team. But then, you allowed yourself to be bribed into passing on information about scenes where crimes had taken place."

"It was just as I told you back then. I'd run up a few debts in a couple of night clubs and needed the money," Morris shuffled his feet as he spoke.

Alan shook his head. However, before he could say anything further, Andrews held up his phone.

"I've finally managed to get through, sir," Andrews said. He glanced at Morris, before looking back at the DCI. "I have the manager on the line."

"Thank you." Alan held out his hand to take the phone. "Meanwhile, take Morris down to the incident room. I'll be there in a few minutes."

Alan waited until his sergeant had escorted Morris from the room and the door was firmly closed, before he spoke. "Leo, this is DCI Johnson. After speaking to one of my detectives, I believe we really need to have a few more words with one of your waitresses. Her name is Rose Arrowsmith. Can you check when she goes off duty? I'll hold on."

It almost seemed that Leo had the the staff rota tattooed in his brain, as he replied immediately without having to look it up. "Rose will be here until seven o'clock this evening."

"Okay, I'm sending a detective to speak to her. Now, listen carefully, Leo. I understand that you like to be open with your employees but, in this case, I don't want you to mention a word of this conversation to Ms. Arrowsmith or any other employee. Let's keep this between ourselves until my man gets there."

Once Leo had happily agreed to the proposal, Alan reached across and replaced the receiver on Andrews' phone. He then sat back in his chair and closed his eyes.

Where the hell he had gone wrong? A DCI was supposed to be an inspiration to his men. Show them how to be good detectives and follow the law while apprehending their man. Yet, in the case of Morris, he had failed. Nevertheless, Alan had overlooked his indiscretion and kept him on. Even so, since then, Alan had never fully trusted Morris and had placed him on desk duty, where he could keep an eye on him, until today. Today, he had given him another chance. However, instead of interviewing a witness dutifully, he had tried to date her.

Was this the time to show Morris the door?

Chapter Six

When Agnes had left the restaurant, Alan and his detectives were still investigating the murder. Slowly making her way back to Northumberland Street, thoughts of what had occurred over the last couple of hours kept running through her head. She really needed to sit down somewhere and think it all through while it was still fresh in her mind.

Strolling into the first café she came to, she found a vacant table and sat down. She glanced at the shelves behind the counter. The thought of a large glass of red wine from the bottle which appeared to be gazing down at her, was certainly very tempting. However, wanting to keep her head clear at the moment, she looked away and ordered an extra strong coffee and a ham and cheese sandwich.

She shivered as she cast her mind back to the moment she had found the lifeless body lying on the cold, tiled floor. Though, quite honestly she wasn't sure why she should shiver. This wasn't the first time she had discovered a body. She had stumbled across a few in the past eighteen months or so. Surely she ought to be getting used to it by now. But then, how could anyone get used to finding a dead body…?

Hurriedly moving away from the actual crime scene, Agnes brought to mind the possibilities she had considered when wondering how the man had ended up in the ladies' room. She recalled that she had ended up with two options. Had the man taken the wrong corridor believing there was an exit down there? Or, had he noticed a man following him out into the corridor and had ducked into the ladies' room hoping to lose him? She had discussed these thoughts with Alan. But, while he appeared to have taken them on board, would he look into them, or simply dismiss her concepts as not feasible?

Agnes looked up as the waitress arrived with her order.

"Thank you," she said, with a smile.

Now however, as she stared down at the large mug of strong black coffee and the pitiful sandwich sitting on the plate together with a gathering of green leaves and half a tomato, she wondered whether a large glass of red wine might have been the better option after all.

* * *

The DCI's team, including Jones and Smithers who were back from their assignment with the superintendent, were gathered around the board when Alan walked through the door of the incident room. He couldn't help noticing that Morris was standing a few feet further back from the rest of the team. Sergeant Andrews, who had been talking to the detectives, hurried over to join him.

"Did Morris say anything further after you both left the room?" Alan whispered, raising his eyebrows.

Andrews shook his head. "Not a word."

"Okay." Alan raised his voice as he turned and looked at the group standing in front of him. "As you are all aware, a man was found dead in a restaurant just off Northumberland Street. He had been shot. The body was found lying on the floor in the ladies' room. And," he added, when there were a few giggles from some of the detectives, "I would appreciate it if you stopped sniggering and took the matter seriously."

Alan held up a photograph of the man's face, before pinning it to the evidence board in front of him. He had taken the shot using his mobile phone while at the scene of the crime and had forwarded it to the IT team at the station, to be copied and printed ready to hand out to his detectives.

"We'll have more detailed photos from the forensic team shortly. However, in the meantime, does anyone here recognise this man?"

Everyone in the room took a few steps closer to the board to see the photo more clearly, but they all shook their heads. Alan had guessed, even before he asked the question, that it was a longshot. But he had absolutely nothing else to go on and was desperately looking for somewhere to start. Once he had gone through what little he knew about the case, and everyone had expressed their thoughts, his phone rang. The call was from the desk sergeant. Apparently Dr Keith Nichols had arrived a few minutes ago and was waiting in his office.

Alan thrust the photos into his sergeant's hand, asking him to pass them around. "Keith is waiting in my office," he said. "Join me the moment you're done here."

But, before leaving, he took the time to give some instructions to Smithers and Jones, telling them to go to Alberto's restaurant and speak to Rose Arrowsmith. He went on to say that she wasn't a suspect, but that she might be able to help with what she saw on her way to work this morning.

While Alan was aware it didn't take two detectives to interview one waitress, he was also mindful of how well the two men worked together. They had a knack for procuring information from witnesses, even when they themselves didn't realise they knew anything of importance.

A few minutes later, Alan arrived back in his office where he found Keith already settled in a chair in front of his desk. The pathologist swung around when he heard someone enter.

"I gather you wanted to see me," Alan said, as he strode over to his desk. "Does this mean you've found something new?"

"Yes. As you are already aware, the man found earlier died due to a bullet to his forehead," he replied, getting straight to the point. "However, I believe the victim was dead before he even hit the floor, which was why there was very little blood found at the scene. Whoever fired the shot knew how to handle a gun. It was *the* perfect shot. There were no other marks on the body."

Alan was about to say something, but Keith held up his hand. "Let me finish. There's more."

Reaching into his pocket, he pulled out two evidence bags. One appeared to be holding a wallet, while the other held what looked like a small black notebook.

"It seems the man is called Robert Jameson, but…"

"Well, at least we now have a name to go on," Alan interrupted, stretching across the desk to take the two evidence bags.

"Hang on a minute." Keith moved his hand away before Alan could take the bags. "You don't think I trailed over here just to tell you that the man died of a gunshot wound, which was pretty obvious at the scene, or to merely give you his name, do you?"

Alan looked up sharply. "You mean you know something more?"

Keith cocked his head to one side and heaved a sigh. "It's just that…" He broke off and swung around in the chair and glanced towards the door.

Alan followed his gaze. He hadn't heard anyone approaching his office, but maybe Keith's hearing was more sensitive than his. However, as no one appeared, he was just about to turn his attention back to Keith, but the pathologist was on his feet and striding towards the door. Pushing it shut, he walked back to the chair.

By now, Alan was really intrigued. He knew that Keith was very discreet about the details of whoever was lying on his slab. But discretion was part of a pathologist's job. They had to deal with the grieving relatives whether the dead person happened to be a thief, a murderer, or someone who had died due to natural causes. However, today, Keith's behaviour seemed a little over the top. Nevertheless, Alan remained silent. No doubt Keith would explain all in due course.

"It seems that Robert Jameson, if that's his real name, could be an agent with MI5," Keith continued, once he had sunk back into the chair. "I came here in person because I didn't want to risk a phone call, or an email, where it could be picked up by someone hacking into… police investigations."

"What do you mean, hacking into police investigations?" Though Alan tried to sound calm, his tone said otherwise. "Why on earth do you think someone might be … " The DCI came to a full stop, suddenly picking up on something Keith had said earlier.

"MI5?" Alan blew a sigh. "Did I hear that right? What the hell is an MI5 agent doing here in Newcastle? Is there something going on in the city we don't know about?" He paused for a moment. "And if so, why on earth didn't the Secret Service keep us in the loop? We would have been discreet and stayed in the background."

Keith shrugged. "Which question would you like me to answer first?" He winked. "But the answer to your questions could be – because it's secret. The answer is in the name," he added with a smile.

He slid the two bags across the desk. "Perhaps there's something in the notebook which will help you figure it out. We've already taken fingerprints from both items and also from everything inside the wallet, so there's no real need for you to worry on that score."

Alan opened his mouth to say something, but Keith got in first. "Yes, before you ask, all the fingerprints on both items matched the victim. No other fingerprints were found. However, that doesn't mean no one else touched the two items. It simply means any perpetrators could have been wearing gloves. And," he added after a brief pause, "there's something else you should know. Both items were carefully concealed in a secret pocket inside the victim's trousers. You'll recall that I didn't find anything of interest in his pockets at the crime scene?"

"Which means the killer must have taken everything they could find, after the shooting took place." Alan muttered.

"It's possible," Keith pulled a face. "But, there's a problem with that," he continued. "Evidence shows that the chain on the window was broken from the outside. Someone had smashed it by pushing it inwards. Also, there are two metal bars fastened into the wall across the window on the outside. Therefore, unless the killer was a really slim person, there was no way they have climbed into the room to take anything from the body."

"And you're absolutely sure that the shot was taken from outside that window?"

"Yes," Keith replied. "A few scratch marks were found on the rubbish bins situated below the window, made by shoes or boots. Someone clambered up onto those bins to reach the window. However, there were no fingerprints found on the glass and the frame. Nevertheless, putting all that aside, the angle of the wound proves that the shot came from somewhere above the victim, so where else could it have come from?"

The pathologist paused for a long moment. "It's possible that the victim had already disposed of anything else he might have been carrying, such as car-keys, cash, or even a phone, before he entered the restaurant. Unless, of course, someone rushed into the ladies' room and took whatever they could find, before scurrying out again. I gather that a man left his table at about the same time as the victim. However, there are so many fingerprints both inside and outside of the room, it is almost impossible to determine one from the other. Nevertheless, we are still working on the assumption that he, or someone else, could have followed the man in there."

After hearing what the pathologist had to say, Alan sank back in his chair. He had been tempted to interrupt a couple of times with questions of his own, but Keith had answered most of them.

"Just supposing the victim had left his belongings somewhere before he entered the restaurant, surely that must mean he was aware his chances of escape were pretty slim." Alan stroked his chin, as another thought popped into his mind. "When you mentioned the man's name earlier, you suggested it might be false. Was that because, being a secret agent, he might use several different names?"

Keith shook his head. "That's certainly a possibility, but in this case – no."

"So, you have some other reason in mind?"

"Yes, it's because…" But just then the door swung open and Andrews burst in.

"Sorry I'm late, sir. I got caught up with a few extra questions in the incident room."

"Well, I better get back to the morgue. There're a few other things I need to look into." Keith said. He rose to his feet and buttoned his jacket. "You'll see what I mean about the name thing when you check out the badge. I'll get back to you if I find anything more."

Keith nodded at Andrews. "The DCI will explain," he said, as he strode out the door.

"Did I miss something important?"

"Yes, Andrews, I'm afraid you did."

Chapter Seven

Meanwhile, still in the café, Agnes took a sip of her coffee as she traced her mind back to when she left the restaurant. At that point, Alan had been about to help Andrews and Morris, by questioning some of the diners. Being a weekday, most of them would need to get back to work. However, she recalled that a few hadn't appeared to be in too much of a hurry to leave.

It could be that they had booked the table in order to discuss a business proposition with a client over lunch. In which case, there would be no need for them to rush back to the office. Though, someone finding a body in the restaurant would be enough to put any client off whatever proposition was on the table. On the other hand, there was a chance that some were too intrigued by the police presence to even think of leaving.

Agnes's mind swept back to the group that were there for a celebration of some sort. She still didn't know what the celebration was all about. Maybe it was a pre-wedding lunch, or perhaps someone had been given a promotion at their place of work. Nevertheless, she thought it a little strange to hold a celebration lunch in the middle of the week. Surely they would have held it on a Friday. Wasn't that when these things usually happened?

According to the restaurant manager, one of the men from the group had left the table at around the same time as the man she had found dead. Was it possible that he had followed the man in order to murder him? Yet, if that was the case, why would he have forced the window open? Unless he wanted the police to think that the shot had come from there. He certainly hadn't left the building by that route as the window was too small for anyone to crawl through, plus metal bars across the centre had been fixed to the wall outside. But, maybe he had wrenched the window open merely to fool the police into thinking the shot had come from outside. Even so, that would have been quite a stretch, as the window was a fair way up the wall.

Agnes nibbled at her sandwich as she continued to think it through. Hopefully, forensics would determine from which side the window had been forced open. It would certainly solve one of her questions. She heaved a sigh. Perhaps she should have hung around at the restaurant for a while longer. Maybe she would have picked up more information. But it was too late to think about that now. Pushing the half-finished mug of coffee to one side, Agnes raised her hand to attract the attention of a passing waitress.

She was going to have that glass of wine after all.

* * *

Back at the police station, the DCI quickly explained to Andrews the reason for the pathologist's sudden arrival. So far, Alan hadn't had a chance to examine either the wallet or the notebook, both of which were still in the bags on his desk. Lying alongside the evidence were photographs the forensic team had taken of the body. Keith had placed them there before he left. The photos showed the victim, both at the crime scene and in the morgue. They were much clearer and more detailed than the ones he had handed out to his team earlier. Hopefully, the IT section downstairs would have received copies to print out for the detectives and uniformed officers. However, at the moment, there was something else Alan needed to fix his attention on. Grabbing some latex gloves from a box in one of the drawers in his desk, he threw a couple across to Andrews.

"I think we should take a look at the wallet and notebook before I hand them over to Superintendent Blake," he said to Andrews. "Forensics have already taken fingerprints from the items, but we can't be too careful. Blake might ask for them to be checked out again."

"Why would he want to do that?" Andrews asked. He looked puzzled. "Surely he'll see from the report that fingerprints had already been taken?"

"But that doesn't mean he won't ask for a further set of prints to be taken, especially when he learns I received the evidence before he even knew anything about it."

Andrews was aware that from the moment Blake arrived at the station, he and Alan had never hit it off. He was about to mention that evidence from the pathologist usually reached the detective in charge of the case in the first instance. However, he was cut short.

"Sergeant, we're wasting time. Just put the damn gloves on!"

Once both men were wearing gloves, Alan opened the bag and allowed the slim wallet to slide onto his desk. Opening the wallet, he found a small card holder on the right hand side. The name showing on the cards was Robert Jamison. On the left of the wallet was a Secret Service MI5 Badge with the same name.

"What are you thinking, sir?" Andrews said, staring down at the badge. The sergeant, who had seen a real MI5 badge only the year before, felt sure this was real. "It certainly looks genuine to me."

"Yes," Alan replied slowly. "I agree. It certainly looks real enough." He took a deep breath. "Yet there was something Keith said that..." He broke off, and looked up to see a puzzled frown on his sergeant's face. "Oh, don't misunderstand. I'm not saying the badge isn't genuine. I'm sure it is. What made me stop and think was, why would an MI5 agent get involved in a street brawl? Surely that would only make his face known to all and sundry, rather than keep his identity secret."

"Oh, I don't know about that, sir," Andrews joked. "You only have to think about James Bond. He gets up to all sorts of capers – even when he's supposed to be undercover."

"Yes, but James Bond is fiction – a character in a series of novels. Therefore, he does whatever Ian Fleming dreams up..." Alan looked back at the wallet he was still holding. "Let's not go down that road, Andrews. What we have right now is a man lying in the mortuary who, according to this ID, is an MI5 agent..." Alan paused. He was still staring down at the badge and card in the holder. "But, no matter how genuine this all looks, for some reason I'm a little sceptical about it."

"Why is that, sir?" Andrews asked. "I thought we both agreed that the badge looked genuine."

"I'm not talking about the badge, sergeant. It's the card that I'm concerned about. There's something that doesn't look right, but..." Alan broke off and looked even closer at the card still in the holder. "That's it! Take another look at the card, Andrews." Alan thrust his forefinger towards the card as he spoke.

"What am I looking for, sir?"

"Just look closely at the damn card, Andrews, then tell me what you see."

Chapter Eight

Once Agnes had finished her glass of wine, she considered whether to continue looking around the shops in the mall, or go back to the apartment. While she had gone off the idea of any further shopping, she didn't really feel like going back to the empty apartment. Very likely Alan would be held up at the station for some time; going over the various statements he and his detectives had taken at the restaurant. That could leave her sitting on her own for ages. But, where else could she go?

In the end, she decided to pick up the purchases she had left at the collection point and call Ben, her favourite taxi driver, to take her home. However, as Ben pulled up outside the apartment building, she glanced up at the tall structure and changed her mind. Asking Ben to wait for her, she swiftly dropped off her parcels in the apartment and hurried back to the taxi.

"Change of plan, Ben," she said. "Drop me off on the quayside."

"Is there anywhere in particular you want to be dropped off?"

"Not really," Agnes replied, absentmindedly. But then she made a decision. "No – wait. Take me to the foot of the Tyne Bridge. I'll make my way along the quayside from there."

"Towards your favourite café near the Millennium Bridge, by any chance?" Ben grinned.

"Oh, Ben, you know me so well." Agnes laughed.

As Ben pulled away from the apartment, she fell silent, recalling the moment she had asked Ben to take her to the estate agent to view the apartment. Back then, he had commented on how she might miss being in the hotel so close to the quayside; how right he had been! Though she loved the apartment, there were times when she missed being able to step out of the door and find herself in the throng of the quayside. Maybe it was because she had stayed at the hotel too long. Perhaps, if she had found the apartment earlier, she wouldn't have missed the buzz of the hotel quite so much. She had really enjoyed talking to the other guests and having everything on tap – meals, room service and, most of all, the quayside just outside the front door.

It was at that moment that she suddenly remembered something she had been meaning to talk over with Ben. Yet, she hadn't managed to find the right time – or place.

"Do you need to hurry away when you drop me off? I mean, do you have another... er, pick-up waiting for you?" She wasn't sure whether that was the right description for people waiting for a taxi.

Agnes grinned at that last thought. Did that mean she could be called a pick-up?

"No, not for another hour, unless I suddenly get a call," Ben replied, without taking his eyes off the road. "Why do you ask?"

"It's just that I've been meaning to talk to you about an idea I've had for a while. Could you spare me a few minutes? We could have a coffee at the hotel, or even the café by the Millennium Bridge?"

Agnes was aware she couldn't offer him anything stronger, as he needed to ferry passengers around for the rest of the afternoon and probably most of the evening, too.

"Okay," Ben answered slowly.

He was a little intrigued at what Mrs Lockwood wanted to talk to him about. Could there be a problem? Had he done something to upset his most fervent customer?

"Coffee in the hotel would be good," he continued. If there was something going on, he needed to know about it. "I've never actually been inside the Millennium Hotel. Though I've dropped you and several other passengers off there many times, I haven't been any further than the reception desk."

"Good, then the hotel it is."

Agnes sat back in her seat for the rest of the journey puzzling over how she could persuade Ben to accept the offer she was about to propose. Being such a proud man, she knew he wouldn't take anything he couldn't pay for. But, on reflection, her late father had been much the same. Once his diplomatic career was over, he had gone into business for himself by using his severance pay to open a small shop in Tottenham. Yet, he had ended up owning a large department store in Knightsbridge. It hadn't been an easy road. He had refused to put the family into debt by not accepting a penny from anyone, unless he knew he could pay them back in the short term, either by paying back the money he owed in full, or in kind. It was that final thought which gave Agnes an idea. Maybe there was a way to convince Ben to accept her offer, after all.

Once they arrived at the hotel, Agnes showed Ben around all the rooms on the ground floor. She even pointed out the shop and the well-stocked library. "And this is the drawing room," she said, at the end of the tour.

Stepping through the door, she was relieved to find it empty, apart from one man snoozing at the far end of the room.

"Take a seat," she said, gesturing to the two cosy armchairs in front of them. "I'll order afternoon tea for two to be served in here."

"Afternoon tea?" Ben questioned, as he sank into one of the luxurious leather chairs. "I thought we were merely stopping off for a coffee."

Agnes shrugged. "Same thing, isn't it?"

He opened his mouth to say something, but was stopped when a waiter suddenly appeared in front of them.

"Nice to see you again, Mrs Lockwood," he said. "Is there anything I can get for you?"

"Thank you, William," she replied. "It's good to be back, even if only for a short while. I'd like to order afternoon tea for two, please. But perhaps we could have a pot of coffee rather than tea."

"How did he know we were here?" Ben whispered, once the waiter had disappeared.

"I don't know. Maybe the ladies on the reception desk saw us come in here and thought we might like a drink or something. Anyway, Ben," she added, changing the subject, "what do you think of the hotel, so far?"

"It's superb," he replied. He sank back into the chair as he spoke. "I could really get used to this," he added, glancing around the lavish furnishings in the drawing room.

Some sofas and armchairs were leather, like the one he was sitting in, while the others were covered in exquisite fabrics.

He looked back at Agnes and cocked his head to one side. "I was really surprised when you moved out of the hotel, Mrs Lockwood. You had everything at your fingertips here."

Agnes didn't reply. Instead, she turned her head towards the large bay window which looked out along the quayside. To the left, another large window showcased the Millennium Bridge. As it happened, the bridge was being raised at that very moment. It was a sight she never grew tired of. Even though she could see it from the balcony which ran around her apartment, it didn't seem to be the same. Here, she was up close and personal.

Agnes sighed heavily as she turned her attention back to Ben. None of that mattered now. Why should it? She had wanted a place she could call home. Yet, there were times when she missed being here in the hotel – like, for instance, right now! But she needed to get a grip. She hadn't coaxed Ben into coming here so she could pour out her woes.

"Ben, how would you and your family like to spend a couple of weeks here, at the hotel?" She paused. "I know you can't go far from home as Alec is having some new treatment, but you could come here and enjoy being able to relax for a while." She laughed. "Then, at the end of the break, you can honestly decide whether you're looking for-ward to going back home, or would rather spend more time here."

Ben stared across at her in amazement. However, before he could say anything, the waiter arrived with a large tray loaded with their afternoon tea.

"If you need anything else, just press the button," he said, pointing towards the wall behind Ben's chair. "I'll be here in an instant."

"That's something new," Agnes said, looking towards the button.

"Yes. There's another, further along, two over there and three on the back wall," William replied, tracing his finger around the room as he spoke. "They were only installed last week. The calls are picked up in the bar. You'll recall they're open most of the day."

"Thank you, William." Agnes slid him some money as she spoke. "That should cover it. Keep the change."

Ben waited until the waiter left the drawing room before he spoke. He hadn't failed to notice how much money had passed between Agnes and the waiter.

"For goodness' sake, Mrs Lockwood, I couldn't afford to spend a day here, let alone two weeks. What are you thinking?"

Agnes picked up the pot of coffee and filled each of the two cups. "Why don't you try this delicious afternoon tea before you decide?" She smiled coyly, as she slid a cup towards Ben.

"Mrs Lockwood…"

"The sandwiches are really wonderful," Agnes interrupted, pointing towards the large selection carefully arranged on the pretty china plate at the bottom of the four tier stand. "And as for the cream scones and the cakes," she continued, allowing her finger to travel up the tiers, "I'll leave you to judge for yourself. Go on, help yourself."

Agnes watched as Ben eyed the food in front of him. He certainly looked impressed.

"Thank you, Mrs Lockwood," Ben replied slowly. He reached across and took the plate she was holding out in front of him. "Yes, as you say, everything looks really tempting – but like I said, I can't afford to stay here."

Agnes remained silent until Ben had chosen a sandwich and was settled back in his chair. She didn't want him to suddenly rush out of the hotel when he heard what else she had to say.

"What if I was to pay for your stay and…?"

But that was as far as she got before Ben broke in. "No! I won't let you do that. You know I don't accept charity."

"If you would just let me finish, we might get somewhere," Agnes replied. "I was going to suggest that if I paid for your stay here, you could pay me back by not charging me when I used your taxi, once you were back at work. Let's say for a couple of weeks."

"But why – why would you want to do this for me… for my family?"

"Simply because I think you work hard for your family. I suspect you work all hours and never once have I heard you complain." She shrugged. "I just want to help you a little."

Ben remained silent as he picked up his coffee and took a sip.

There were just a little over two weeks remaining before the school holidays ended. While both Ben and his wife really needed a break, at the same time, they couldn't go far from home at the moment. Not that they could afford to go anywhere, even if they wanted to.

While Agnes was waiting for Ben's reply, she glanced towards one of the large mirrors which reflected the whole reception area. Maybe there was something happening out there that would keep her interested for a few minutes. However, the place was deserted, apart from the two receptionists on duty. But then, just as she was about to look away, a man entered the hotel. He was wearing a beige casual jacket, with similar coloured slacks. The top buttons on his white shirt were open at the neck and he had a black rucksack slung over one shoulder.

Without stopping at the reception desk, he made his way straight across to the lift. As he wasn't carrying any luggage apart from the rucksack and didn't stop at the desk, Agnes assumed that he was either already a guest at the hotel, or might be visiting someone. Though, as far as she knew, visitors normally stopped off at the reception desk to announce themselves. Nevertheless, that wasn't what had set Agnes thinking. It was because she felt certain she had seen this man some-where earlier in the day, but couldn't remember where.

Had Agnes been sitting on her own, she would have grabbed her bag and hurried out to 'accidentally' bump into him; thus enabling her to get a closer look at his face while making the necessary apologies. But, as Ben was with her, it wasn't appropriate to leap up from her seat and leave him sitting there. Maybe a quick word with the reception staff before she left might shed some light on the matter.

"Okay, Mrs Lockwood, I'll have a word with Amrita, my wife." Ben's voice interrupted her thoughts. He glanced around the room for the umpteenth time. "But, let me say this, it's going to take more than a couple of weeks' free taxi service to pay for a two week stay here – it's probably more in the region of twenty-four months!"

"Okay, Ben, whatever you say," she said.

Nevertheless, Agnes knew she would never allow that to happen.

Chapter Nine

Back at the police station, Sergeant Andrews stared down at both the card and the badge.

"It doesn't exactly leap out at you," he pointed out. It was only after comparing the two items for some time that he had discovered what the DCI was getting at.

The words on a separate pin, half hidden beneath the badge, named the man as Robert Jamison. However, on the card, the surname was spelled differently: Robert Jameson. Both sounded the same when spoken aloud. Anyone being shown the badge briefly, to verify the status of the agent, might never have noticed the discrepancy.

"Which now leaves us with the question of which is right, the card or the badge? Myself, I would say the badge is correct," Alan continued, answering his own question. "I would think getting a new pin printed would be difficult. But a card, well that would be a simple matter for anyone with access to a computer, even though they got the spelling wrong. Now we need to find out who this imposter really is."

"Obviously the victim isn't a local man, as none of the team recognised him," Andrews said. "Jones and Smithers tend to get all over the place and see new faces every day. Yet neither recalled seeing him before."

Alan nodded. He hadn't really been listening, but when his sergeant's words finally sunk in, he looked up sharply. "What about Morris?"

"What about Morris? Sorry, yes, I see what you mean. Well, it seems Morris didn't know him, either. He saw the photographs along with the rest of the team."

While they were talking, Andrews had been thumbing through the notebook. There were several dates shown. However, the writing alongside had been abbreviated into initials. They could be of a person, or even a place. Some dates showed several initials next to them, while others only had a couple.

"This is going to take some puzzling out," he said, holding the book in front of the DCI.

Just then the phone on Alan's desk rang. After a few words with the desk sergeant, he slammed down the phone.

"This will all have to wait," Alan said, as he took the book from Andrews and swiftly placed both pieces of evidence back into the bags. "I'll get someone to puzzle it out once the superintendent has seen them. Meanwhile, grab your coat."

"What's happened now?"

"There's been a robbery at the jewellers on Northumberland Street," Alan replied.

* * *

Once they had finished their afternoon tea, Ben suggested he drop Agnes off at her apartment. However, Agnes had other plans. She really wanted to have a word with the reception staff about the man she had seen entering the hotel earlier. Therefore she declined, saying she was going to take a stroll along the quayside before going home.

"The sun has finally come out, so it looks quite pleasant out there now," she told him.

It was true. The sun had suddenly appeared from behind the large cloud where it had been hiding for the best part of the day.

"Okay, but if you need a taxi, give me a shout."

Once Ben's taxi was well out of sight, Agnes strode back into the hotel and headed straight for the reception desk. She hadn't failed to notice how quiet the hotel was today. Usually, if it was wet outside, guests chose to hang around inside the hotel. Yet, while she and Ben had been in the drawing room, no one had entered or left the hotel, apart from the man she wanted to question the reception staff about. Even the drawing room had been empty, except for that solitary figure, an elderly gentleman who was slumbering in a chair in the far corner, and he had still been there when they left.

"Good afternoon, Mrs Lockwood. What can we do for you today?" The question came from one of the women on the desk.

"Hello, Sally," Agnes replied with a smile. "I just need a little information, if you don't mind." She paused. "I appreciate that you aren't supposed to divulge information regarding the guests. However," Agnes cocked her head to one side in an almost pleading position, "if you could help me just this once, I'd be most grateful."

Sally glanced around the reception area before answering. "Certainly, Mrs Lockwood, what do you need to know?"

"The thing is," Agnes began, but then paused for a moment when Pauline, Sally's colleague, suddenly joined them. "While I was sitting in the drawing room, I saw a man enter the hotel," she continued. "However, he didn't stop at the reception desk to check in, or even announce himself as visiting a guest. Therefore, I assumed he was already staying here. He had a rucksack. Do either of you know who he is?" She watched the two receptionists glance at each other, before adding. "If it would help to jog your memory, I could add that no one else has passed through the reception area since his arrival."

"Yes, we know exactly who you mean." Pauline replied. "His name is Robert Jameson."

Agnes thanked them both for the information.

She was about to turn away from the desk, but stopped when Pauline spoke again. "Actually, neither of us knows much about Mr Jameson – apart from his name. He only arrived last night." Pauline glanced at Sally for a moment, before continuing. "He only booked a room yesterday morning. I suppose he was lucky to get accommodation at such short notice, especially at this time of the year."

Agnes nodded in agreement. Yet, while she was aware it was a busy time of the year for hotels in the area, after spending almost eighteen months here, she had picked up several things about the hotel business. In this particular instance, she had learned that at least two rooms were kept free at all times on the off-chance that someone might need to find accommodation at short notice. Either the two receptionists didn't know that, which was most unlikely, or they had no idea how much she had learned during her stay.

"Come to think of it," Pauline added, tapping her chin, "he must have arrived very late, as even the evening reception staff had signed out. He was checked in by the new security officer." She shrugged. "We only recognised him because he was pointed out to us this morning when he happened to walk through the reception area during our catch-up session."

Pauline went on to explain that when she and Sally came on duty each morning, they were given updates as to what had happened in the hotel after they had both signed out. "You know the kind of thing I mean – who arrived late, who checked out ahead of schedule leaving rooms up for grabs?"

"Yes, I understand." Agnes paused. "You mentioned something about a new security officer. What happened to the other man? He was so helpful. He certainly helped me out of a couple of tricky situations."

"Yes, he was really nice," Pauline replied. "But he decided to take early retirement. He said that he and his wife were going to take a long cruise while they were both young enough to enjoy it. We organised a party for them both before he left."

"What about the new man?" Agnes asked. "How do you get on with him?

"Fred's okay, I suppose." Pauline sniffed. "He's certainly not as friendly. But he does the job and keeps his head down, so Mr Jenkins is happy enough. Maybe he'll open up a little, once he gets to know the staff better."

As Pauline was speaking, Sally moved across to the computer and tapped on the keyboard. "Robert Jameson is on the first floor – room number 106," she said. "Actually," Sally added, peering more closely at the computer, "his surname is spelt with the letter I in the centre. Until I looked him up, I would have spelled it with an E. I have an uncle with the same name, but his name is spelled with an E. Anyway, getting back to what I was about to say, it seems he particularly requested a room overlooking the bridge." She lifted her eyes from the computer to glance at Agnes. "But that's nothing unusual. Most people request a room overlooking the river – though we can't accommodate every-one's demands. It's usually a first come, first served scenario. Also," she continued, looking back at the computer, "though the booking is for five nights, a notification has been added. It seems the room is not to be re-booked until the guest has finally checked out." She shrugged. "But again, that's nothing new. It tends to mean that the guest is in Newcastle on business and might need to stay on until their deal is finally settled. Or," at that point she winked at Agnes, "it could mean that someone likes the place so much, they can't bear to leave us!"

"By that, I guess you're referring to me," Agnes replied, with a grin. She couldn't argue. She would be the first to admit how much she had enjoyed staying here.

"Right then," Agnes continued, realising the two women were watching her. She clasped her hands together. "I'll leave you to get on with whatever you were doing before I interrupted."

As Agnes turned to move away, she glanced towards the lift and was surprised to find that it wasn't anchored in its usual position on the ground floor. Normally, Larry Parker, the senior lift attendant, would have been standing outside the open doors waiting to escort a guest to their floor. Only a few months ago, Larry had been accused of a terrible crime but Agnes had helped prove his innocence.

Turning back to enquire why the lift wasn't in its usual position on the ground floor, Sally beat her to it, having noticed the puzzled expression on Agnes's face.

"If you're wondering about Larry, he's off on holiday this week," she said. Glancing across towards the lift, Sally screwed up her eyes and shook her head. "I don't think Andy, Larry's new assistant, has got the message about how the lift should be brought back to the ground floor once a guest has been dropped off. He tends to park it somewhere upstairs – maybe wherever he dropped off the last guest."

"And what has Mr Jenkins to say about that?" Agnes asked, after making a mental note that the lift was now stationed on the first floor; the floor where he had most likely dropped off Robert Jamison. Perhaps they were still chatting about something.

Agnes was well aware of the hotel manager's obsession that the lift should be returned to the ground floor and the doors left open once the guests had alighted. Mr Jenkins had also given similar instructions to the people running the hotel shop and the library; the doors were to remain open during working hours. "Closed doors in the reception area make the hotel look dull and uninviting," he had said on several occasions.

"We understand that the manager has brought up the subject with Andy a few times. But, though he apologises to Mr Jenkins and promises he'll stick to the rules in future, he continues to do things his own way." Sally sighed. "But, he'll be sorry when he loses his job. The manager won't allow him to carry on like this for much longer."

"You're right. By the way, is Mr Jenkins in his office?"

"Yes," Pauline said, glancing down at what Agnes thought might be a copy of the manager's diary, lying somewhere out of sight of prying eyes. "And, from what I can see, he's alone at the moment. Would you like me to let him know you want to see him?"

"Don't bother," Agnes laughed. "I'll surprise him."

Chapter Ten

As Agnes was walking towards the manager's office, she caught a glimpse of Sue Matthews. A few months ago, she had been the victim of a stabbing only a short distance from the hotel. Apparently, at that time, she had signed the off-duty roster and was on her way to meet up with a few other members of staff at a coffee shop on Newbridge Street when she was attacked from behind.

However, while in the ambulance on her way to the hospital, there had been a setback and if it hadn't been for both the paramedic and Dr Keith Nichols, she would never have pulled through.

Sue was at the hospital the last time she had seen her. Back then, she had looked well, despite what she had been through. But today, she looked absolutely amazing. As staff liaison officer, Sue had always set out to be an example to the rest of the staff. However, today Agnes couldn't help noticing that the light blue suit Sue was wearing, together with the neat white blouse, made her look even more elegant than usual.

"Sue, you're looking great, I'm *so* pleased to see you!" she said, as she hurried across to greet her.

"Thank you," Sue said. "It was quite a harrowing experience, but thankfully, I'm okay now."

"So I see," Agnes said, giving Sue a hug. She then took a step backwards to look the young woman up and down. "More than okay, I would say – you look wonderful. I really didn't think you'd be back at work yet, otherwise I would have come down to your office and..."

"Then you wouldn't have found me," Sue interrupted. "I'm in a new post and a new office..." She gave a huge smile. "I've been promoted. You are now looking at the Millennium Hotel Staff Supervisor – what do you think?"

"What do I think?" Agnes exclaimed. "I think that's absolutely brilliant! I'm so happy for you. And I know you'll do a great job," she added.

"Thank you, Mrs Lockwood."

"Please, call me Agnes. After all, I call you Sue."

"I don't think we're allowed to call guests by their first names."

Agnes grinned. "But I'm not a guest – well, not a paying guest. I only dropped in for afternoon tea. Besides, we're friends, aren't we?"

Sue nodded. "Yes, we are – Agnes."

"That's better," Agnes replied.

The two women laughed.

"So, how is your young man, Sue?"

"Keith is fine," Sue replied. "We're getting on so well together. He can be so much fun."

Agnes raised her eyebrows. She had never thought of Keith as a fun person. Though, on reflection, the day she met him at the hospital when she was visiting Sue, he had come across as quite amusing. Maybe she had always related his personality to his job. After all, he did have a rather sombre occupation. Yet, thinking about it, if everyone's personality was linked to their job, Alan would be one of the grumpiest men on the planet, especially if an investigation wasn't going well. But he wasn't grumpy when he arrived home, as he always pushed whatever he was working on to one side the moment he stepped through the door. Unless there was something about it that was really bothering him – then he would talk it through with her, rather than spend the whole evening brooding over it alone.

"He's one of the most fun people I've ever met," Sue continued excitedly. "From the moment I was discharged from the hospital, Keith has spent every minute possible with me and he always managed to find something to make me laugh, especially on the days when I was feeling down." She paused, before turning serious. "It wasn't easy for me to come to terms with the fact that someone I worked with wanted to kill me." She closed her eyes for a second. "I also know that if it hadn't been for Keith and the paramedic in the ambulance, I wouldn't be alive today. I have a great deal to thank them for. But that's not the only reason Keith and I are still together. Something clicked between us while I was in hospital and, from that moment, we both realised we were meant for each other."

Agnes knew she couldn't even begin to argue. All she could do was nod her head and blink back the tears, as she cast her mind back to the very day she first met Jim, the man she had later married. Like Sue and Keith, something had 'clicked' between them. Love at first sight, as the saying goes, though some would have doubts about that in this day and age. Nevertheless, she and Jim had enjoyed a wonderful life together – until his life had been cut short.

"So you see," Sue added, interrupting her thoughts, "Keith and I are planning to set up home together." She paused. "Now, I suppose you're going to tell me that it's all a bit sudden, and we should wait a while to make sure we're doing the right thing."

"Not at all, Sue." Agnes threw her arms around Sue as she spoke. "If that's how you both feel, then who am I to tell you differently? I wish you both all the best for the future."

"Thank you, Agnes. I do hope you'll accept the invitation to our wedding."

"I wouldn't miss it for the world," Agnes replied, trying not to show her surprise that the young couple were planning to marry. Nowadays, when someone talked of setting up a home with their partner, it didn't always mean a wedding was on the agenda.

Sue took a step backwards and smiled. "But now I must get on, otherwise Mr Jenkins will think I'm shirking my duties. I was on my way to a meeting with the bar staff."

Agnes watched Sue head off towards the bar, before turning her attention back to the reason she was still here in the hotel. She heaved a sigh and looked towards the manager's office. A few minutes later, she tapped on his door and entered.

"Can you spare me a few minutes?"

"Absolutely, Mrs Lockwood, please sit down." Pressing the 'save' button on his computer, Jenkins leaned back in his chair and gestured towards the seat opposite him.

"I hope I'm not interrupting anything," she said, nodding towards the computer.

"Not at all. I was just going through last month's figures before they're sent to head office. It's nice to see you again. I hope you've settled into your apartment," he added, with a broad smile.

"Yes," she replied. "It's exactly what I was looking for. But I still miss being here."

Agnes told him how she had enjoyed afternoon tea in the drawing room. "It was like old times." She then went on to say how good it was to see Sue back at the hotel. "She told me about her promotion to staff supervisor."

"Yes, Miss Matthews did exceptionally well in the post of staff liaison officer – it was only fitting that she should get the promotion. Though it means I need to find a new liaison officer." Relaxing deeper into his chair, he formed a steeple with his fingers. "I did consider Larry Parker for the job. He's a good man and well-liked by all the staff. But..." he paused. "Who would I put in his place? The young man on duty at the moment is useless. I'll be handing him his notice once Larry is back."

Agnes had listened carefully while the manager poured out his thoughts. She guessed he was talking to her as a businesswoman and seeking out what she would do in a similar situation, rather than ask her outright.

"I agree with you. It's a difficult decision," she replied. "But, if I were in your shoes, I would need to ask myself whether I wanted to keep Larry Parker at the hotel, or lose him to another company."

"I'm not sure I understand, Mrs Lockwood. Lose him? Why would I lose him?"

Agnes took a deep breath. "I believe that if you don't even consider Larry for promotion – which, I may remind you, is the policy of the hotel when a job becomes vacant – then I feel he might seek employment elsewhere." She paused. "Look at it this way. What would you do if you were in his position – a young man trying to make his way up the ladder? Would you stay here, at a hotel where the manager wouldn't even consider you for promotion because he needed you to stay where you were? Or would you look for a job elsewhere?"

Jenkins nodded. "Thank you for that. You're right. I'll speak to him on Monday." He leaned his head to one side. "But, Mrs Lockwood, I'm sure you didn't come here to advise me on my staff problems. So tell me, what can I do for you today? There's nothing untoward going on at the hotel, is there?"

* * *

Agnes glanced at the clock on the wall, as she stepped out of the manager's office. She hadn't meant to stay with Mr Jenkins for so long. She had only gone into his office to request that all charges to Ben and his family were to be added to an account she would set up in her name, should he decide to accept her offer to stay at the hotel. However, after their discussion about Andy, it was late in the afternoon when she left his office.

Now, slowly walking towards the entrance, Agnes knew that if she were to leave right away, she could grab a cab, head home and start preparing something for their evening meal. Yet, at this precise moment, she had no desire to rush back to the apartment and think about what to have for dinner, let alone set about cooking it. But then, as she swept her eyes away from the hotel entrance, they fell on the sign pointing the way to the dining room, which gave her an idea. Maybe she could book a table for dinner and Alan could join her when he was able to get away from the station. With this new case now on the agenda, who knew how long he would be kept there?

As Agnes reached the reception desk with the intention of booking a table for dinner, another question rose to mind. If Alan was tied up with the case for several more hours, would he really feel in the mood to drive back to the apartment after they had finished their meal? Agnes smiled as she looked across the desk towards Pauline.

A new idea had suddenly popped into her head.

Chapter Eleven

It was around five-thirty when Alan pulled up alongside the Millennium Hotel. He had made the decision to call it a day and suggested his sergeant do the same. "We're getting nowhere with either case," he said. "We'll make a fresh start tomorrow."

The manager of the jewellery shop had been in a state of despair when the DCI and Andrews had arrived. It had taken them some time to calm him down enough to explain that the items stolen were of extreme value. Nevertheless, he was able to give them a photograph of the jewellery. The manager had taken the picture as a memento. He had gone on to point out where the items had been kept under lock and key. During the day, they were in a bullet-proof glass case where people could admire them. However, once the shop had closed, they were moved to a vault at the back of the building. The only time the case had been opened was when the young assistant had dusted out the cabinet earlier that morning in readiness for the inspection later in the day.

"It's only done periodically because, as you can see, it's almost dust-proof," he had said.

He also assured the two detectives that the door to the case was firmly locked after she had finished. "I even tried it myself, as I passed by to get to my office. Yet, as you can see, the case is not broken. Therefore, how the hell did they steal the items?"

Photographs and fingerprints of the scene had been taken by the forensic team, but Alan guessed that the thief would probably have worn gloves. Also, it appeared there had been a few problems with the CCTV over the last couple of days. It had shut down for a few minutes the previous afternoon and again this morning. Someone was coming to check it out later that day. Even so, it was still a mystery as to how anyone could have stolen the jewellery while the shop was open for business without being seen by anyone, especially as the manager had told them they had been rather busy that morning.

Alan sighed as he locked his car. He would have much preferred to have gone straight back to the apartment, rather than come here for dinner. Back there, he could have curled up with Agnes on the sofa and watched the television. But, as Agnes had sounded so happy about the idea when she rang, he hadn't voiced his thoughts. However, feeling thoroughly despondent after a non-satisfying day, he wished he had said something to discourage her. But it was too late now. No doubt the table had already been booked and she would be waiting for him in the drawing room.

Clambering out of his car, Alan locked the doors and shoved the keys into his jacket pocket before straightening his tie. Though he would like to have had the opportunity to freshen up a little before dinner at the hotel, he knew that he was suitably attired. While the hotel did not have a strict dress code for dinner, unless there happened to be a special function, the management did stipulate diners should be appropriately dressed. In other words, T-shirt and jeans were frowned upon.

As he walked into the drawing room, he looked around and spotted Agnes sitting on a sofa in one corner of the room, her head stuck into a magazine.

She looked up when he slumped down beside her.

"Poor you," she said, rubbing his arm. "You look so tired. I booked the table from six o'clock onwards as I wasn't sure what time you would get away. But, as you are here early, it means you have plenty of time to unwind with a glass of something." She paused. "Maybe

I was being too presumptuous when I called you? Perhaps I should have talked it through with you before I booked the table."

"I thought you *had* talked it through with me before..." Alan broke off. There was no point going down that road. He had agreed to come – end of story. "It's okay," he continued, wrapping his hand around hers. "It's just been one hell of a day. No one recognised the dead man, not even Morris, and if that..." But then, suddenly remembering he wasn't in the solitude of their home, he looked around the drawing room.

"It's alright, Alan." Agnes reassured him. "We're alone, everyone has either gone out for the evening or else they're in the bar. *And if that...*" she prompted him to continue where he had left off.

"If that wasn't enough for one day, there was a robbery at the jewellers on Northumberland Street." Alan continued, once he was sure they weren't being overheard.

"Gosh! By that, do you mean a sort of hold-up?" Agnes said.

"No, nothing like that," Alan replied. He told her that the items stolen had been in a case on display in the shop. "I understand that they were very expensive and were only on loan to the shop. Yet, no one had even noticed the stuff had gone until a few hours later."

"How could they not notice that a case of jewellery was missing?"

"I believe it had been replaced by copies."

"So, getting back to the murder case, you particularly mentioned Morris not recognising the dead man," Agnes said.

"When he and the rest of the team were shown photographs of the victim, Morris stated that he hadn't seen him before. Just when I thought this would be the one time I could rely on him, he let us down."

"Why were you so certain that John would recognise the dead man?" Agnes enquired.

"Because, if you recall, Morris has had connections with a few shady places in the city since he arrived in Newcastle," Alan replied. "I had this idea that he might have seen the man propping up a bar somewhere. At the very least, it would have given us somewhere to start."

"Okay," Agnes said slowly, suddenly realising that, even after so many months, Morris was still not a favourite in Alan's court. However, never having been one to be put off so easily, she swallowed hard and continued. "But, if Morris had been given the opportunity to see the victim in the flesh, so to speak, might that have jogged his memory?"

"No. I don't think so. Why would it?" Alan replied. "You see a face and either you know it, or you don't." He paused. "For goodness' sake, where is this going, Agnes? Morris said he hadn't seen the man before! What are you thinking?"

"Right," Agnes said, pulling her hand from Alan's grasp. Leaning forward, she plucked up the cushion behind her and plumped it up, before throwing it back in place and flopping against it. "You asked me what I was thinking – well, let me tell you. I think you are being a little hard on Morris because he didn't recognise the victim from the photo you showed him. However, as I see it, you're saying he let you down, rather than talking him through a few of the places he'd been to in recent weeks, all because you have a thing against him. Okay, I agree," she continued, before Alan could interrupt. "The man needed taking down a peg or two. But you can't just dismiss everything he says because…"

Agnes bit her lip and swung around towards the window. If she wasn't careful, this was going to end up in a row and she had hoped they would have a wonderful evening together in the hotel.

"But we don't need Morris," Alan gloated. He slid back into the sofa and stretched his legs out in front of him. "You see, we already have the victim's identity. We now know his name to be Robert Jamison. By the way, his surname is spelled with the letter I, instead of the usual E. I gather that's an unusual way to spell the name. Most people with that name spell it as Jameson. Therefore, I'm sure we'll be able to trace him without any help from Morris."

"Really?" Agnes, who had already begun to turn back to face Alan before he announced the man's name, was now peering straight at him. She raised her eyebrows. "That's most interesting. Tell me more."

"Actually, it was down to Keith Nichols. He found an identity card and an MI5 badge in a pocket secreted inside the man's trousers. But when Andrews and I looked at it closely, we picked up a discrepancy."

He went on to explain how the badge and the identity card each spelled the name differently.

"So, you see," he said, slapping the palms of his hands on his knees in triumph, "we don't need Morris's help."

"Is that so?" Agnes said. "Well done."

Without moving a muscle, Alan retained his gloating stance as Agnes slowly picked up her glass from the table and took a sip of wine. During his years as a police officer, he had seen this carefree action many times before. Very often, the suspect sitting in front of him in the interview room, or wherever else the interview was taking place, would take a drink from a glass or cup in front of them, before admitting that the DCI was right after all. No doubt, Agnes was about to do the same, once she had gently placed the glass back onto the table. However, his hopes fell apart a few seconds later.

"Well, I've got a feeling you might need to think again," Agnes replied. "And, on doing so, you may find that you need Morris after all."

"Why on earth would I still need Morris?" Alan spluttered, pulling himself upright. "For goodness' sake, didn't you hear me? I just told you – we now have the victim's name. He was called Robert Jamison!"

"Yes, Alan, I heard you perfectly," Agnes replied, calmly. "However, you might be interested to know about something I learned today. You see, I just happened to see a man walking into the hotel, at least two hours *after* the murder was committed and…"

"So?" Alan interrupted. He flung his arms into the air in frustration. "People walk into this hotel all the time. Okay, so a man walked into the hotel today. What the hell this man has got to do with our murder case?"

"I don't know!" Agnes retorted. "Maybe nothing at all!"

For a moment, she was sorely tempted to walk out of the room and leave him sitting there. If anyone else had spoken to her like that, she would have been gone by now.

However, taking a deep breath, she tried again. "But, at the same time, he might know something about it, or he could even be involved. However, as you aren't interested, just forget it. We'll move on."

Agnes turned away and picked up the dinner menu that was standing on the coffee table in front of them. Even at a glance, she could see that there was a rather extended menu this evening. Perhaps there was something going on in the hotel she hadn't heard about. Occasionally, the hotel hired a comedian or a singer to appear in the large room at the back of the hotel. But when that was the case, the information was plastered on boards all over the reception area. Yet she hadn't noticed anything.

"What would you like to have for dinner, Alan?" she asked. "There seems to be a number of your favourites on the menu..."

"Forget about dinner, Agnes," Alan said. Grabbing the menu from her hands, he thrust it down onto the table. "What did you mean – the man you saw might have something to do with the case?"

Agnes stared down towards where the menu had fallen. That was the second time within a few minutes that Alan had humiliated her. She closed her eyes and counted to ten. How much more would she take before she stormed out?

"What I was about to tell you, Chief Inspector," Agnes said slowly, "was that the man I mentioned happens to be booked into the hotel under the name of Robert Jamison. And, before you go off on another tantrum, let me add that the spelling of the surname is exactly as you quoted earlier."

Picking up the menu from where it had landed, she held it out in front of Alan, while trying to hide a smile of triumph.

"Why don't you take a look, Alan? As I said, they're serving a number of your favourites this evening."

Chapter Twelve

It took a moment or two before Agnes's news sank in. But when it did, Alan quickly leapt to his feet and yanked his phone from his pocket. He called Andrews and, pacing up and down the floor of the drawing room, he ordered his sergeant to join him at the Millennium Hotel right away.

"I suppose that means our dinner together this evening is off." Despite being really angry at his attitude towards her, Agnes tried to sound calm, hoping to ease the tension a little.

Unfortunately, Alan didn't pick up on her relaxed tone of voice. "What the hell do *you* think?" he barked. "Come to think of it, Agnes, why didn't you tell me this earlier? You could have mentioned something about seeing this Jamison person when you called asking me to join you here for dinner? Andrews and I could have been here in a flash and …"

"Because, *Alan*, if you recall," Agnes interrupted, icily. "When I spoke to you on the phone, you didn't say a word about having learned the victim's name. Even when I asked whether you had anything new on the case, you said no. If you knew the man's name at that time, which I now believe you did, then why didn't you say something? I could have told you there and then that a man was staying here under that name. At least it would have saved all this mess, argument, embarrassment or whatever else you want to call it."

Alan didn't reply. Instead, he turned away and focused his eyes on the window which looked out onto the straight, narrow road that ran along the quayside from the hotel to the bottom of the Tyne Bridge.

Agnes was right. When she had spoken to him on the phone, she had asked whether there was any further information on the case. While he had been on the brink of saying that they had now learned the victim's name, he had remained silent. Why? Agnes had helped him solve a few cases recently. Even today, when she called him about finding the body, she had followed his instructions to stand guard outside the door of the room and stop anyone from entering before the police arrived. So why had he been so evasive about answering her one simple question? He heaved a huge sigh of relief when he caught a glimpse of Andrews's car heading towards the hotel. He had been saved from having to explain it to himself, let alone Agnes.

"My sergeant is here," he said, as he headed towards the door leading out into the reception area. But then, glancing behind him, he saw Agnes was about to follow him. "Where do you think you're going?"

"Don't worry, I'm not following you. I'm going to the restaurant," Agnes replied. "Where else would I be going? In case you've forgotten, I have a table booked for two." She paused. "By the way, if Sandra hasn't yet eaten, tell Sergeant Andrews to give her a call – she might be in the mood to join me. It seems you both have other plans."

Alan heaved a sigh as Agnes marched off towards the restaurant. Their conversation hadn't gone at all well. Yet, he felt sure he would be able to set things straight with her later. But, for the moment, he needed to focus on the case. Hopefully, the guest staying at the hotel under the name of Robert Jamison would be able to answer some of the problems surrounding their investigation. Who knows, he could be the killer and let something slip. Then they could arrest him. If so, at least one case would be closed.

Turning his attention towards the entrance of the hotel, Alan saw the doors slide open, allowing his sergeant to stride in. However, he was rather surprised to find that Andrews wasn't alone; he was accompanied by his fiancée, Sandra. Both were dressed as though they had planned an evening out together.

"Okay, what's happened?" Andrews asked, as he approached the DCI. He paused, and gestured towards Sandra. "I do hope this won't take long. We were just about to go out for dinner when I got your call."

"It will take as long as I say, *sergeant*," Alan replied, stressing the last word to put Andrews in his place. He hadn't failed to notice that his sergeant had been a little cocky of late; even more so, if Sandra was in the vicinity.

Turning towards Sandra, he smiled. "I'm sorry about this. But these things tend to happen from time to time. Perhaps you'd like to join Agnes in the restaurant. She has a table booked for two."

Though it might have sounded more like a question to anyone listening close by, it came across to both Michael and Sandra as more of a statement.

"Very well," Sandra replied, after a brief glance at Michael. "That sounds like a good idea."

"Okay, what's this all about, sir?" Andrews asked, once Sandra was out of earshot.

Alan quickly explained what Agnes had told him, as they walked across the reception.

"She also learned that he was staying in room 106," he added, as they reached the lift. However, as it appeared to be stationed on the first floor, Alan pointed towards the stairs. "I understand Larry's on holiday," he continued. "Perhaps the new guy hasn't quite grasped the hotel rules – in that the lift should be brought back to the ground floor once it has been cleared of passengers."

"What's so difficult to understand about that?" Andrews asked, as they began to mount the stairs.

Alan placed a finger to his lips as they approached the first floor. A quick scan told him that room 106 was only a few doors away. However, before taking the last two steps up the staircase, he glanced towards where the lift was stationed. Though the doors were open, there was no sign of the attendant. Could he be standing at the back of the lift; out of sight? Alan nudged his sergeant and pointed two fingers at his own eyes, before pointing to the lift.

Andrews nodded. He understood that his DCI wanted him to creep along the landing and take a look inside the lift. Once he was close enough to peer inside, he turned back to DCI Johnson and shook his head. There was no one there.

Alan nodded and beckoned his sergeant to rejoin him.

"So where the hell is he?" Alan whispered, once Andrews was back with him. "He's supposed to be on duty."

Andrews shrugged. "I don't know," he replied, keeping his voice low. "He could be on a tea break."

"I don't think so," Alan said. "I know for certain that while the lift attendant is away from his post, someone is assigned to take over until he returns. The rules come from head office, which means the manager will have made darn sure that the lift attendant was aware of them." He paused. "Let's face it, Jenkins, the manager, has found himself in enough trouble over these last few months, what with thefts and murders, without allowing a lift attendant to swan off somewhere before securing a replacement."

"Yes, I suppose so." Andrews nodded in agreement. "But, don't you think that having a lift attendant in this day and age is a bit old-fashioned?" he added, casually. "Surely people are capable of using a lift on their own." He paused. "Though, I suppose the London hotels are different. They tend to look on that kind of thing as the norm – what do you think?"

"I think you should shut up, Andrews. We need to find Jamison! We can sort out a solution to your problem about the need for a lift attendant at a later date." Even though Alan kept his voice low, his frustration at his sergeant's useless observations still showed through.

Andrews remained silent as he followed the DCI along the corridor towards room 106.

"I only hope he hasn't gone out somewhere," Alan said, as they approached the door. "Like I said earlier, Agnes told me she saw him turn up at the hotel and didn't see him leave. Yet, who knows? He could have slid out of the hotel when she had her back turned."

"When has Agnes ever had her back turned where a police investigation is concerned? If you recall, she likes to be included in everything." The words had spilled out of his mouth before he could stop them.

Andrews fully expected a reprimand for his remark. Yet, at the same time, he had meant every word. In his mind, Agnes was a busybody and wanted to be involved in all their cases. He didn't dislike Agnes; he would just prefer her to stay out of police investigations. Today, once again, it was she who found the body. Therefore, there was no doubt that she would insist on being included in any findings in the ongoing inquiry. But more than that, he was annoyed that Sandra had joined Agnes for dinner. They would probably be talking about the case right now. The last thing he wanted was for Sandra to get involved.

The DCI had been on the point of disciplining his sergeant for his remark. However, after taking a deep breath, he held his tongue. This was neither the time nor the place. He would confront Andrews later. In the meantime, they really needed to speak to Robert Jamison.

Now, standing outside the room, Alan glanced at his sergeant, before tapping lightly on the door.

When there was no reply, he knocked a little harder, causing the door to move slightly. Alan looked at his sergeant before pressing his hand against the door.

"Hello!" he called out, when the door opened a little further.

Again, there was no reply. Alan took a few steps into the room with Andrews following closely behind. A swift glance around the room showed that it was empty.

"Do you think he's made a run for it?" Andrews asked.

Alan didn't answer. He was concentrating on a suitcase perched on top of the wardrobe. Pulling open the wardrobe doors, he discovered several items of clothing hanging neatly inside. Without saying a word, the DCI looked at his sergeant and gestured towards the contents of the wardrobe.

Andrews raised his eyebrows when he saw the row of expensive suits hanging on the rail. If Jamison had left the hotel, his departure couldn't have been planned. Otherwise he would not have left these suits behind. Therefore, either he was still in the city or, if he had left the area, it had been on the spur of the moment.

Swinging around to take another look at the room, the sergeant's eyes fell on a jacket looped over the back of one of the chairs by the table in front of the window.

Giving the DCI a nudge, he motioned towards the jacket.

Alan nodded. "We'll take a look, but we'd best check out the bathroom first," he whispered.

Andrews tapped on the door. When there was no reply, he slowly turned the handle and carefully pushed the door open a few inches. Seeing no one in his line of sight, he pushed the door open further and stepped inside. A fleeting glance told him no one was there. He turned back to the DCI and shook his head.

"Okay, Andrews, it's time for us to take a look at the jacket."

* * *

"So what's going on?" Sandra asked, once she caught up with Agnes. "I couldn't help noticing that Alan seemed rather uptight about something. What's happened?" She glanced back at the two men just in time to see them hurrying towards the staircase.

"Alan is uptight with me," Agnes replied calmly, once they had been shown to the table she had booked. She clicked her tongue. "Or, should that be because of me?

Either way, I'm somewhere in there."

Taking a closer look at Sandra's dress, Agnes realised that her friend was dressed more for an evening out with her fiancé, rather than meeting up with her at the hotel.

"Can I say that your dress and jacket are absolutely wonderful – they really suit you," she said. "Obviously you and Michael were going out this evening. I'm so sorry that your evening has been spoiled."

"We'd planned to go out for dinner, but Michael suddenly received a call from Alan to drop everything and come here."

"These things happen, Sandra." Agnes smiled. "Maybe not often, but they do happen."

Feeling at a loss as to what to say next, Agnes picked up her menu and pretended to look at choices for the evening. She had seen them earlier and knew already what she was going to choose.

"Let's see what's on the menu tonight."

"I must say there's a wonderful selection," Sandra replied, gazing at the menu. "I'm spoilt for choice. But…"

"This is on me, Sandra," Agnes interrupted, guessing that the prices might be a tad higher than Sandra had expected. "I hate dining alone," she added, "and the outcome of our evening isn't quite what either of us had anticipated. Therefore, why shouldn't we enjoy this meal together?"

Once they placed their order, Agnes glanced around the dining room. It was quite full, even though it was still rather early in the evening.

Casting her eyes to the far corner of the room, Agnes saw a table set for one person. However, it was still vacant. About to turn away, she saw a man following the head waiter towards the table. It was same man she had seen sleeping in the drawing room earlier today. Moving her head slightly, she found that most of the other tables were occupied in that quarter of the room. However, sweeping her eyes further towards the centre of the room, Agnes stiffened when she spotted a man sitting alone at a table set for two. She was unable to see his face clearly as he was peering down at something on the table; probably the local newspaper. Nevertheless, despite him having changed from the outfit he was wearing earlier, into a rather expensive dark grey suit, Agnes felt sure he was the man she had seen entering the hotel earlier. The man booked in under the name of Robert Jamison.

At that moment, the man looked up to beckon a passing waiter, giving Agnes the opportunity to see his face more clearly. Yes, it was definitely Jamison, and she was even more certain that she had seen him somewhere earlier in the day – but where? She still couldn't remember. If banging her head on the table in this busy restaurant would have helped, she would have done so, but...

"What's so interesting about him? Is he your type?" Sandra joked. She had watched her friend closely for the last few minutes and couldn't help noticing that Agnes's eyes were focused on one man in particular.

Agnes swung back to face Sandra. "Keep your voice down," she hissed, before looking back at the man out of the corner of her eye.

However, it appeared he hadn't overheard Sandra's remark. Having spoken to the waiter, Jamison had turned his attention back to whatever it was he was reading.

"That man certainly isn't my type," Agnes continued. "Don't look now, but he's Robert Jamison, the man Alan and Michael are looking for at this very moment." She heaved a sigh. "I suppose I should call Alan and tell him that they are wasting their time up there and get down here right away – or I could wait until..."

"Wait!" Sandra broke in before Agnes had finished her sentence. She leaned across the table and lowered her voice. "I think we should hang on and see who turns up to join him."

"How did you know what I was going to say? And, come to think of it, what do you mean by, *we*?"

Sandra cocked her head on one side. "I was just guessing – but I'm right, aren't I? As for your second question, you want to wait and so do I."

"Yes, I would wait if I was sitting here on my own, especially after my encounter with Alan earlier. I..."Agnes broke off. There was no need to spill out the details of what had happened between them. "Look, I just want to say that, at the moment, I'm concerned about you and Michael. I don't want to do anything to jeopardise your relationship."

"Don't worry about that. We've had a few problems of our own lately. Besides, when they don't find anyone in the room upstairs, I imagine they'll stride in here before we've had the chance to see who joins Jamison at his table."

"But we'd still be here, Sandra. We'd be in the position to see who-ever joins him." Agnes hadn't failed to pick up a note of disappoint-ment in her friend's voice. "There's no way either of the detectives, or their merry men could move us out of here."

"Yes, I realise that. But it would be much more exciting if we were in the position of being able to pass on information to Michael and Alan *after* they arrived." Sandra paused and neatened the lightweight jacket draped over her shoulders. "I suppose this is all run-of-the-mill stuff to you, Agnes. You've been involved in so many different police investigations, whereas this is still new to me. Yet I really want to be included."

"But I thought you and Michael were now working together, as a team, so to speak."

A few months back, Alan had mentioned that his sergeant was con-sidering leaving the police force. It appeared that Sandra was unable to come to terms with the number of hours he had to work. At that point, Alan had made the suggestion that his sergeant could include Sandra by asking her opinion about certain aspects of whatever investigation they were working on at the time. Though it went against the rules, there were times when even the police needed a little help.

"Yes, he did." Sandra screwed up her eyes. "Well, sort of. But, he never really told me very much, and then he began cutting me out altogether."

Agnes totally understood. Though she had helped Alan with sev-eral of his cases in the past few months, today he had held back from passing on the name of the dead man; deciding to keep that piece of information to himself.

"Right, that's settled," Agnes whispered. "We'll wait to see who joins Jamison, before we call the detectives – unless, of course, they happen to arrive here in the meantime." She grinned, as a thought popped into her mind. "But then, how would they know the man sitting at the table over there is who they were looking for, unless we decide to tell them?"

"Well, I'm certainly not going to say a word," Sandra uttered. "I'm with you on this one. Let's do it!"

Agnes had been on the point of giving Sandra a high five, when she suddenly saw a young woman appear in the doorway of the restaurant. For a moment, Agnes was rather surprised that she had missed seeing the woman enter the hotel. Even though she had been conversing with Sandra, she was facing the large mirror close to the door of the dining room. Being slightly tilted, from her position it showed a full reflection of the main entrance and part of the reception area.

However, when the woman stepped further into the dining room, Agnes noted that she wasn't wearing a coat or even a jacket over her elegant, beige coloured, off-the-shoulder dress. As there was a slight chill in the air this evening, surely the matching wrap draped around her shoulders wouldn't have been warm enough. Therefore, could she be staying at the hotel? Agnes was still admiring the woman's outfit when Alex, the headwaiter, hurried across to greet his latest customer. After a brief exchange of words, Alex nodded and led her across to the table where Jamison was sitting.

Having picked up on her arrival, Jamison leapt to his feet and pulled out the chair facing him. Once the woman was seated, he instructed Alex to bring a bottle of champagne to their table.

Agnes swung back to face Sandra, intending to bring her up to speed about Jamison's companion. However, there was no need as Sandra raised her glass and nodded, indicating that she had seen everything for herself.

"Cheers," Agnes said, lifting her glass. "Here's to us."

"Cheers," Sandra echoed. "I'll drink to that!"

* * *

Upstairs, Andrews had checked the pockets of the beige jacket slung across the back of the chair. The DCI, who had followed him across the room, checked the trousers he found strewed over the seat of the same chair. Recalling the pathologist's words, Alan also made sure there weren't any secret pockets hidden somewhere inside the trousers.

However, they found nothing to identify the man booked into this room under the name of Robert Jamison. By now, Alan was so frustrated at the lack of information that he went even further, deciding to almost ransack the room by searching through the chest of drawers and instructing Andrews to go through the pockets of the clothes in the wardrobe, as well as checking under the bed. But again, they found nothing to go on.

Alan was well aware that even if they had found something incriminating, it probably wouldn't have stood up in a court of law. Their search would have been described as illegal as they weren't carrying an appropriate warrant. Even though the door to the room was open when they arrived, the suspect's lawyer would have had a field day in court. Yet Alan was so desperate to find something to help their investigation, he had been willing to take the risk.

"No passport, no credit cards and, can you believe it, no money," Alan fumed. He paused, while he thought for a moment. "I've just remembered," Alan clicked his finger and thumb as he spoke, "the hotel now has a safe installed in every room. Andrews, check the bottom of the wardrobe – that's where the safes have been fitted. If it's locked, there's a good chance it'll hold something of importance – though we won't be able to open it without the code."

Andrews bent down and fumbled through the numerous pairs of shoes and other items stored in the bottom of the wardrobe. "I've found the safe… " he began, excitedly. But then he broke off and, pulling himself upright, he closed the wardrobe doors. "Yes, like you said, there's a safe in there – it's fastened to the wardrobe floor. However, it wasn't locked so I was able to take a look – it's empty."

"Well, that's it." The DCI blew a sigh. "There's nothing more we can do here. We've hit a dead end. I think we should go back downstairs and join the ladies – bring them up to speed."

Alan was anxious to get back to Agnes and try to make up for the episode in the drawing room. However, his sergeant was less than keen.

"No!" Andrews said, pushing the DCI to one side. "We must have missed something," he said, yanking the wardrobe doors open again. "I don't want Sandra involved in this or any other case. We need to look again. There has to be something..."

"Michael!" Alan hissed. He grabbed his sergeant's arm. "Get a grip, man! What the hell's the matter with you?"

The sergeant, who had been about to tear a suit down from the rail in the wardrobe, turned to face his DCI. "I'm sorry, sir," he said. "I don't know what's wrong with me." He heaved a sigh, and sat down on the edge of the bed. "No, that's not true," he corrected himself. "It's about Sandra."

"What about Sandra?" Alan reached out and placed his hand on Andrews's shoulder. "She's okay, isn't she? I mean, she isn't ill?"

"No, it's nothing like that. She's fine, health-wise." Andrews looked away for a moment. "I suppose it's all down to me, really." He took another deep breath. "I did as you suggested a few months ago and began to talk through a few things about the case with Sandra. Or at least I tried to. But..." He broke off.

"Wasn't she interested after all?"

"Quite the opposite, she was *too* interested. She kept coming up with really worthwhile suggestions – things I'd never thought of and I just couldn't come to terms with that. So..." he broke off.

"... So, you decided to give up talking to Sandra about our inquiries because her suggestions made you feel inadequate?" Alan finished the statement for his sergeant. He thought for a moment. "Does that mean some of the things you came up with in the past few months, might have come from Sandra?"

Andrews nodded. "Yes."

Alan blew a sigh. Where had he heard that before? He had done much the same thing a few times, today being the latest. If only he had mentioned the name of Robert Jamison when he was speaking to Agnes on the phone that afternoon, things could have turned out very differently. For a start, he and his sergeant could have arrived earlier and found the man in his room. Secondly, and more importantly from his point of view, there would have been no reason for the argument he'd had with Agnes earlier that evening.

Alan glanced towards the door. It was very slightly ajar, exactly as he and Andrews had found it when they arrived. It hadn't rebounded and slammed shut the way it was meant to once the occupier had either entered or left the room. The doors of the guest rooms were set up that way as a security measure should the guest leave in a hurry. Obviously, the mechanism above this door needed readjusting.

"Okay, Andrews, I think it's time we got out of here." He quickly straightened the duvet where his sergeant had been sitting, before glancing around the room to make sure everything looked exactly as they found it. "We'll talk it over, but not here."

"Where?"

"Anywhere, just not in here, okay? Now, move!"

Alan almost knocked his sergeant off his feet as he pushed him out of the room. After making sure the door was firmly closed, he looked back at Andrews, totally unsure as to what he could say to help his sergeant. How on earth could he advise him about something that he himself had fouled up on only an hour ago?

"We're no further forward with the case, are we, sir?" Andrews asked, once they had taken a few steps away from the door.

"No, we're not," the DCI replied, firmly.

Pausing for a moment, Alan looked over his sergeant's shoulder and saw that the lift was no longer parked up here. A glance at the indicator above the doors told him it was now situated on the ground floor.

"But, that's down to me," Alan continued, turning back to Andrews. He held up his hands in a surrender-like pose. "I guess, as detectives on a case, we think of ourselves as being in command of any situation. Yet, at the end of the day, we aren't. We send out our detectives to seek information from the public, showing them photos, etcetera, and if it wasn't for something one person had seen or heard, we could end up with nothing and the killer could go free."

Alan went on to explain how he had held back from telling Agnes he had learned the victim's name. "Darn it, Andrews. If only I had passed on that piece of information, we could have been here hours ago and found Jamison in his room. But instead, I messed up and now…" Alan broke off.

"… And now you and Agnes have had a bit of a row." Andrews finished the sentence for his DCI.

"Yes. Quite a big row, actually." Alan gritted his teeth. Those last few words had been thoughts swimming around in his head. He hadn't meant them to spill out. "So you see," he quickly continued, "you and I are in the same boat. We're both reluctant to share anything that threatens our ability to solve a case without help from our partners. Yet, there are times when it's in our best interests to ask for help. At the end of the day, Andrews, we rely on the public to help us find a suspect and whichever way you look at it, our partners are still members of the public."

"I guess I didn't look at it from that point of view, sir."

Alan glanced towards the stairs. There was no point in standing around here any longer. Jamison could be gone for hours. Maybe they should just go downstairs.

"Come on, Andrews. It's time to go and join the ladies."

* * *

In the dining room, Agnes and Sandra were still trying to listen to the conversation between Jamison and the attractive young woman who had joined him. However, they were too far away to hear very much; especially as the couple seemed to be keeping their voices low. Or, could it be that the chatter in the dining room had risen to a higher level after everyone had had a few drinks?

Nevertheless, they had learned that the lady's name was Deborah because Jamison had said it out loud when he had leapt to his feet upon her arrival. Once they had sat down, both had been quite casual; he had called her Debbie a couple of times. Now, they sat with their arms stretched out across the table, holding hands.

Still watching the couple, Agnes felt that something wasn't quite right. Picking up her glass of wine, she twirled the stem between her fingers as she continued to observe the pair. As it happened, she was in the ideal position to see them both as she was almost facing their table. Even if she turned to face Sandra, she only had to move her eyes slightly to the right to see what was happening at Jamison's table.

"So what's going on now?" Sandra asked.

Sandra wasn't able to see the couple as clearly as Agnes without turning her head slightly. However, she didn't want to do that too often. Yet, at the same time, she was keen to know what was happening.

"Nothing." Agnes shrugged. "Well, they're acting all lovey-dovey. But we're too far away to hear exactly what's being said. Yet, there's something about the whole set-up that doesn't ring true."

Before Sandra could question Agnes about her last remark, the waiter arrived with their first course.

"Now this really looks good," Sandra said, looking down at the plate in front of her.

"It does indeed," Agnes replied.

However, before the women had a chance to pick up their cutlery, Alan and his sergeant swooped in front of them.

"Any chance we can join you?"

Without even waiting for a reply, Alan swung around and grabbed a chair from a table nearby and placed it at the table. He gestured towards his sergeant to do the same.

"That looks good," Alan added, eyeing Agnes's plate.

"My guess is, everything didn't go as well as you'd expected," Agnes said, raising her eyebrows as she spoke. "Jamison wasn't there."

"Why would you think that? We..." Alan broke off and sighed heavily.

He had been on the verge of lying by telling her that they'd had a chat with Jamison, but then realised he was only digging himself and Andrews into an even deeper hole.

"Yes. You're right. The room was empty."

"I see. So you didn't find anyone in the room," Agnes replied.

"Didn't the DCI just say that?" It was Andrews who replied, in a rather icy tone.

"Does that mean you burst into his room when he didn't answer?" Sandra said, joining in the conversation.

"No! Sandra, you've got it all wrong." Michael reached across and took her hand. "We didn't burst in – the door was ajar. It simply hadn't closed properly."

"Yet, I bet you took the opportunity to search his room whilst you were there." Sandra pulled her hand away from his grasp as she spoke. "Otherwise, why did it take you so long to get back down here? Come to think of it, why are you here at all? Why aren't you out there questioning the reception staff as to whether they saw him leave?"

Agnes shrank back into her chair at Sandra's sudden outburst. After their earlier conversation, she was aware that Sandra was annoyed at Michael's reluctance to even talk to her about a case. However, until this moment, she hadn't realised quite how riled her friend really was.

"I've just had a thought," Agnes said, drawing herself back up in her chair. "It might be a good idea if you men found another table – that is, if you're still feeling hungry. I'm sure the waiter would find you a table – somewhere."

"You know something, don't you?" Alan nodded his head as he spoke. He glanced at Sandra. "You both do."

"What on earth makes you think that?" Agnes asked. "You saw us both come in here and, might I add, we've been here ever since. What could we possibly know that you and Michael don't?"

"Sandra. For goodness' sake, can't we talk about this?" Michael asked.

He reached out to take his fiancée's hand again but she was too quick for him and moved it away before he even got close.

"What is there to talk about?" Sandra said. "Look, Mike, you usually don't want to talk to me about your cases, so why the sudden change of heart? Why don't you just go away – and let me enjoy my meal."

"Yes, let us get on with our meal," Agnes intervened. "I think we've all said enough for the time being."

Despite the heated conversation, Agnes had still been keeping an eye on the couple at the table a short distance away. Right now, the waiter was clearing away the dishes from their first course. Agnes was keen to see where the couple went once they left the dining room. But at this rate, they would be long gone before she and Sandra had had even a few bites of their food.

"Right, then. I'll see you back at the apartment." Alan stood up as he spoke.

"I doubt it," Agnes replied. "I'm not planning to return this evening. I have somewhere else in mind."

Alan glared at her for a long moment before returning the chair to the nearby table, but he held back from saying what was on his mind.

"We'll talk more when you get back to your flat, Sandra," Michael said, as he rose from his chair. It sounded more like a statement than a question.

Sandra had been on the verge of nodding in agreement, mainly because she didn't have any other option at such short notice. However Agnes, who was taking a sip of her wine at the time, looked over the top of her glass and cast her eyes towards the ceiling a couple of times, indicating that Sandra could spend the night at the hotel.

"No, I don't think so, Mike," Sandra replied, slowly. "I think I might visit a friend after dinner. With all the news I have to tell her, it's possible I'll end up spending the night there."

Agnes and Sandra smiled at each other as the two men stormed out of the dining room.

"You do know we're going to have to apologise to the men the next time we see them, don't you?" Sandra said, with a sigh.

"Really?" Agnes asked. She shrugged and gave Sandra a huge grin. "No, I don't think so. Surely that would be a sign of weakness."

"I know where that came from," Sandra laughed. "But I couldn't agree more."

"Then I guess we both enjoy watching Gibbs in *NCIS*!"

* * *

"Well, that didn't go well," Alan uttered, the moment he and Andrews stepped out of the hotel. He wrapped his arms around his upper body.

Even though he was wearing his overcoat, the cool air still bit into him. "I had hoped Agnes might have caught a glimpse of Jamison leaving the hotel. With a bit of luck, she might even have noticed whether he was on his own, or with someone else. And, knowing Agnes the way I do, I guess she would have even taken note of which direction he'd headed."

"If you recall, I wanted to stop at the reception desk to ask the receptionists those very same questions. Yet you held me back," Andrews said. He had been staring along the quayside, but now he suddenly swung back to face Alan. "Why the hell did you stop me? One of the two women on duty might have been able to give us some useful information. For goodness' sake, you'd have thrown the book at any one of the detectives on your team if they had allowed something as easy as that pass them by."

The sergeant broke off. He was aware he had overstepped the mark with his last quip. However, he wasn't in the mood to apologise. Pulling up the collar of his jacket, he turned away and huddled beneath the canopy that sheltered the large sliding doors leading into the hotel. Then, as the doors began to open to admit a couple of guests, he moved away, back into the chilly breeze. He should have worn something warmer, but standing around anywhere in the city, especially next to the River Tyne had never been on his agenda, otherwise he would have thrown an overcoat into the car.

Earlier in the day, before the body had been found in the restaurant, Andrews had called Sandra, suggesting they went out for a quiet meal together that evening. Once she had happily agreed, he had gone on to book a table at a local restaurant and get in touch with Ben, Agnes's favourite taxi driver, to pick them up at Sandra's flat. He had even told Ben that he would also need him to collect them later. For that reason, Michael hadn't even considered wearing an overcoat when he left home to pick up his fiancée. However, just as Ben pulled up outside Sandra's flat, Michael's mobile phone had rung. As it turned out, the call was from the DCI ordering him to get to the Millennium Hotel right away. While Michael had gone out to send the taxi on its way, he had left Sandra to call the restaurant and cancel the booking. Once that was done, they had both clambered into his car. Though he had tried to persuade Sandra to stay home, saying that whatever was going on at the hotel could take some time to sort out, she had insisted on accompanying him, suggesting that there might still be time to go somewhere else from there. Yet, it had still crossed his mind that it might simply have been an excuse for her to be included in the case. Even so, he had still hoped he might persuade her to take a taxi home once they arrived at the hotel. But the DCI had ended that idea the moment he suggested Sandra should join Agnes for dinner. Now, standing out here in the cold, Andrews was furious at the thought of Sandra having dinner with Agnes in one of the most expensive hotels in the city. It was *he* who should be having dinner with his wonderful fiancée this evening; not Agnes. He had planned to talk to Sandra about setting a date for their wedding...

"Yes, I would!" Alan burst out, interrupting his sergeant's thoughts. "But only because I wouldn't have understood the situation."

"What do you mean – you wouldn't have understood the situation?" Andrews retorted. "What's so different about this situation to any other? We, as detectives, either look into all options at the time of the inquiry, or else we're wasting our time, *sir.*"

The sergeant gazed up towards the sky. The light was fading fast. Any minute now, the streetlights would automatically switch on, shortly followed by the colourful lights on both the Tyne and Millennium Bridges – or was it the other way around? Did the lights on the bridges come on first? He couldn't remember. But, at that moment, he didn't care. If they didn't come on at all tonight, it wouldn't bother him. He had more to worry about than whether the damn lights came on. At this moment, it was possible he was in the process of losing his job; but, more importantly, he could have already lost the only woman he had ever loved.

"I need a drink!" Andrews declared.

Even as he spoke, the sergeant shoved his hands into his trouser pockets and sloped off down the steps leading from the hotel. He didn't want to go back to his lonely flat and he definitely had no intention of returning to the station, which was what usually ensued after visiting a suspect; whether they had actually interviewed the person or not. All Andrews really wanted to do was find some pub where he could blend in with the crowd and get drunk.

Alan watched his sergeant reach the bottom of the steps before pulling to a halt. After a slight hesitation, Andrews strode off towards the pleasant café-cum-restaurant just around the corner.

It had been in that very café, almost a year ago, that Agnes had first broken the news to Alan that she was happy for them to be together as a twosome. Until then, though they had been out for dinner together several times, he had always felt there was something standing in the way of their relationship. He still had absolutely no idea how or why Agnes had suddenly made the decision at that particular moment and he had never asked; believing she would tell him in her own time. Yet, so far, she had never mentioned it.

Alan shivered. Even though he was wearing a heavy overcoat, the damp chill was still filtering through the thick material. Andrews must be almost at freezing point in the suit he only wore on special occasions. It was only then that Alan realised that tonight was to have been such an occasion for his sergeant. He recalled hearing Andrews on the phone earlier that day, reserving a table at a restaurant, followed up a few minutes later by booking a taxi. At the time, he hadn't thought too much about it. But now, Alan realised that tonight was to have been a special evening for his sergeant and his fiancée.

"Where're you going for a drink?" Alan called out, even though he had already guessed. "Don't forget, the hotel has a bar," he added, throwing his thumb back over his shoulder.

"I've no idea where I'm going but I'm certainly not going back into the hotel," Andrews replied, without turning around. "I'll probably go to the café by the Millennium Bridge," he continued. "It's just a few yards away."

"Do you mind if I join you?"

"Do you *have* to, sir?" Andrews stopped walking and swung around. "I *can* find my own way there."

"Yes, I know that, sergeant. However, my real concern is whether you'll be in a fit enough state to find your way back."

Chapter Thirteen

By a stroke of luck, Agnes and Sandra finished their meal at the same time as Jamison and Deborah. However, it was mostly because they'd almost wolfed down the last course to keep up with them. Still keeping an eye on the couple, Agnes did manage to overhear Jamison suggest that they retire to the drawing room for coffee. There were a few other words that followed that she didn't pick up, but at least she was aware that the drawing room was to be their first stop.

Neither Agnes nor Sandra really felt they could eat or drink anything else. Both had eaten too much, while the wine had certainly overflowed. Yet, as it would be a good excuse to follow the couple into the drawing room, Agnes ordered coffee to be served there.

"Now, if only we could start a conversation with the couple, we might learn something about them," Agnes said, as they left the dining room. "You know the kind of thing I mean – why they are staying here? Is it for work or pleasure? However, the answer we're really seeking is whether he really is called Robert Jamison. But it could be a little difficult to interrupt their conversation, as they're trying so very hard to show themselves as being totally in love."

"Do you think they're putting on an act?" Sandra asked. "They looked like a real couple to me. She was all over him." She coughed. "If you see what I mean."

Agnes tapped her lips, as she traced her mind back to when she saw the couple holding hands across the table. "Yes, I understand what you're saying. But I have a feeling that what we're seeing is not the real thing – at least not in his case."

Sandra nodded. "So, you think he's pulling the wool over everyone's eyes – including Deborah?"

"Yes, I do. But it's only a thought buzzing around in my head." Agnes broke off for a second. "Anyway, I believe we need to talk to this couple before they head off into the sunset, or wherever else they're going. Yet, we can't just plonk ourselves down in front of them…"

"It's okay, I get the picture," Sandra replied. "Leave it to me." And she strode off.

"Wait!" Agnes said. But it was too late; Sandra was already making her way into the drawing room.

"This really is the most wonderful hotel, Agnes," Sandra spoke out loud, as she burst into the room and threw herself onto one of the plump sofas positioned only a short distance from where Robert and Deborah were sitting.

"Thank you so much for inviting me to join you this evening," she added, as Agnes slipped gracefully into the sofa next to her. "I simply can't understand why on earth my fiancé has never suggested bringing me here for a meal."

Gazing around the drawing room, Sandra allowed her eyes to fall on the couple she and Agnes had followed in here. They were both staring at her.

"Oh, my goodness," Sandra said, flinging her hand across her mouth. "I'm ever so sorry for disturbing you. But you see, I have never been here before and am a little overwhelmed."

Robert nodded. "That's okay. Yes, it is a wonderful hotel. I came here a few years back and enjoyed it so much that now, I come back here two or three times a year."

"You do?" Sandra replied, clapped her hands together, excitedly. "In that case it *really* must be good." She paused. "Have you come far?"

"No. Well, at least not too far. I live in London." Jamison laughed. "It's not as though I live in Australia, is it?"

"No!" Sandra laughed. "Australia! Now, that's somewhere I would really call too far to travel for a brief stay here on Tyneside."

Agnes sat quietly and watched, as Sandra turned her attention to Deborah.

"I'm really sorry for my intrusion," Sandra continued. "But, like I said, I was so excited at being here that I didn't notice you both sitting there. Please enjoy the rest of your evening." She paused. "Perhaps you'd allow me to buy you both a drink to make up for my interruption."

Agnes had to admit, Sandra was either very clever, or a darn good actress. So far, she had gained the information that Robert Jamison lived in London, yet came to this hotel on a regular basis.

Agnes held her breath while Robert and Deborah considered Sandra's offer. If they were to agree, then the couple would have to at least continue the conversation for a little longer, if not reciprocate in kind.

A moment later, Robert turned back to Sandra and thanked her for the offer. "However, there's no need," he continued. "Besides, we've already ordered coffee to be served here in the drawing room."

"Yes, we did the same thing," Sandra replied. "We felt it was getting a little too warm in the dining room." She flapped her hands in front of her face as she spoke. "But maybe that's due to the amount of wine we drank over dinner."

"In that case, perhaps you'd both care to join us." Deborah pointed at the sofa opposite where they were sitting.

"Yes, we'd love to," Sandra replied, glancing at Agnes. Though her glimpse had been swift, she had found time to raise her eyebrows at her friend.

It took less than a minute for the two ladies to gather up their belongings and settle themselves on the sofa opposite the couple.

"My name is Sandra, and this is my friend, Agnes. This is my first time at this hotel..." She giggled. "But of course you must know that by now. However, my friend has stayed at the hotel several times. In fact, Agnes stayed here for several months until she found herself a lovely apartment."

At that point, Sandra stopped talking and swung around to face her friend as though indicating that it was now her turn to carry on the conversation.

"That must mean you lived here at the hotel for quite a while," Deborah said. "How wonderful – but tell me, what made you decide to stay at this hotel in the first place? Did someone recommend it to you?"

"No. Not at all," Agnes replied, slowly. "I think I should explain. I was simply visiting the area to catch up with my past." She lifted one shoulder. "You see, I was born here in the northeast, but my family moved away when I was a child and I had never been back. Therefore, when I had to choose where to stay, I hadn't a clue. In the end, I simply closed my eyes and stuck a pin into a list of hotels shown on a leaflet which had fallen out of a magazine I happened to be reading at the time."

"Gosh," Robert said, taking a deep breath. "I don't think I could compete with that. My first visit here was…"

However, before he could say anything further, he was interrupted by a waiter suddenly appearing in drawing room.

"Coffee is served," he said.

Agnes couldn't quite decide whether the look which had suddenly spread across Robert's face was one of relief, or annoyance at the interruption.

"So sorry for the delay," the waiter continued. "They were a little snowed under in the kitchen. Several guests turned up at once."

He set the tray down onto the coffee table and began to lay out the crockery and the two pots of coffee. However, Deborah intervened, telling him that she would see to it. After Robert had slipped him a tip, the waiter disappeared out of the door.

"Now, where was I?" Robert turned his attention back to Agnes and Sandra, while Deborah set about pouring out the coffee. "Oh yes, I was going to tell you how I found this hotel." He sat back in his chair. "Well, the truth is, I didn't really find it myself. It was chosen for me by the company I work for. They do that when they need to send a member of their staff to another part of the country." He shrugged. "It was as simple as that – and, as they were footing the bill, I couldn't really argue with them. However, as it turned out, I was delighted with their choice on that particular occasion."

"Does that mean you've found yourself in some dismal hotels in the past?" Agnes asked, thoughtfully.

If this man was an undercover agent with MI5 or some other secret service department, then it was more than likely that he would have had to bed down in some squalid conditions in the past.

"Yes, indeed I have," Robert replied.

"Then I guess we were both lucky that we ended up here," Agnes replied. She smiled at Deborah, who was sliding a cup of coffee across the table towards her, before turning her attention back to Robert. "What line of work are you in?"

Agnes was well aware that, if he really *was* a secret agent, there was no way he would reveal that piece of information to her, or anyone else. Nevertheless, as they had been getting on so well, she had felt that her question wasn't totally out of line. It was possible that she could learn something useful, either from what he said, or how he said it.

Without taking his eyes from Agnes, Robert leaned forward and picked up his coffee and took a long drink, before replacing it on the saucer.

"I think we should change the subject and talk about something that will include the other two ladies. We seem to have taken over the conversation."

"Yes. You're absolutely right," Agnes replied.

She looked across the coffee table towards Deborah. "Is Robert your fiancé?"

Deborah glanced at Robert and smiled. "No, we're just good friends. By the way, my name is Deborah, Deborah Swift."

"Sorry if I spoke out of turn. But you just look so good together, I thought that you were an item – as they say." Agnes replied. "I take it that you live and work locally?"

"Yes. Actually, I work for Rent-a-Temp, the temporary staff agency. It's quite fun, really. You never know where you will be next."

"Gosh, you must have a number of skills under your belt," Sandra said. "I'm a secretary in a large organisation."

Deborah nodded. "Yes, I do office work most of the time, but there have been times when I've helped out in market stalls, staff canteens – I've even stood in for shop assistants. I tend to be able to put my hand to anything now."

Agnes couldn't help noticing that Robert looked a little uneasy, though she couldn't think why.

"Well done. I'm most impressed" Agnes said, looking back at Deborah. "But I'm sure you don't want to talk about your work during your time off." She paused. "Do you both have plans for the rest of the evening?"

"Yes, we're going to the theatre," Deborah replied, excitedly. "You might have heard that the West End show, *Les Misérables,* is touring the country and it's showing at the Theatre Royal at the moment. I did try to book seats for us both when I realised that Robert was going to be in Newcastle this week. But they had sold out." She paused and glanced at Robert. "However, when I mentioned it to Robert, he said he would ring them and he managed to get two tickets in the front row of the Circle at the very last minute. I really don't know how he did it. He's a star. But then, he did the same thing once before…"

"It's really quite simple." Robert interrupted. "There's no reason to make a big deal out of it, Deborah." He shrugged. "I just happened to ring the theatre at the right time. Apparently, a couple had phoned in to cancel their seats only a few minutes earlier. It was pure luck that I called the ticket office when I did." He then turned his attention to Deborah. "I think we should be making a move, Debs," he said, rising to his feet. "We don't want to miss the opening and, don't forget, I promised you a special drink in the bar before we took our seats."

"Did you? I don't remember you saying anything about…"

"Of course I did!" Robert interrupted, sharply. "And, may I add, you were all for it, at the time. But now, since we got talking here," he gestured towards Agnes, "it appears you've forgotten about me and everything I said."

"Sorry, Robert. Yes, I remember now." Deborah took Robert's outstretched hand and rose from the sofa. "I guess you weren't the only one to have had a little too much to drink over dinner," she added, looking down at Sandra.

"I think you're right. I better hold on to you, otherwise you're likely to fall over." Robert replied. "At least I've put our coats in the car, so it saves you having to struggle with the stairs."

"You have?" Deborah looked surprised.

"Yes. I came and collected your coat, while you were still deciding what to wear. Don't you remember that, either?"

The moment he finished speaking, Robert took Deborah's arm and led her towards the door.

"Enjoy your evening," Agnes called out as they left, "and Deborah, if I see you in the morning, you must tell me all about the show. I might even try to get tickets."

"I'll be sure to look out for you at breakfast," Deborah replied.

If she said anything further, it was lost as Jamison almost dragged her out of the drawing room.

"Well, what do you make of that?" Sandra asked, once the couple had disappeared. "He seemed to be in a hurry to get Deborah away from us."

"Actually, I think he was in *too* much of a hurry," Agnes replied.

Sandra thought for a moment. "I suppose if he had promised Deborah a drink before the show, they would need to get a move on."

Agnes nodded. "But, what if he hadn't mentioned anything about going into the bar before the show? You have to admit, Deborah appeared to be most surprised when he mentioned it. Even when she claimed she had simply forgotten about his suggestion, her face still showed a slight expression of disbelief. But then, there is the coat thing."

"What about the coat thing?" Sandra asked. "Didn't Robert explain that he had collected her coat while she was still getting dressed?"

"Yes, that's what he said. But think about it for a moment, Sandra. There's no way he could have gone to her room and collected her coat while she was there, without her remembering. Therefore, *if* he had her coat in the car, then he must have gone into her room without her knowledge."

Sandra's jaw dropped. "So, you think he was lying and she covered for him yet again? Why on earth would she do that?" She paused. "Maybe she'll explain it all when we see her at breakfast tomorrow morning."

"I think you mean, *if* we see her at breakfast tomorrow morning," Agnes replied, thoughtfully.

Chapter Fourteen

In the restaurant, only a short distance away from the hotel, Alan and his sergeant were having dinner together. When they walked through the doors, the thought of having a meal hadn't even crossed Andrews's mind. His only intention had been to sit in the bar and get drunk while feeling sorry for himself. However, his DCI had insisted on accompanying him and, while ordering the drinks, he had asked for a menu.

"For goodness' sake, Michael, this is just a tiff between you and Sandra. It'll all blow over in the morning when you apologise to her – unless, of course, you want to drag it out by getting drunk and being thrown out of here." Alan looked around the restaurant. "They could even call the police!"

Michael laughed. "I am the police, or have you forgotten?"

"Then act like a police officer," Alan replied, sharply. He waited a few moments before continuing. "Look, let's enjoy the meal, and then we'll go back to the apartment and talk it through. I'm sure we'll find a solution to your problem."

"You're a good one to talk, sir," Andrews said, thinking back to earlier in the evening. "If I remember rightly, Agnes also put you in your place a short while ago. To my mind, we're in the same boat."

"It was all a misunderstanding. I've already admitted that I was wrong and should have mentioned the name of the victim..."

"Yes. We both know what you should have done." Andrews cut into the large, juicy steak on his plate as he spoke. "Nevertheless, you didn't do it. You didn't apologise to *Agnes* for your outburst." He paused and looked up at his boss. "I'm assuming there was an outburst from you – yes, of course there was. That's how you work when things aren't going your way. Anyway, instead of apologising – and maybe picking up a little further information from Agnes – you stormed off in a tantrum. But, not only that, you called me and ruined my evening."

Andrews looked up when there was no reply and found Alan staring down at his plate. "It sounds to me as though that boat we're stuck in is somewhere way out at sea," he added.

Alan heaved a sigh but then, catching the eye of a passing waiter, he ordered two extra-large whiskies, before turning back to Andrews. "Yes, I guess we are – but only for tonight," he said. "Tomorrow we'll both head for the shore."

"And then what?" Andrews asked. After what he had said to his DCI, he would be lucky if he still had a job tomorrow.

"We'll pull down the sail and make a landing."

* * *

Still sitting in the drawing room, Agnes suddenly began to feel very tired. No, it was more than that, she was exhausted. It was hard to believe it was only at lunchtime today she had found a body in the restaurant. So much had happened since then. She would like to have spent more time talking to Sandra about their recent conversation with Deborah and, more importantly, with Robert Jamison; if that was his real name. Apart from him having the same name as the dead man, there was something else about him that bothered her. Yet she couldn't put her finger on it. But what annoyed Agnes even more was that she still couldn't remember where she had seen him earlier in the day. Had she imagined it?

"Are you okay?" Sandra reached across and placed her hand on Agnes's arm. "You looked miles away."

"Yes, I'm fine, Sandra. It's just that I feel so tired. It's been such a long day. I think I need to go up to my room and settle down for the night. But first," she added clapping her hands on her knees, "we need to get a room sorted out for you."

"I could just take a taxi back to my flat, if that would make things easier. I doubt if Michael will go there now since I told him I wasn't going home."

"Nonsense, there's no need for that. I'm sure there'll be a room available. But, if not, then you can spend the night with me. Problem solved."

However, due to a cancellation, there was a room vacant and it was only a few doors along from Agnes.

"The room comes ready equipped with most things you need for an overnight stay – soap, toothpaste, toothbrush and towels etcetera," Sam, one of the evening receptionists, explained.

"And I'll probably have anything else you'll need." Agnes grinned. "When I nipped home earlier today, I brought back enough stuff to keep me going for a few days."

"I can vouch for that," one of the porters said, as he passed the desk. "I took Mrs Lockwood's luggage upstairs. I recall thinking that a trolley might be needed," he added, with a grin.

Agnes had gone a little over the top for a one night stay. But, secretly, she had hoped Alan might agree to stay at the hotel for a few days. Therefore she had packed two suitcases of their clothes.

"It wasn't that bad," Agnes laughed. "Anyway, Sandra, if you need anything, it's more than likely I'll have it." She paused. "Unless you want to take a taxi back to your flat and grab a few things. Anyway, I'm sorry, but I really must go to my room. I feel shattered. But don't let me stop you from enjoying your stay here. Order whatever you like and put it on my tab."

"I can't do that..."

"Yes, you can. No arguments. I'll leave you to check in, but I must go upstairs to my room before someone needs to carry me there."

* * *

Once in her room, Agnes made sure the door was tightly closed, before sliding the security chain firmly into place. She had never forgotten the night she had been drugged while in the bar downstairs. Back then, she had been followed into her room, simply because the door hadn't closed quickly enough. Since that night, the hotel had called in a firm to make sure the door mechanism was set to swing the doors tightly shut once someone entered or left their room. Nevertheless, Agnes always checked it for herself. Once bitten, twice shy – as the old saying goes.

Satisfied that the door was securely locked, Agnes threw her bag and key-card onto the bed and slumped down into a chair by the window. Though her body felt drained and ready to switch off, her brain was still active. She couldn't stop thinking about how Jamison had kept turning the conversation around the moment it became his turn to explain something about himself. But more than that, there was the rather over-the-top performance he gave when Deborah couldn't remember him mentioning anything about a drink in the bar before the show.

Agnes shook her head as she thought back to that moment. Talk about being dramatic; his performance would certainly have wooed a West End theatre audience. Nevertheless, she had seen through his showmanship. He was behaving like man desperate to get Deborah out of the room before she said something he wanted kept secret.

Heaving herself out of her chair, Agnes moved closer to the window and peered down onto the brightly lit quayside. She looked at a group of young people wandering towards the café-restaurant near the Millennium Bridge. If she could have found the strength, she would have gone down to the quayside herself – not to join the young set; she was well past that stage. No. It would have been to unchain herself from the quiet life to which she now felt bound. Though, on the bright side, she was due to go to London shortly.

A meeting of the board of directors of Harrison's Department Store, which she had owned since her parents' death, was to be held very soon and she needed to attend. A trip to the bright lights of London would bring back the much needed sparkle to her life. It wasn't that she didn't like being here on Tyneside; she loved it. But, since she and Alan had moved away from the hotel into the apartment, her life seemed to have taken three or four steps backwards.

The thought of Alan made her wonder what he was he was doing at this moment. Had he gone back to their apartment, or had he found something else to occupy his mind? But, at this moment, did she care what he was doing? Not a damn!

Stepping away from the window, Agnes looked across at her bed. It was starting to look more inviting than ever. Maybe her brain was beginning to respect how the rest of her body felt. Without a moment's hesitation, she pulled the curtains, quickly undressed and almost fell into the bed. Maybe she could consider the rest of the case as she lay in bed.

However, that wasn't about to happen, as she dropped off to sleep the second her head hit the pillow.

* * *

Once the doors of the lift swept shut, taking Agnes up to her room, Sandra gave the necessary details to Sam, the receptionist.

"Perhaps I should take a look at my room," she said, glancing down at the key-card in her hand. "Fourth floor, you said?"

"Yes," Sam replied. He glanced at his colleague. "Will you be okay for a few minutes while I show Miss Anderson to her room?"

"No problem, take your time, it's rather quiet at the moment."

Upstairs, Sam escorted Sandra along the corridor until they reached room 409.

"Here we are," he said. "Mrs Lockwood is only a couple of doors away," Sam added, sweeping his hand back the way they had come. "So you have a friend nearby." He opened the door and stepped inside. "Nevertheless, don't hesitate to ring downstairs if you need anything," he added. "Now, would you like me show you around the room?"

"No. It's okay, thank you," Sandra replied.

Once Sam had headed back downstairs, Sandra peered around the room. It was everything she had imagined it would be, and more. Television, sofa, small refrigerator, table and chairs by the window and even a complimentary bottle of red wine sitting on a tray with two glasses. The room had everything she could possibly want, everything – except Michael. Maybe she shouldn't have been so harsh downstairs. Yet, at the same time, he should stop treating her like a child. Surely that was no way to start married life! Casting those thoughts aside, she stepped across to the window to take a look at the view and was delighted to find that it looked down onto the quayside; slightly to the left of the Millennium Bridge. Having booked in at the last minute, she had envisioned the room would face out onto a large collection of garbage bins in the hotel's back yard.

Still staring down at the quayside, Sandra thought she caught a glimpse of Deborah. She couldn't quite make out the woman's face as she was too far away, but it was the outfit she was wearing that had caught her eye. It certainly looked like the one Deborah was wearing earlier that evening. Then she dismissed the notion. Both Deborah and Robert would be at the Theatre Royal now. Besides, if it was Deborah strolling along the quayside, surely she would be wearing her coat.

Sandra stepped away from the window and deliberated over whether to go back to her flat to pick up some clothes. She was due a few days off work, and it would be so nice to spend them here – even though it would cost her a tidy sum of money. Brushing the cost to one side, she decided to collect some clothes from her flat and book the room for a further few days. Or, maybe that should be the other way around. Perhaps she should make sure the room was free for the next few days, before heading off to her flat. Someone else could have already booked the room in advance.

Why was it that the simplest of things always ended up being so complicated?

Chapter Fifteen

Agnes opened her eyes the next morning and turned to look at the clock. It was only seven o'clock; fortunately she hadn't overslept. She had felt so tired the previous evening, it wouldn't have surprised her if she had slept until midday. She lay quietly for a few minutes before flinging the duvet to one side and leaping out of bed. A nice warm shower was exactly what she needed now.

A short while later, Agnes was seated in the dining room reading the local daily newspaper. She had told the waiter that she was waiting for someone to join her, before ordering breakfast.

"Did you sleep well?" Sandra asked, once she had joined her friend.

"Absolutely, I went out like a light. And you?"

"Yes, I slept very well." Sandra paused. "Actually, I decided to go back to my flat and pick up a few things."

"So I noticed." Agnes smiled. "You're wearing a different outfit this morning and it's certainly not one of mine."

"But that's not all." Sandra swallowed hard. "I've also extended my booking into the hotel for a few days."

"Yes, I thought you might." Agnes paused. "Actually, so have I. After bringing so many clothes yesterday, I thought why not enjoy a few days here? I spoke to the staff when I came downstairs this morning."

At that moment, the waiter reappeared.

"Can you give us another couple of minutes, please?" Agnes asked. She gave the waiter a huge smile. "We've been chatting so much we haven't had a chance to look at the menu."

"Yes, of course, madam. I'll come back later."

"It was a last-minute decision," Sandra said, once the waiter had left. "I hadn't really planned on spending extra time here. But that was before I saw the room. It is so spacious and has everything a guest could possibly want."

"I agree. But now we must look at the menu and decide what we want for breakfast before the waiter reappears. Then, you and I can crack on with the case – if you're still up for it."

"You try to stop me!"

Once they had finished their breakfast and were leaving the dining room, Agnes saw Keith Nichols entering the hotel.

"Don't tell me you're here because there's been a murder!" Agnes asked, feigning an expression of horror. She had already guessed that the real reason for his visit was to see Sue.

"No." Keith held up his hands and laughed. "Relax. Sue said she might have a couple of hours off, so I thought I'd surprise her."

"I'm sure she'll be delighted to see you," Agnes replied. "This is my friend, Sandra," she added. "She just happens to be staying here for a few days."

"Nice to meet you, Sandra," he said. "But, if you ladies will excuse me, I need to find Sue."

"Then you don't need to look very far, Keith."

They all swung around to see where the voice came from, only to find Sue walking towards them.

"I'd just been going through a few figures with Mr Jenkins," Sue explained. "But as I came out of his office, I saw you standing here and couldn't help overhearing your remark."

"I must say, you have excellent hearing," Agnes said.

Sue laughed as she drew closer to the group. "It comes in handy sometimes. So, what are you doing here," she added, turning her attention to Keith.

"You mentioned having a couple of hours off – I just thought that as I was free, we could have a coffee together. What do you say?"

"Yes, that would be lovely. But we'll have that coffee somewhere away from the hotel." Sue looked around. "If I am anywhere in the building, the staff assume I'm on duty. I'm just surprised that no one has pounced on me already." She laughed. "There's rather a nice place just around the corner." She looked at Agnes. "I believe it's your favourite haunt."

Agnes was about to reply when she caught sight of one of the domestic staff, hurrying down the stairs. Reaching the reception area, the woman paused and looked around, before making her way to the reception desk. After a quick word with Pauline, she hurried across towards Sue.

"I think you might have spoken too soon, Sue," Agnes said, nodding towards the woman rushing towards them.

Now that the woman was closer, Agnes noticed that her auburn hair was untidily bunched up at the back of her head. Her cap, part of the domestic staff uniform, was tilted towards one side of her head, rather than positioned neatly on top, while the rest of her navy-blue uniform looked as though it could do with a good wash. Agnes couldn't recall seeing this woman while she had been staying at the hotel. She would certainly have remembered. Therefore, she assumed she was a new member of staff.

Sue didn't have time to reply, as the young woman suddenly sprang in front of her.

"I need to talk to you, Miss Matthews," she said. "It's important."

"What is it?" Sue asked. "Tell me, has someone upset you?"

"No. It's not that."

Sue drew the woman to one side. "Okay, tell me what's happened."

"Upstairs. In one of the rooms, I saw a man – he was in bed." She hesitated for a second. "I didn't just barge into the room – I knocked first. I only went in when there was no reply. I don't want anyone thinking that I burst into his room unannounced."

"Yes, I understand," Sue said. She placed her arm around the woman's shoulders in an effort to calm her down. "But tell me, what about the man in bed?"

"I think – I think he might be dead! You see, when I tried to apologise for walking into his room, he didn't answer, so I moved a little closer to the bed and tried again. But there was still no sound or movement from his direction." The young woman pulled a handkerchief from her pocket and wiped her eyes. "That's when I came out and closed the door. I couldn't let anyone see him like that, could I?"

"You did the right thing. Tell me, which room is this man in? My friend," Sue added, gesturing towards Keith, "is a doctor. He'll go up and see to him."

"Err... Sorry... It's on the first floor, room 106," the woman replied, stuffing her handkerchief back into her pocket.

Though she was standing some distance away, Agnes had picked up every word. But it was hearing the room number that made her glance towards Sandra. That was Robert Jamison's room. By the time Agnes looked back, Sue had retrieved the master key-card from the room cleaner.

"You'd better get up to room 106 right away, Keith," she said, handing him the card. "Take this, mine is in my office. I'll follow you in a few minutes."

Once Keith had headed off towards the stairs, Sue escorted the young woman across to the reception desk.

"Pauline, could you take this young woman to my office? She's had a bit of a shock."

"Yes, of course," Pauline replied, as she walked from behind the desk.

"Once you're there, make her a large mug of hot, sweet tea. Be sure to stay with her until I get back. And please, don't either of you speak to anyone about this."

Pauline nodded and began to lead the woman down the corridor to Sue's office.

"Is it okay if we come with you?" Agnes asked, as Sue began to hurry across the reception towards the stairs.

Though the lift was now back on the ground floor, the word was that the young man who was standing in while Larry was away loved to gossip. For the time being, at least, Sue needed to keep the news of a death in the hotel under control. Swinging around, she looked back at Agnes. If it had been anyone else, she would have said no. But Agnes had helped the police solve a few cases in recent months.

"Yes, of course."

Once they had reached the first floor, they hurried along the corridor to room 106. Sue was surprised to find that the door was slightly ajar. Stepping inside, they saw Keith bent over the bed.

"I didn't hear you open the door," he said, looking up at the three women.

"There was no need, the door was already open," Sue replied. "I thought you had left it ajar for us."

"No. I gave it a push once I was in the room. Though I thought these doors were meant to close automatically. Anyway," he added, turning back to the man lying on the bed, "I can confirm that the woman was right – the man is dead."

The three women moved a little further into the room to take a look at the man in the bed. He was lying on his back and, as he looked so peaceful, it was more than likely the poor man had simply died in his sleep.

Nevertheless, without raising their heads an inch, Agnes and Sandra glanced at each other for a brief moment.

Though this was Robert Jamison's room, this was not the man they had met in the drawing room the previous evening.

* * *

Shortly afterwards, the three women left the room, leaving Keith alone with the body. While Sue hurried off downstairs to inform the manager of the news, Agnes and Sandra remained in the corridor a little way from Robert Jamison's room.

Just before they left, Agnes had asked Keith if he could tell her the time of death. After some deliberation as to whether he should pass on such information at this stage, he finally stated that he believed the man had been dead for at least twelve hours.

"But that didn't come from me," he had added, firmly.

Agnes had been more than happy to oblige, suggesting he didn't mention to the DCI and his sergeant that he had seen either of them.

"Where do we go from here?" Sandra was the first to speak. "This is the last thing I expected."

"Me, too," Agnes replied. "It's bad enough for the hotel that a man has been found dead in bed. But, when it turns out that it's not even the man who should be in the bed... well, that's going to take some working out."

"No doubt Alan and Michael will be here in a few minutes. I suppose we'll have to confess that the dead man in Jamison's room isn't actually Jamison," Sandra said, thoughtfully. "Then they'll start laying down the law about how we should have told them that Jamison was sitting across from us last night. I can almost see Michael wagging his finger at me, as though I was a 'naughty little girl'."

"Yes, I agree," Agnes replied. "Not about Michael wagging his finger at you, only the bit about them laying down the law. But that could only happen if they were able to find us. I think we need to have a little time to think this through before we see them. Plus, we must also try to find Deborah before she hears this news from the police. She must be staying here, so the first thing..."

"Wait!" Sandra interrupted, suddenly remembering she had seen Deborah last evening. "There's something I need to tell you about her first." She thought for a moment. "Look, why not grab your coat and anything else you would normally take with you while on a shopping trip and join me in my room. If Alan *does* go to your room, he'll think you've gone out on a shopping spree and aren't even aware of the body found in the hotel."

"Brilliant idea," Agnes replied. But then she had a thought. "Won't Michael come to your room? I mean, he might enquire at the desk as to whether you're staying here."

"He can enquire all he likes, but the answer he'll receive will be no. You see, I took the precaution of using my grandmother's maiden name, Anderson, when I checked in." Sandra grinned. "I know I told him I was going to stay with a friend, but I did wonder whether he might check at the desk, just in case."

"Sandra, you would make a great detective," Agnes said, clapping her hands on her friend's shoulders. "But now, we must get upstairs."

Once they had reached the fourth floor they parted company. Agnes rushed into her room to grab a few things, while Sandra hurried on to her room, further down the corridor. A short while later, Agnes carefully peered out of her door to make sure no one was lurking around before creeping along the corridor to her friend's room.

"I must say this is all very exciting," Sandra said, the moment Agnes was safely in the room.

"Yes, it is," Agnes replied. "But we must keep our voices down. We don't want anyone to know there are two people in this room."

"I'd already thought of that," Sandra said. She went across to the television and switched it on. Flicking through a few news channels, she eventually found one showing an old episode of *NCIS*. "I think Gibbs, calling the shots, should cover our voices, especially if we sit over by the window – well away from the door."

A few minutes later, Sandra began the discussion by going through what she had seen the previous evening.

"The clothes the woman was wearing certainly matched Deborah's. But I dismissed the thought for two reasons." She went on to say why she had decided it couldn't be Deborah.

Sandra looked at her friend, who hadn't said a word during her dialogue.

"You're very quiet, Agnes. What are you thinking?"

Chapter Sixteen

Alan and his sergeant leapt from the car and hurried into the hotel. Once they had received the call about a body being found in the Millennium Hotel, they had rushed out of the office, only pausing to grab their coats.

Inside the hotel, they found Mr Jenkins pacing the floor in the reception area.

"The body was found on the first floor – room 106," he said. Pulling a handkerchief from his pocket, he wiped his forehead. "I haven't been up to the room. However, I understand Dr Nichols has checked the man and has confirmed that he is dead." He pointed towards the lift. "I see that the lift is on its way down. It'll be here in a moment."

"Thanks, but we'll take the stairs," Alan called out, as he hurried across towards the staircase.

"How the hell did Keith get here before us?" he mumbled to his sergeant, once they were well out of earshot.

"I have no idea, sir," Andrews replied.

At that moment, the sergeant really didn't care who might have got there before them. He had woken up with the most frightful headache and it was still bothering him. The bright lights in the reception hadn't helped. *Did they really need such bright lights at this time of the morning?* Andrews was aware that it was due to having too many drinks the previous evening. Yet, despite the DCI trying to stop him, he had caught the waiter's eye at every opportunity. Now, he could only hope the pathologist would find the person had died through natural causes. Then he could return to the office and slump in his chair.

By the time Andrews reached the first floor, Alan was already tapping on the door. "Come on, sergeant, get a move on," Alan called out.

"I'm coming, sir," Andrews puffed. How could a man almost twice his age mount the stairs so quickly? "It's just that the stairs…"

Whatever else he was planning to say was lost when Dr Nichols opened the door.

"Come in, but take care, the scene hasn't been checked out yet," Keith said, as he led them into the room. But then he stopped and swung around. "By the way, make sure the door closes properly behind you. There seems to be a fault with the mechanism."

"Yes, we already know about that. We found it ajar yesterday, when we…" Andrews stopped abruptly when he saw the DCI's icy glare.

Keith looked amused as he glanced at each of the two detectives in turn. "So, you guys have been in here before. But don't worry, sergeant," he added, lifting a finger to his lips. "I won't say a word."

"We just wanted to talk to the man, but the door was open and…"

"… And you walked in," Keith interrupted. "Yes, I get it. Perhaps you should stop talking, Michael."

Shaking his head, Andrews took a small step backwards, unable to believe he had given away the fact that he and the DCI had searched the room illegally. For goodness' sake, how much *had* he had to drink last night?

By now, Keith had turned his attention back to Alan. "I'm afraid I can't tell you very much at the moment. I need to get him back to the lab. However, from what I can see, I believe he died about twelve hours ago."

"Twelve hours!" Alan blew a sigh. "The killer could be well away from the area by now. They could even be out of the country…"

"Hang on a minute," Keith interrupted, "aren't you getting ahead of yourself? I didn't say he had been murdered. He could have died in his sleep. Until I do the post-mortem, even I don't know for sure how he died."

Alan looked down at the bed again. Keith was right. The man did look very peaceful lying there.

"Yes, sorry about that," Alan blustered. "I guess that after the last person by the name of Jamison was murdered, I took it for granted that much the same thing had happened here." He glanced back down at the bed. "Have you pulled back the duvet, Keith? I'm just a little curious about what he's wearing." He gestured towards the bed. "From what I can see, he appears to be wearing a T-shirt. Is that part of the modern day pyjamas-cum-lounge wear, as they call it, or might he have been out jogging and simply leapt into bed when he got back?"

"No, I haven't pulled back the duvet," Keith replied. "Like I said, I don't want to touch anything in this room until my team arrive." He frowned. "For heaven's sake, Alan, photographs, fingerprints and other things need to be taken before anything is touched. You know that! You would be furious if someone tampered with a crime scene before forensics arrived. But," he added, in a more quiet tone, "I believe T-shirts and joggers are part of the nightwear scene now."

"Okay," Alan replied, sullenly. He hated being put down by someone younger than himself. "However, I have another question. As you're here on the scene, Dr Nichols," he added, raising his eyebrows, "might I ask why your team aren't here, too? As I recall, you all usually arrive together."

The pathologist grinned. "Why are you asking me that? Surely you don't think I had anything to do with this?" Keith stared at the chief inspector's stern expression for a moment. "My goodness, you do, don't you? You damn well think I'm involved with this," he said, gesturing towards the body. "I hate to disappoint you, but I had only just arrived at the hotel this morning when the body was discovered. I called to speak to Sue Matthews about the two of us having a coffee together. It was while we were talking that one of the domestic staff interrupted, claiming there was a dead body in one of the rooms." He paused. "Are you satisfied, or do I need to contact a solicitor?"

"Keith, I didn't think you had…" Alan began awkwardly. But, before he could apologise, a knock on the door stopped him from saying anything further.

"That'll be my team," Keith said, crisply. "Perhaps you and your sergeant could let them in on your way out."

* * *

"Well, that didn't go well. How could you possibly think that Keith was involved in the death of…?"

The sergeant broke off and pulled a face. He hadn't meant to sound so judgemental. But, as he himself had fallen foul of everything he had done over the last twenty-four hours, it felt good to know that even the DCI could put his foot in it sometimes.

Alan remained silent as he stomped down the stairs towards the reception area.

"But I'm sure Keith will have realised you didn't mean anything by it. He was probably upset at having to put off having his date with Sue," Andrews added, trying to smooth over his previous remark.

Though Alan was aware his sergeant was droning on about something, he wasn't really listening. These last two days had been a nightmare. Two men had been found dead. One was murdered, while the second – well, they didn't have information on that. Though, he had to admit, it did look like natural causes. Then there was the robbery at the jewellers, which Jones and Smithers were looking into at this very moment, as well as the argument he had had with Agnes and now, he had almost accused the pathologist of murder. Nevertheless, despite all that, it was his outburst at Agnes which concerned him the most. It was possible that she might never want to speak to him again.

"Are you all right, sir?"

His sergeant sounded concerned. Andrews had expected to be chastised after his comments a few moments earlier. Yet Alan had remained silent.

"Yes, of course I am. I was just mulling over the case," Alan lied. By now, they had reached the ground floor.

"Then, where do you think we should go from here, sir? As I see it, we're at a dead end until Dr Nichols is able to get back to us about the body found earlier this morning." Andrews paused. "But Jones might have some news regarding the robbery."

Alan heaved a sigh. His sergeant was right. They had nothing at all to work on until Keith was able to give them any further news – unless... By now, The DCI's mind was working overtime. Was it possible that Agnes had learned something since their last meeting in the dining room the previous evening? Or, more to the point, might she have known something even then, but had kept it to herself?

Alan swung around to face Andrews. "I think we should find Agnes and Sandra. I think they might know something."

"No! I'm sure Sandra would have told me if she knew anything..." The sergeant broke off, reflecting how he and Sandra had parted the previous evening. She hadn't wanted to speak to him about anything, let alone the case. "But, maybe you're right," he agreed, in almost a whisper.

Alan didn't say anything further. Instead, he marched towards the reception desk, his sergeant following lamely behind.

"Mrs Lockwood booked a room here yesterday. I understand it was for one night," he said, the moment Pauline stepped up to the desk. "Has she has checked out yet?"

"Let me see." Pauline looked at Alan and smiled sweetly, as she very slowly tapped the keys on the computer. She wasn't used to being spoken to in such an abrupt manner. Visitors at such a prestigious hotel as The Millennium were usually more polite. "It will only take a moment," she added, as she continued to tap her fingers on the keys.

Pauline was well aware that Mrs Lockwood had changed her booking arrangements, thus enabling her to stay on indefinitely. But she wasn't about to pass on that information so quickly.

"By the way," she said, looking up from the keyboard. "Might I ask who you are? You must understand that information regarding our guests is not passed on to the general public."

"I am Chief Inspector Alan Johnson as you, and your colleague, very well know," Alan replied, holding up his badge. "This is my sergeant," he added, gesturing towards Andrews, who was standing some way behind him. "Now, can you get on with it?"

"Yes, I think so," Pauline replied, with a hollow smile. "But I'm sure that you, of all people, will be aware that hotels in the region were recently requested to check out anyone making enquiries regarding the guests. I understand the idea came from Deputy Chief Superintendent Blake." She looked back at the computer. "I've found Mrs Lockwood. It appears she changed her plans yesterday afternoon. From what I see here, she has booked the room for the unforeseeable future." Pauline looked up at Alan. "Does that help – Chief Inspector?"

For a moment, Alan was too staggered to speak. Yet, he managed to regain enough composure to ask the receptionist to call her room and inform her that he wanted to speak to her. "Tell her it's urgent."

"There's no reply," Pauline said, replacing the receiver. "Perhaps you might care to try again later."

"What about Sandra Williams," Michael intervened, suddenly stepping forward. "Is she staying here?"

Again, Pauline slowly turned her head to look back at the computer and tapped in the name. "No," she said. "I'm afraid not. There is no one by that name staying here at the moment."

As the detectives moved away from the desk, Alan pulled out his phone and called Agnes. But there was no reply.

"Try calling Sandra, they might be out somewhere together," Alan suggested.

Andrews nodded and took out his phone. When there was no reply and it went to voicemail, he tried again; maybe she hadn't heard her phone the first time. "I'm afraid there's no reply," he said, stuffing the phone back into his pocket. "It could be that she's at work."

"Then why don't you try calling her office?" Alan snapped.

While Andrews punched in the number to Sandra's office, Alan stepped back to the desk. "Tell me, is Mrs Lockwood's room booked in her name only, or is my name included?"

Pauline tapped a few keys on the computer. "Yes, Chief Inspector Johnson, your name does appear on the original booking." She glanced at the screen again. "It doesn't seem to have been deleted since she updated her stay."

"Then, might I have a key to the room?"

"Yes, of course." Pauline opened a drawer and took out a key-card. After adding the room number through some device hidden beneath the desk surface, she handed it to Alan. "Enjoy your stay."

Alan turned back to Andrews, only to find him slumped on the sofa at the other side of the reception.

"What's happened?"

"Sandra isn't at the office. She rang in this morning to say she was taking a few days off. They also told me that she didn't say why or where she was going." Andrews took a deep breath. "This is all my fault. I should have been more understanding."

"Look, Andrews, moping around on the sofa isn't going to get you anywhere. I have the key-card to Agnes's room. If we find her, she might know where Sandra has gone. So come on, let's take a look."

A few minutes later, the two detectives were upstairs in Agnes's room.

Alan had heaved a sigh of relief when he entered the room. The bed had been made and, thankfully, no one was lying in it. He had been concerned that he might find Agnes dead; struck down in her room like the man in room 106. Though, as far as he knew, she had no connection to either of the victims. Pulling open the wardrobe doors, he found that her coat, scarf and handbag were missing. Obviously Agnes was out somewhere; probably the Eldon Square shopping mall.

"Maybe Sandra is with her," he added, trying to reassure Andrews. "You know how they enjoy shopping together. I'll try calling Agnes again later," Alan said, closing the wardrobe doors.

"When you came up here, did you think she might be hiding in her room and not answering your calls, sir?"

"No, of course not, Andrews. I just wondered whether she had brought any of my stuff when she decided to stay here for a few days," Alan lied.

"And had she? Brought any of your clothes, I mean," Andrews persisted.

"No!" Alan mumbled, as he headed towards the door. "She hadn't."

Chapter Seventeen

Upstairs, in Sandra's room, a mobile phone rang.

"That's my phone," Agnes said, recognising the ring tone. "It'll probably be Alan wondering where I am. Yes, it is Alan," she added, pulling the phone from her pocket.

"Are you going to answer?" Sandra asked, as she watched Agnes stare down at her phone.

"No," Agnes replied. She laid the phone down on the table.

After the bust-up the day before, Agnes wasn't ready to talk to him. She had been so angry the previous evening that she hadn't even bothered to unpack his suitcase. Instead, she had placed it at one side of the wardrobe.

A couple of minutes later, Sandra's phone rang and, like Agnes, she ignored it when she saw the call was from Michael.

"Now, where were we before we were interrupted?" Sandra asked, placing her phone back into her pocket.

"I don't think we'd come up with very much, actually," Agnes replied, with a sigh. "You told me about seeing someone outside the hotel last night, who, at first sight, you thought to be Deborah. But then you changed your mind."

"Yes," Sandra replied. "I thought it was Deborah mainly because of what the person was wearing – the woman's dress was certainly the same colour. But then, I realised Deborah would have been wearing a coat. Robert told her that it was already in the car. Besides, they would both have been at the theatre at that point." She paused. "But I told you all this earlier, Agnes and you didn't seem to think it was important."

"Yes, I know," Agnes replied, thoughtfully. "However, I've given everything a great deal more thought and I now wonder whether they really *were* going to the theatre. Jamison could have made the whole thing up."

Sandra sounded doubtful. "Surely Deborah would have known whether or not they had seats booked at the Theatre Royal? She must have seen the tickets as she appeared to know exactly where they would be sitting."

"Yes, that's true," Agnes said slowly, as she thought back to the previous evening. "Nevertheless, I still picked up vibes telling me that Jamison was lying about several things, giving me the impression he was making things up as he went along."

Agnes sat back in her chair and thought for a few minutes.

"Look," she said. "I know we went through all this last night, but it could be worth us giving it another shot. We might remember something we missed earlier. Take, for instance, when Robert suddenly reminded Deborah they were having drinks in the theatre bar. She looked surprised. But then, more importantly, when he told her that both their coats were already in the car, she looked alarmed."

"Yes, I agree. Deborah did appear to be surprised, bewildered, even – but *alarmed*?" Sandra shook her head. "This is getting beyond me. I know it's still early in the day, but I really could do with a glass of something."

Agnes looked at her watch. It was later than she thought. But perhaps still a little too early to open a bottle without something to eat. "Yes, me too," she replied. "But maybe we should go downstairs and have some lunch. They do room service here at the hotel. Yet, I think it would do us good to get out of the room."

"Good idea." Sandra picked up her handbag and was about to head for the door, when Agnes stopped her.

"Sandra, aren't you forgetting something?"

Sandra spread out her arms as she glanced at herself in the mirror. "No, I'm fully dressed. I have shoes on my feet and a bag in my hand – what else do I need?"

"Your coat."

"My coat?" Sandra looked puzzled. "But we're only going downstairs. Why would I need my coat?"

Agnes picked up her own coat from the bed and slipped it on. "For the same reason you gave me earlier. If Alan was to come back to the hotel, for whatever reason, I would like him to think I had been out when he called. As for you, if Michael was also present, I'm sure he would notice that you didn't have a coat with you and..."

"Yes, I get the picture," Sandra nodded. "He would wonder whether I might be staying at the hotel after all. Okay, good thinking, Agnes. I'll get my coat."

A few minutes later, they were making their way towards the stairs.

* * *

"Now, would you please explain to me what you meant just before we left the room?" Sandra asked, once they were both seated in the bar. "Why on earth would Deborah be alarmed because Robert had put her coat in the car? Surprised, maybe, but *alarmed*?"

Agnes rested her arms on the table and looked around to make sure no one was close enough to listen in to their conversation.

"I think there was more to it than merely being surprised. I really believe Deborah was alarmed, or even, frightened."

"But why would she be?" Sandra leaned forward in her chair. "For goodness' sake, why get upset because he'd put her coat in the car?"

"I think it was more because he'd been *able* to put her coat in the car," Agnes replied. "From the way Deborah spoke, I took it to mean that she wasn't sharing a room with Jamison. Therefore, she was probably shocked to learn that he had gained access to her room without her knowledge."

"But how do you know that she wasn't sharing a room with Jamison? I thought they were a twosome! It certainly looked that way to me."

"That's exactly what he wanted everyone to think. I admit he's certainly a good actor. But, as to how I knew they weren't sharing a room, that's simple – I checked it out."

Sandra chewed her lip while the headwaiter removed the cork from a bottle of wine. He was about to add some to each of their glasses but Agnes thanked him and said she would see to it.

"I won't ask where you found such information – I think I can guess," Sandra said, once the waiter had left. "But, isn't it against the rules of the hotel for anyone to pass on information about the guests?"

"Probably, but then there are a number of rules people overlook. For instance, there are people who book into hotels under a false name," Agnes replied, as she picked up the bottle of wine and poured some into each glass. "I think that is frowned on in some hotels, especially in London."

"*Touché*," Sandra replied.

Both women laughed.

"Right," Sandra said, when their laughter died down. "Getting back to Jamison and Deborah, if they had separate rooms, they should only have had one key-card each – the one to their own room. Yet, if your theory is correct, some way or another Jamison was able to gain access to Deborah's room to pick up her coat."

"Yes and maybe find anything else he was looking for," Agnes replied, thoughtfully.

"What could he be looking for?" Sandra sounded surprised. "Secret messages from another boyfriend, perhaps? Okay, I think Jamison was a bit over the top, but surely he didn't believe she had another man in tow? From where I sat, I got the impression that Deborah was rather smitten with Jamison and, don't forget, she was ready to lie for him. Incidentally…"

Sandra paused when the waiter arrived with their lunch.

"Do you need anything further?" the waiter asked.

"No, we're fine," Agnes replied, after an enquiring glance at Sandra. "What did you mean by – 'anything else'?" Sandra continued, once the waiter was out of earshot. "She's a young woman enjoying life, what could she possibly have to hide?"

"I have no idea – at least, not yet," Agnes admitted, as she picked up her cutlery. "But that's at the top of the list of things we need to find out."

Chapter Eighteen

"I'm sorry about what happened earlier today, Keith. I really don't know what came over me. But, if it helps, you're not the only person I've upset recently – I seem to have it in for everyone at the moment."

At the station an hour or so earlier, while the DCI had been talking to the detectives about the body found in the hotel, Andrews had handed out a photograph Alan had taken at the scene. Yet, no one recalled having seen the man before.

At that point, Alan had been just about to lose his temper. Surely someone had learned something? It was then he decided to call into the laboratory in the hope that Keith might have some news. He was aware the pathologist hadn't had much time to examine the body thoroughly. But the DCI was feeling desperate. So far, they were no further forward with the murder at the restaurant, let alone the second body found at the hotel. And there was still the jewellery robbery to solve. He was starting to feel a bit overwhelmed.

"I'm sure I'll get over it – in time, Alan," Keith replied. He grinned to himself as he turned back to look at the body stretched out on the table. "However, I don't think I can help you very much at the moment. All I can say is that there are no knife or gunshot wounds on the body and, so far, I haven't found any problems with his organs – though I haven't finished my examination. Meanwhile, tests are being taken of his stomach contents as we speak." He paused. "As for your question about what he was wearing at the time of his death – the top certainly looks like a T-shirt, while the bottoms could be called joggers. But, in this day and age, they are often called nightwear. Anyway, they are being tested for DNA just in case someone else put them on the body either before or after his death – though the predator could have been wearing gloves. Nevertheless, the results should be here very soon."

"I hope so," Alan replied. He scratched his head. "As you know, we now have two men claiming to have the same name. Both have been found dead. One was shot in the forehead in a restaurant, while the other appears to have died in his bed at the hotel… though we don't yet know the cause of his death."

"Did any of your team happen to find anything tucked away in the victim's room that might help us?" Andrews asked.

"Not really." Keith turned his attention to the sergeant. "Nothing had been disturbed and any ID found in the room, credit cards, driver's license, etc., were all made out in the name of Robert Jamison. However, there is one thing that might interest you. A woman's beige scarf was found on the floor at the other side of the bed. I say scarf, but it's quite large, so it may be something women drape around their shoulders. But whatever it is, it's being checked out for DNA along with the other things I mentioned. I'm waiting for the results from forensics as we speak."

"Why the hell didn't you tell me about this scarf thing when we were with you earlier?" Alan blurted out the words before he could stop himself. He hadn't meant to sound so irritated.

"Because, Chief Inspector, if you recall, I told you that I hadn't gone any further into the room. Therefore, I didn't know the scarf was there," Keith replied, calmly.

Keith turned to Sergeant Andrews. "Might I and the DCI have a moment?"

Andrews nodded and quickly headed towards the door.

Once Keith was sure that Andrews had closed the door behind him, he turned back to the DCI.

"I think you need to stop and think about what's going on with you, Alan. Maybe it's this case. Perhaps it's beginning to get to you." Keith paused as he considered his last remark. "But I don't believe that's the reason," he added slowly. "I've known you for a good few years and I've never known you to allow any case to get in the way of your relationship with your friends and colleagues." He placed a finger on his chin as he thought for a few seconds. "Therefore, I believe there's something else bothering you."

"Have you decided to add psychiatry to your list of achievements, Keith? Or are you merely taking a guess?" Alan gave a broad smile as he spoke, trying to make a joke of the whole thing, though, truthfully, Keith had hit the nail on the head.

"Life is good for me at the moment," he continued. "What on earth could be 'bothering me'?" He made quotation marks in the air as he spoke.

"Then I'm happy for you, Alan, long may it last," Keith replied, though he didn't sound convinced that the DCI was telling him the truth. "But, getting back to the case, rest assured I'll be in touch as soon as I learn anything further."

Alan heaved a sigh as he left the room and went in search of his sergeant. He had managed to talk his way out of the situation with the pathologist, or at least he thought he had. But Keith was right. There *was* something bothering him, causing him to lash out at his friends and colleagues and that something, or, to be correct, that *someone*, was Agnes. He had treated her badly, almost screaming at her the other evening and he hadn't yet got over it. Thankfully, she was a strong woman and could stand up for herself. Otherwise, she could well have been on the next flight to Australia to rejoin her two sons and he might never have seen her again. Yet even knowing that didn't really help. He needed to meet her privately and talk things through with her. Maybe if...

"Is everything okay, sir?" Andrews interrupted his thoughts as he sidled up to the DCI.

"Yes. Of course it is, sergeant. Why wouldn't it be?"

"No reason," Andrews mumbled.

"I think it's time we got back to the station to find out whether anyone has managed to come up with something helpful."

However, when Alan started the engine of his car, he didn't pull away from the kerb. Instead, he sat back in his seat for a long moment.

"Are you okay, sir?" Andrews sounded concerned. "Would you like me to drive?"

"No. I'm fine, sergeant, but there's been a change of plan."

"There has? I guess that means you have had a sudden inspiration." Andrews rubbed his hands together in anticipation, as Alan flipped the car into gear and moved out into the road. It wouldn't be the first time the DCI had suddenly come up with a great idea, which had led them to solving the case. "Don't keep me in suspense, sir. If we aren't going to the station, where *are* we going?"

"To the Millennium Hotel, Andrews, I need to catch up with Agnes."

* * *

"Why don't we take a stroll along the quayside," Agnes suggested, once she and Sandra had finished their lunch. "The fresh air might do us both good and give us some inspiration."

"Good idea," Sandra replied. "Besides, despite all my prods, you still haven't told me why you think Deborah had a secret to hide."

It was true. Agnes had evaded the question a few times during lunch, mainly because she didn't really have an answer. It was just a feeling that had niggled away at her, since she and Sandra had met up with the couple in the drawing room the previous evening. How could she explain something to anyone, when she wasn't even clear about it herself?

Outside, the air was cool and smelled invigorating. Obviously, the tide had turned inwards at the coast and was bringing a welcome breath of fresh air to the city.

"You'll have to let me work it out for myself first," Agnes replied. "At the moment, it's just a feeling I have. Yet I feel sure I'm right. Let's sit over there for a few minutes," she added, pointing towards a bench overlooking the river.

"There are so many things bothering me with this case, and I can't seem to get my head around any of them," Agnes continued, once they were seated.

"Would it help if we talked them all through?" Sandra suggested. "You know how the saying goes – two heads are..."

"... better than one," Agnes chanted the last three words, in time with Sandra. "Okay, I'll lay out what's troubling me."

Before Agnes could say another word, a car horn bellowed out from somewhere behind where they were sitting. Both she and Sandra swung around, half expecting to see two drivers shaking their fists at each other. Instead, what they found was Alan parked at the kerbside, with Andrews sitting alongside him. Both men were waving at them.

"We'll talk about this later," Agnes told Sandra, "and don't forget, if the subject comes up about how we happen to be together – we bumped into each other while out shopping this morning."

Sandra nodded, before rising to her feet. She didn't have time to say anything further as, a few moments later, Michael landed in front of her.

"I've been so worried about you, Sandra," he said, flinging his arms around her. "Where were you? I tried calling your mobile, but I couldn't get through."

"That's probably because I was at the shopping mall earlier today," Sandra said, when Michael finally withdrew his arms. "You know how difficult it is to hear your phone ring while you're in there. Anyway, Agnes and I just happened to bump into each other and after a quick chat, we decided to have lunch together. Then, we thought a stroll along the quayside would be good." She paused. "Actually, Mike, it's been quite fun – doing my own thing for a change."

"What do you mean by that?" Andrews asked, glancing at the DCI as he spoke. "You *always* do your own thing."

"No, I don't think so," Sandra replied, slowly. "You *do* like to have a say in whatever I do. Last night, the idea of me spending the night with a friend rather than rush home with you, seemed to bowl you over. If I hadn't stuck to my decision, you would have whipped me back to my flat and made some lovey-dovey excuse to stay with me to make sure I didn't attempt to contact anyone."

"I wouldn't do that, Sandra. Why would I?"

"Because, Mike, you want to keep me under your thumb." Sandra paused for a moment and looked at where Agnes had been sitting, only to find that Alan, having parked the car, had joined Agnes and they were standing a few feet away.

"Anyway, how are you both getting on with the case?" Sandra asked, changing the subject.

"It's not going very well, Sandra." It was Alan who answered, having overheard her question. "Actually, that's the reason we stopped by," he added, turning to face Agnes. "I was rather hoping that you might have picked up the odd snippet or two about the man who was found dead in his room at the hotel early this morning." He hesitated. "But of course, if you've been out all morning, you won't have heard about it."

Agnes was aware Alan was testing her; the tone in his voice gave him away.

Knowing her the way he did, he would know that if a body had been found in one of the rooms, she would never have left the hotel to go shopping. Luckily, Agnes had prepared herself for this moment, though she hadn't expected it to come quite so soon. She looked at Alan for a few seconds, giving the impression that maybe she hadn't heard him correctly.

"Are you saying a man was found dead in one of the rooms?" Agnes uttered, clutching her chest with one hand, while the other was tucked neatly in her coat pocket with her fingers crossed. "Oh, my goodness, no, I didn't know about that. It must have happened after I left. I did leave rather early." She paused and shook her head slowly for effect. "Who was he?"

Alan was watching Agnes closely while she spoke. Her reaction to the news looked quite genuine.

"It seems the man was Robert Jamison. His body was found by one of the domestic staff," he said, after a long pause.

"Jamison…" Agnes repeated the name slowly. "Yes, he was the man I saw walking into the hotel yesterday afternoon." She looked up at Alan. "I believe he was the man you wanted to speak to. But, due to rather unfortunate circumstances, he'd already left his room before you arrived."

Agnes knew she was rubbing salt into the sore wound. Nevertheless, she couldn't resist having a dig. Besides, she was sure Alan had only come to see her in an effort to gain further information.

"How did he die – or don't you know that yet?" she added.

Alan shuffled his feet. "No, I'm afraid not. Keith is still doing the post-mortem. However, he did mention that when Jamison was found, he had been dead for at least twelve hours. Other than that, we have nothing to get us started."

"Don't forget about the lady's scarf found at the scene," Andrews reminded him, "and the man's wallet and credit cards."

"Yes," Alan agreed. "But they're all still with forensics. I just wish they would hurry up."

"They found a lady's scarf in his room?" Sandra queried, feeling she had been silent long enough. "Perhaps he was sharing the room with a woman, in which case it could have been hers."

"No. We enquired at the desk. Apparently Jamison was booked into the room alone. Though I suppose he could have had a visitor at some point," Andrews admitted. "Anyway, it was Keith who said it was a woman's scarf. He said it was beige and described it as a large, silk-like scarf. Apparently it was found lying on the floor on other side of the bed, which was probably why we didn't see it when we were in the room. We needed to stay close to the entrance for fear of contaminating the scene." He paused for a couple of seconds. "In the meantime, we are also investigating a robbery at a jewellery shop on Northumberland Street…"

Andrews looked at his boss, hoping he hadn't said too much. Though the DCI wasn't scowling, he didn't look too thrilled.

"A robbery in the centre of Newcastle?" Agnes said, now turning her attention to Alan. "It sounds as though you have your hands full."

"Yes," Alan replied. "But I have other detectives working on that case."

"Even so, I would like to hear a little more about it."

Alan shrugged his shoulders. "There's nothing much to say. I understand that the jewellery, a prized collection on loan from a foreign court, was touring the country's jewellery shops. When it finally reached London, it was due to go on show at a large gallery. However, one minute the jewellery was in the case waiting for a party of the region's jewellery experts to see it and the next, it had disappeared. But, if it is so expensive, how on earth is the thief going to sell it?"

"Unless the thief already has a buyer," Agnes suggested.

"Yes, you're right," Alan replied. He had already thought of that, but wondered whether Agnes would come up with the same idea.

"This whole thing tends to take me back to the jewellery thefts at the hotel," Agnes continued, recollecting the events that had taken place when she had first gone to stay at the Millennium. "But back then, there was something even more expensive at stake than someone's necklace, though nobody realised that at the time."

There was a short silence, before Agnes spoke again.

"However, getting back to the man found dead in the room, I guess there really isn't much for you go on, assuming the man was murdered, of course. If he had died of natural causes then it would be case closed – well, at least *this* case would be closed. You'd still have the first Jamison case to investigate, as well as the robbery."

Alan turned away and rested his elbows on the railings. Clasping his hands together, he peered across the river towards the Sage building. He and Agnes had spent some great evenings together at various concerts held there. His life, after meeting up with her again after so many years, had changed for the better. They had even bought an apartment together. But now, since their argument, would things ever be the same again?

Agnes came alongside him and they glanced at each other for a moment, before they both looked down at the river. Alan was the first to speak.

"Agnes, tell me, do you recall seeing Jamison in the hotel at any time, other than your initial sighting in the reception? This could be really important to the case."

Agnes swallowed hard. That statement was something she hadn't been prepared for. She knew it was time to pass on everything she and Sandra had learned – especially the part about the dead man not being the Jamison she had seen the previous evening. But surely Alan and his team would learn that for themselves, once the results of the DNA tests taken from both the body and other items in the room came back from forensics. Therefore, she was left with two questions. Was it her duty to tell the police what she knew? The answer to that was yes. The other question, rattling around in her head, was did she really *want* to tell him what she knew?

Might this be the right time to come clean?

Chapter Nineteen

Once the two detectives had climbed back into the car and driven away, Agnes and Sandra slowly made their way back to the bench and sat down.

"I certainly wasn't expecting to see Mike and Alan descending on us," Sandra said. "Though I must admit, it has cleared the air a little between the two of us. But what about you and Alan – did you manage to make it up? You both looked deep in conversation so I assumed things were a little better."

"No. Not really," Agnes mumbled.

Sandra looked towards the slowly flowing river for a long moment, before turning back to Agnes. "I'm sorry to hear that. I always thought that you two were good together."

"He wanted to know whether I had seen Jamison since yesterday afternoon."

"And you said you hadn't?"

"Yes. However, I must say I did give it some thought before I made the decision. But in the end, I just wasn't prepared to give in to him."

"Why? Surely it was the perfect opportunity for you to overcome the problem dividing you both."

"Sandra, the problem dividing Alan and I was caused by him. He still hasn't apologised for the way he spoke to me." Agnes paused for a moment. "Anyway, the moment he asked the question after all his pussyfooting around, I realised that the only reason he had sought me out today was to seek out information. Normally, I would have been happy to help, but today I decided against it. Nor did I tell him that the man found dead in the room wasn't Jamison – well, not the one we saw, anyway. But they'll learn that once the DNA results come back." She smiled. "Who knows? Maybe he's called Jamison, too. That would certainly add more confusion." Agnes took a deep breath. "But, I'm pleased that all went well with you and Michael," she added, changing the subject.

"Yes." Sandra pressed her lips together and shook her head. "He was all over me – apologising for this, that and the other. But when he asked whether I would be at my flat tonight, I told him no, as I had already promised to meet a friend for dinner and then spend the night back at her place." She paused. "By the way, we didn't talk about the Jamison case, just in case you were wondering."

Agnes smiled. "I guess Michael has a lot more on his mind at the moment than just the police investigations." She glanced out across towards the river for a few moments. It looked so peaceful; certainly not like the way she felt. Her world had been turned upside down recently.

"Right, Agnes, enough about the menfolk." Sandra clasped her hands together as she spoke. "Getting back to where we were before we were interrupted, I believe you had something bothering you regarding the case."

"Yes, you're right." Agnes leaned back in the seat and took a deep breath, while she collected her thoughts together. "You'll recall me telling you about the man I found dead in the restaurant, and how I later learned he had a small wallet in a pocket concealed inside his trousers."

Sandra nodded. "Yes, you said Alan had told you about the different spellings of his surname."

"But then, later that day, a man turned up at the Millennium hotel while I was there. I had a feeling I'd seen him earlier, but couldn't re-member where – I still can't, actually. Anyway, moving on, I learned from the receptionists that his name was Robert Jamison with exactly the same spelling. Therefore, which one is the real MI5 agent – that is, if either of them really are MI5 agents? The way this case is going, there could still be another Robert Jamison out there somewhere." Agnes paused. "Sorry, I'm getting carried away. Are you still with me?"

"Yes," Sandra replied. "Carry on."

"Then, earlier today, we both learned that the second Robert Jamison, the one staying at the hotel, was suddenly found dead in his room. But, when we saw him, we found it wasn't the Jamison we had met. So who is this person and what was he doing in Jamison's bed? At the moment, we don't know his cause of death. Yet," Agnes clicked her tongue, "despite him looking so peaceful, I can't help wondering whether he, too, might have been murdered. Maybe the killer suddenly realised that he or she hadn't killed the right Jamison in the first place and had tried again. And now, just to add a little further confusion, we were told that a beige wrap was found in his room. We both know that it could be Deborah's – she had a beige wrap draped over her shoulders when we saw her last night. But we can't simply assume it belonged to her – we would need to see it for ourselves to be sure." Agnes fell silent, believing she had come to the end of her statement.

But then she had another thought. "Also, it might be helpful to know where the first Robert Jamison, the one I found dead, was staying. I doubt he was booked into the hotel, as I'm sure Sally or Pauline would have mentioned it – unless the two Jamisons were acting as one. Though I admit they didn't look alike." Agnes heaved a sigh. "And then there's the robbery at the jewellery shop."

"Do you think the robbery has anything to do with the murders?"

Agnes shrugged. "I have no idea – but I'm keeping an open mind."

"Gosh, Agnes, it's certainly one big problem."

"I think it's gone beyond that stage, Sandra. It's more what I'd call one big mystery!"

* * *

"Did you believe her?" Andrews asked his DCI.

By now, the two detectives had almost reached the station. They had discussed the case during the short journey from the quayside, even though they didn't really have anything new to share. Both were at a total loss as to where to even start the investigation. It was only when Alan turned into the road leading to the station that he had mentioned asking Agnes whether she had seen Jamison since her first sighting of the man the previous afternoon, but she'd said no.

"Yes, of course I believe her," Alan replied, pulling into the parking space marked for the DCI. "Why wouldn't I? I agree Agnes and I have had some differences lately, but she understands that this is a murder inquiry. She wouldn't lie about something so important. Besides," he added, switching off the engine, "I was watching her closely from the moment we met up, and I feel sure she was telling me the truth."

Alan opened the door of his car and stepped out onto the freshly-laid tarmac. He heard something crunch beneath his feet as he locked his car and headed towards the station entrance. Though he had tried to sound robust in his reply to Andrews, he couldn't really be sure whether Agnes had told him the truth or not. She could be so clever at keeping secrets. He needed to get this problem between them solved once and for all. But had it gone too far? Not once had she even hinted that he should join her at the hotel. Problems between them had arisen before, but they had certainly never been as serious as this.

"Are you sure it's okay to park here?" Andrews lifted his left foot and grimaced when he saw tarmac clinging to the sole of his shoe. He glanced at the empty spaces around the DCI's car. "Didn't we get a message asking us not to park here until the tarmac had set?"

"Did we?" Alan shrugged, without even looking around. "I don't re-member – maybe I missed it. For goodness' sake, Andrews, get a move on. We need to find out whether anyone has come up with anything which would help our investigations. Also, Jones and Smithers might have some news on the robbery."

Alan had been disappointed when the two detectives hadn't learned anything further from the waitress in the restaurant. Though she did confirm that she was sure she had seen him in a fight in Northumberland Street. "But he wasn't wearing a suit," she had told them. "He was in a pair of grey trousers and a scruffy shirt."

Now, inside the incident room, everyone shook their heads when the DCI asked the all-important question – had anyone anything further to report regarding the death of the two Robert Jamisons, or the robbery.

"For heaven's sake!" Alan roared, slamming his hand onto the notice board showing photographs of the two men. "Surely someone out there must recognise these men? Why on earth hasn't anyone come forward to identify them? Especially the first Jamison – his face has been plastered all over the newspapers and TV since his body was found. If he really *was* an MI5 agent, which I very much doubt due to the discrepancies found in his identity wallet, surely someone from London would have been in touch with the chief superintendent, even if only to stop any further news being passed to the media."

The DCI took a breath before continuing. "Also, we know that a man was peering through the window of the restaurant at about the same time as the victim headed towards the corridor." He pointed at another part of the board where an E-Fit face, as described by the woman at the restaurant, was displayed. "I appreciate that the rest of his description, torn jeans, etc., could fit a number of men wandering around the city. However, surely the ring through his nose could be a clue. The lady who described him said it was rather large. But…"

"He could very easily have removed it by now, sir," one of the team volunteered.

"Yes. Thank you, Grayson – I was just about to mention that. Yet," the DCI added, turning back to the rest of the group, "if he didn't know he was being watched, there would be no reason for him to remove it. Therefore, I suggest you still keep your eyes peeled for anyone matching that description. Though, at the same time, don't haul every man you see wearing torn jeans with a ring through his nose back to the station, or the desk sergeant will have a fit."

That statement brought a roar of laughter from the detectives.

"Take it easy, lads, or we'll have him up here to see what he's missing."

Mathers, the current desk sergeant, was an excellent police officer. Nevertheless, he ran a tight ship and wouldn't take kindly to droves of men being brought into the station, only for them to be released a few minutes later.

Now pointing to the photo of the second Jamison, Alan went on to say that they were still waiting to hear from the pathologist as to the reason for his death. "Dr Nichols was still working on the body when we left the laboratory," Alan continued. "All he could say at that point was that there were no signs of injury to the body, meaning the man hadn't been shot, stabbed, or strangled."

"Then surely it must mean the man died of natural causes," one of the detectives called out.

"That's what the sergeant and I first thought. But we'll have to wait for the full post-mortem before we can be sure. In the meantime, I want you all..."

It was at that moment that Alan's phone rang. Pulling the phone from his pocket, he saw that the call was from Dr Nichols. "I've got to take this, it's from the pathologist. I'll get back to you all in a few minutes. Andrews – with me," Alan called out, before heading towards the door.

"Give me a minute, Keith. I'm on my way back to my office," Alan spoke into the phone, as he hurried along the corridor towards his office. "Does this call mean you've finished the post-mortem?"

"Yes," Keith replied.

By now, both Alan and his sergeant had reached the office. Andrews made sure the door was firmly closed behind him before he strode across to his desk.

"Okay, Keith, what have you got for us?" Alan asked. He set his phone on speaker mode and laid it on his desk.

"Since I last spoke to you, I've been informed that there were no traces of poison in his stomach contents, though I gather he had drunk a large amount of alcohol the previous evening – by that, I mean a *really* large amount of alcohol. Also, after finishing my investigation of the body, I found that he had suffered a massive stroke, which…"

"So you're saying that this man died in bed from natural causes?" Alan interrupted, relieved that the man's death wouldn't instigate another murder inquiry.

However his reprieve was short-lived.

"No, I wasn't saying that at all, Alan. If you'll let me finish, I was about to tell you that I believe he was murdered."

"But how could he be…?" Alan began, but stopped when he realised that he should first hear what Keith had to say. "Okay, sorry, you were about to tell us before I interrupted. Please, carry on."

"Thank you." Keith took a deep breath. "What I was about to say was that I strongly believe air or gas was injected into the victim's veins. Then, when it reached his brain, it caused the stroke."

He paused, but, when neither of the detectives spoke, Keith recalled that, not being trained in the field of medicine, this would be totally new to them.

"Perhaps I should explain," he continued. "In layman's terms, if air is injected into the veins, it will form into an impenetrable bubble in the blood. This bubble of air, now tucked neatly inside the bloodstream, will be carried around the body. It is known as venous air embolism. Only if something was to burst that bubble, would the air blend in with its surroundings. If that were to happen, it's unlikely it would cause harm to the person involved. However, if the bubble isn't stopped, it will be carried with the blood flow until it reaches one of the organs of the body, which could lead to death. One single bubble of air in a syringe can cause a major problem to any organ. That's why you see nurses and doctors flicking a finger at a syringe before injecting a patient. They're simply making sure that any air trapped in the syringe is eliminated."

There was a long silence while Alan and his sergeant absorbed what the pathologist had just told them.

"How can you be so sure that air was injected into his body to cause the stroke?" Alan was the first to speak. "It still could have been due to natural causes."

"Yes, it could. That's why, on finding the victim had died of a stroke, I was more than surprised I hadn't come across any of the usual symptoms in my initial examination. For instance, the mouth wasn't drooping at one side. I state that because it's the most obvious sign of a stroke, but there are others. It was because those signs were missing that I decided to re-examine the body even more closely. It was only then that I found a tiny pinhole at the base of his skull – slightly above the hairline. This is where I suspect he had been injected."

Again there was a long silence.

"Halloo – are you guys still there?" Keith called down the phone. "You *do* realise I have another life outside of this laboratory."

"Sorry, Keith, I think Andrews and I were both a little knocked over by your findings," Alan said. "However, from what you're saying, it would suggest that whoever killed the man had some medical knowledge – right?"

"Could be," Keith agreed.

"But why didn't the victim wake up and call for help when the needle went into him?" Andrews asked. "Surely he must have felt the injection. I would have done." He stroked his left arm as he spoke. He'd had a few injections in the past and, even now, the thought of a needle piercing his flesh gave him the shivers.

"Good question, Andrews," Alan said. "However, going back to the amount of alcohol found in his stomach, it's possible he was too drunk to feel anything and slept right through the whole thing. Or perhaps, by the time the victim realised what was happening, it was already too late. But I rather think it was the first option."

"Exactly," Keith replied.

"Okay, I guess we've come full circle. Thank you, Keith. We'll leave you to get on with whatever you have to do next. Meanwhile, my team and I need to begin a new murder inquiry."

"So, where do we begin?" Andrews spoke the moment the DCI switched off his phone. "We have no idea who this second Jamison is, or why he was here in Newcastle in the first place."

"I agree. But then, we still don't know much about the first one, either. I guess I should get back to the incident room and bring the team up to date."

Sighing heavily, Alan rose from his chair and moved across to the window to peer down at the road below. The traffic was starting to build up. People were going home after a day at the office, or wherever else they worked. For them, their working day was over. But, for him and his team, it was only just beginning. Not literally, only insomuch that they had another murder case to solve on top of the one they were already working on and, so far, they were still in the dark. Also, there was the jewellery robbery.

In the past, gazing out of the window had helped to give Alan something positive to work on. However, today, it was letting him down badly.

"Back in the day," Alan said, as he slowly walked back to his desk, "catching a criminal was so much easier than it is now."

"How was that possible, sir? Surely we have more technology in this day and age. A click on a button of a computer by the right person at the right time can yield so much information."

"I agree," Alan replied. "But that goes for the criminals, too. They also can click on a button and hack into police computers to learn what the police have learned. No, give me the old days any time."

"I don't understand. What could be easier than checking a computer to find a suspect?"

Alan grinned. "Because all we had to do back then was round up the usual suspects. One of them would be our man – or if not, one of them would be able to point us in the right direction."

The DCI sighed. "But now I think we should get back to the incident room and bring the team up to speed."

Chapter Twenty

"Have you ever been inside Betty Surtees House, Sandra? It's a little way up the road over there, then the first road on the left." Agnes pointed towards a road leading off the quayside.

"No, I've never been inside. But I do know the story of how Betty Surtees climbed from a window in order to elope with her boyfriend."

"Yes, that's it. I found the story most interesting, so I went to take a look around the house shortly after I arrived in Newcastle…" Still gazing at the road leading to the historic house, Agnes suddenly stopped walking. "But then something happened…" She fell silent.

"For goodness' sake!" Sandra stepped in front of Agnes. "You can't just leave me hanging. What happened inside the house?"

"Nothing – nothing happened – at least, not while I was in the house." Agnes paused. "It was something I saw late one night when Alan and I found a body lying on the pavement outside the house."

"Yes, I recall Michael saying that you and Alan had found a body on the pavement." Sandra swallowed hard. "That alone would have bowled me over. So, what else did you see?"

"While Alan was checking whether the person was dead or not, I saw a face at an open window. But then, whoever it was pulled the window shut. Actually, it was the window Bessie Surtees climbed out of the night she eloped. Yet, no one came forward to say they had been inside the house at the time we found the body and when the key holder arrived, he swore that no member of staff had any reason to be in the building at that time of night. Nevertheless, the police searched inside looking for any intruder, but no one was found – and all the doors and windows were locked from the inside."

"Gosh, Agnes, do you think it might have been a ghost?"

"I feel sure it was a ghost. However, I've been in the house since then and I didn't see or even feel anything unnatural. I mentioned it to the man on the desk before I left, but he said that no one had ever said anything about seeing a ghost." Agnes laughed. "But I think the idea of a ghost wandering around his place of work gave him the shivers, as he kept looking over his shoulder while I was talking to him."

"I'm not surprised. I would have done the same." Sandra paused. "Are you suggesting that Betty Surtees House is somehow involved in this police investigation?"

"No, of course not. I just happened to glance in that direction and the memory of what happened that night came flooding back to me." Agnes sighed. "But, getting back to the case, I wonder whether Alan has heard anything further from Keith regarding the second death. Though, the way things stand between us, I doubt he'd pass on any information to me. Yet, if we're going to get anywhere, we need to know, and we need to know now."

"Can't *you* ask the pathologist, Agnes? I mean, you're quite good friends, aren't you?"

"Yes, we are, but only to a certain extent. I don't think our friendship extends to the point of him revealing the results of his post-mortem to me." Agnes fell silent.

After a few seconds, Sandra opened her mouth to say something, but Agnes beat her to it.

"Wait wait, Sandra," Agnes said, flapping her hands as she spoke. "I'm thinking."

"So am I," Sandra said.

"Okay, I've had an idea. But you first, what were you thinking?" Agnes asked.

"I'm thinking you're starting to sound a lot like Abby Sciuto!" Sandra laughed. "Now it's your turn."

* * *

"I'll have a word with him, though I'm not sure he'll tell me anything." Even though she was in the confines of her office, with the door tightly closed, Sue kept her voice low as she spoke into her phone. It wouldn't do for anyone to know she was about to ask Keith to breach the rules of his job by passing on information regarding his latest post-mortem.

"But if I do find out anything, you must promise me that you won't tell anyone where the information came from."

"I promise, Sue,"Agnes said, pressing the phone tightly to her ear. She and Sandra were still out on the quayside and the breeze was whistling around them, making it difficult to hear what Sandra was saying. "Get back to me the moment you learn anything."

"Do you really think he'll tell her anything?" Sandra asked, the moment Agnes ended the call. "It's a bit of a long shot."

"Yes, I agree. But we can only hope, as we've got absolutely nothing else to go on." Agnes paused. "Keep your fingers crossed."

* * *

"Keith didn't say anything about whether they had found anything on either the scarf or the garments the victim was wearing," Alan said.

The DCI and his sergeant were back in the office after informing the detectives that they now had two murder cases to solve.

"I guess they're still being examined."

"Yes, I agree, but it does seem to be taking quite a while. In the meantime, we're sitting here twiddling our thumbs instead of being out there – arresting the killer."

"Well, at least the lads are out showing the photos to everyone they meet."

Alan didn't reply. He was aware that Andrews was trying to sound positive. But, as far as the DCI was concerned, the sergeant needn't bother. The detectives had spent the last two days walking around the city, presenting the photo of the first Jamison to everyone they met, yet not one person had even shown the slightest sign that they recognised the man. Therefore, the way things were going, it was more than likely that the same thing would happen again with the photo of Jamison Number Two.

Alan rose from his chair but, instead of walking across to the window, he began to pace up and down the office while rubbing his hand up and down the back of his neck. This was another of his habits while thinking through a major police problem.

"One of these days, you're going to wear out that piece of carpet." Andrews grinned.

Alan stopped walking and looked down at the floor. "I doubt it, sergeant. I think I'll have given up the job long before that happens."

Chapter Twenty-One

Once the call to Sue had ended, Agnes and Sandra continued their walk along the quayside. The breeze, which had given a rather cool feel to the air a short while earlier, had dropped rather suddenly, so it now felt much warmer.

"I now understand why you love being here on the quayside," Sandra said. "It's been quite a while since I was last here, but after these last couple of days, I now realise what I've been missing."

"Wait until I introduce you to the wonderful café just around the corner from the hotel. You'll love it! On a fine day, you can sit outside with a glass of wine, or whatever takes your fancy." Agnes replied. "While I was staying at the hotel, I used to pop in there all the time. But," she sighed, "I don't get there so often since I moved out."

Sandra thought for a moment. "I might be totally wrong about this, Agnes, but you're giving me the impression that you're sorry you decided to leave the hotel and buy an apartment."

There was a long silence, leaving Sandra about to apologise for her intrusiveness. But then Agnes began to explain the reasoning behind the move.

"No. Don't misunderstand me, Sandra. I really do enjoy being in the apartment, just not all the time. I also love being at the hotel. If only we could split our time between the two..." Agnes shrugged. "You see," she continued, "in the apartment, once Alan goes off to work I'm left on my own all day, unless I decide to go out to the shops. But at the hotel, there is always someone around to chat to, even if it's only the staff." She held up her hand when Sandra opened her mouth to say something. "I know what you are going to say – I should have given the idea a great deal more thought." She shook her head. "You aren't the first to say that. Even Ben, the taxi driver I often use to get around the town, said much the same thing. But did I listen? No!"

The mention of the driver's name reminded Agnes about the offer she had made to him. So much had happened in the last twenty-four hours, she had almost forgotten about it. She really needed to get in touch with him and find out what he and his wife had decided. Though she felt she had won Ben over when she made the offer, he still had to convince his wife.

"And now, with this ongoing conflict between Alan and me, I'm not sure where we stand," Agnes continued. "It's all such a mess."

Sandra remained silent as they both continued to stroll along the quayside. Agnes's admission regarding her relationship with Alan had given her reason to consider her current situation with Michael. She did love him, even though he could be rather dominant at times, and he often told her how much he loved her. But, would he ever love her enough to confide in her? The way things stood at the moment, it would appear the answer to that question was a definite 'no'.

"I think I'll pop back to the hotel and see whether there's any sign of Deborah," Agnes said, suddenly swinging around to face the direction they had walked in.

"I'll come with you," Sandra offered, a little half-heartedly. She was lapping up the pleasure of seeing the quayside in a whole new light.

"There's no need, Sandra. You carry on and enjoy your new experience while you can." Agnes grinned. "Why not take a look around Betty Surtees House, or stroll up the road leading to Grey Street?"

"Thank you," Sandra said, peering at the steep road Agnes was pointing out.

"No need to thank me, just enjoy it. You can tell me all about it when we catch up later."

* * *

Agnes had almost reached the hotel when her phone rang. Pulling it from her pocket, she saw that it was a number she didn't recognise.

"Is that Agnes Lockwood?"

Though she believed she recognised the voice, she wasn't taking any chances.

"Who is this?"

"It's Keith Nichols – the pathologist."

"Hello, Keith." Agnes paused. "I suppose you're going to reprimand me for asking Sue to pry some answers from you."

"Yes, I am. Therefore, consider this a severe scolding." Keith paused. "I would rather you asked me yourself. I don't want Sue to be suspected of passing on privileged information."

"You're right, I shouldn't have involved Sue," Agnes replied. "It seemed a good idea at the time, but I admit I was wrong and I do apologise."

"I'm rather surprised you didn't ask Alan for the information. I passed on the latest developments to him and his sergeant only a short while ago."

"I'm afraid that Alan and I are experiencing differences of opinion at the moment."

Agnes had been tempted to make up some cock-and-bull story about how she hadn't been able to get in touch with Alan as he was out making inquiries into his recent cases. But she swiftly changed her mind and told him the truth.

"Not again! Don't you and Alan ever sit down and talk like you used to?"

"It would appear not. And," Agnes added, "I'd be grateful if you didn't mention this conversation to him."

"No problem there. I don't really want to get involved in your problems. However," Keith continued, "I'll bring you up to speed by giving you a few details."

"Thank you, Keith." Agnes moved across the pavement and sat down on a bench overlooking the river.

"As I explained to the DCI earlier, the dead man was murdered."

"Murdered?" Agnes echoed. "You're saying that someone killed him? But he looked so peaceful! Are you sure he didn't simply die of natural causes while he was asleep?"

"Yes, I said he was murdered and, yes, I'm sure he didn't die of natural causes," Keith replied, before going on to explain the details of how he had come to that conclusion.

Just then, there was a sharp tap on the door to the lab, before Phil, head of the forensics team, walked in, carrying a folder.

"Hold on a minute, I might have some further news," Keith said.

Phil held up the folder as he drew closer to the pathologist. "There's something in there I think will interest both you and the police." He thrust the folder into Keith's hand, before turning to leave. "Have a nice evening," he called out, as he closed the door behind him.

Agnes took those few moments to allow the news of the man's murder to sink in. Even though she had considered murder was a possibility, she was still rather taken aback.

"Okay, I'm back," Keith's voice came down the phone. "I've just been handed information you might be interested to hear. It's about a scarf which was found at the scene of the crime, and also the garments the man was wearing at the time of his death." He paused. "It appears that DNA *was* found on the scarf, but it doesn't match the victim. Nor, unfortunately, does it match anyone in our system."

"What about the clothes he was wearing?" Agnes asked.

"I was coming to that. You're beginning to sound like Alan," Keith joked.

"Sorry. I do tend to get carried away." Agnes forced a laugh, though humour was the last thing on her mind at the moment.

"Right," Keith replied with a chuckle. "It appears that the only DNA found on the clothes the victim was wearing, were from the victim himself. However, that doesn't mean the man actually put on the clothes himself, before climbing into bed. It could be that the murderer was wearing gloves when he entered the room and, once the victim was dead, he changed the man's clothes. But that is mere speculation on my part. There's no proof to say that's what happened – and, come to think of it, why would the murderer even bother to change the victim's clothes in the first place? It isn't easy to change the clothes of a dead man. Therefore, why not just leave the man wherever he was and get out of the room as fast as possible?" Keith scratched his head, waiting for some response from Agnes.

"It could be because the murderer wanted everyone to believe the man had died in his sleep," she replied, slowly. "That would mean there was no murder to solve and he, or she, could safely walk away without the fear of having to look over his shoulder for years to come."

Agnes fell silent after her last statement.

"Are you still there?" Keith asked.

"Yes, I'm here," Agnes replied.

"There's something else you should know," Keith took a deep breath. "The DNA found on the wallet and the credit cards in the room doesn't match the victim."

Agnes didn't reply. That was one piece of news she *had* expected to hear. At least she was off the hook. Alan would soon learn that the dead man wasn't the man who had booked the room. But then another thought entered her head. Was it possible that the dead man *had* booked the room, but the man she and Sandra had seen in the hotel had checked in before the victim arrived?

"Are you okay?" Keith sounded concerned when she didn't reply.

"Yes, I'm fine," Agnes said. "I just need a little time to go through what you said and try to put it all together. But thank you for talking to me and I promise not to say I heard anything from you." She was about to close her phone, when something else popped into her head. "Incidentally, Keith, I understand there was a robbery in one of the jewellery shops in the city centre yesterday."

"Yes. From what I've heard, the stolen jewellery was rather valuable."

"Yes, but isn't it unusual for a chain jewellery store to display such expensive pieces? I thought such items were only put on display in places where they could be well guarded." Agnes paused. "I gather fingerprints were taken from the case where the jewellery was kept. Do you happen to know whether they matched anyone other than the staff?"

"Only a few fingerprints were found and they all matched the staff on duty that morning." Keith paused. "I don't know why I'm telling you this, Agnes. It's supposed to be for police ears only."

"It's because you like me, Keith." Agnes laughed. "But seriously, I do appreciate you confiding in me. So," she continued, before the pathologist could change the subject, "you're saying that there weren't any prints from customers? Don't you think that strange? People tend to touch a cabinet when looking at something inside."

"Yes, that's true. However, we learned that the case had been cleaned, both inside and out, a short while earlier. The jewellery was due to be seen by various historians and experts of such collections, at around one o'clock."

"Thank you for that, Keith," Agnes said. "Now I'll let you to get on with whatever you were doing before I interrupted you."

"Before you go, can I ask why you're suddenly so interested in the robbery?"

"You know me, Keith. I like to dabble in all police investigations, just to keep the detectives on their toes."

Once their conversation had ended, Agnes thought through what had been said. Keith's first statement, 'the dead man had been murdered', hadn't really taken her by surprise. She had wondered about that from the moment she had seen him. Nevertheless, she had been interested to learn how he had died, even though some of the details had gone over her head. Then there were the DNA results; they did not match the dead man. It was then that another thought crossed her mind; had any clothes been found in the wardrobe or the chest of drawers? Only a wallet and a scarf had been mentioned.

Had Deborah and Jamison returned to his room after the show, before deciding to go on to some late night club? Nevertheless, even though that sounded plausible, given the timing of the man's death, it didn't sound possible.

Agnes stared out across the river, still trying to make sense of what she had learned. Where on earth should she go from here? Maybe finding both Deborah and Jamison should be at the top of the list. But, on reflection – what list? There was no list. Neither she nor Sandra had found anything to even start making a list with. Yet, the more Agnes considered it, the more convinced she became that finding even one of the couple was of great importance to solving the case.

For a start, had they even gone to the theatre? Sandra had told her that she had seen someone resembling Deborah on the quayside when she should have been in the city centre, well away from the area. What if it *had* been Deborah after all? Maybe Robert had been with her, but just out of Sandra's line of sight. Was it possible that the whole discussion about them going to the theatre had been a ploy?

But then there was the robbery. Agnes had no idea why that had suddenly popped into her mind, but now that it was there, maybe she should give it some thought. According to the news bulletin on television, valuable jewellery had been stolen from a shop in the city centre; Northumberland Street, to be exact. Surely such a shop, one of a chain of jewellery shops throughout the country, would never have had kept expensive items instore? For a moment, she cast her mind back to almost a year ago, when a jewellery robbery at the hotel had led her to finding the thief and almost getting herself killed. But Agnes knew that the man who had committed those crimes was now in prison. Therefore, was it possible that someone was copying him?

Keith had told her that the case holding the jewellery had been cleaned inside and out the morning of the robbery. That sounded fair enough; the manager would want everything to look perfect when the visitors arrived. Keith had also mentioned that the manager had checked the door to the case to make sure it was locked after the young woman had finished. Again, fair enough. Everything appeared to be in order. Yet, something had still gone wrong.

Keen to get back to her room in the hotel now, Agnes made her way back along the quayside. She was almost there when she saw Ben lifting someone's luggage from the back of his cab before carrying it up the steps and into the hotel.

Once the couple had paid the fare and moved away, Agnes hurried across to speak to him. "Have you and your wife made a decision, Ben?"

"Yes." He shuffled his feet before he continued. "If the offer's still open, then we would like to take you up on it. I have to say, my wife was stunned when I told her. Like me, she was a little uncomfortable about accepting such a generous offer of two weeks at this hotel. But when I explained that I would be repaying you via free rides, she agreed."

"I'm delighted, Ben. So, tell me what date suits you and I'll make the necessary arrangements."

Ben gave her the date, which was only a few days away. "It's a bit short notice, so I'm not sure that they will have a room for us. It will have to be big enough to accommodate Alec as well." Alec, Ben's son, had severe health problems.

"Don't worry about that!" Agnes grinned. "They'll have a room ready and waiting for you."

A few minutes later, Agnes stepped into the hotel and made her way across to the reception desk.

"What can we do for you, Mrs Lockwood?" Pauline asked.

Agnes explained that she wanted to book a room for some friends. "I would like them to have a really large room, where a single bed can be added without the guests falling over it every time they want to walk across to look out of the window. And," she added, almost as an afterthought, "the room must face out over the river. By that, I mean the front of the hotel, where they can see the Millennium Bridge, not tucked away around at the side where all they can see is the river flowing away downstream."

"That could be pretty pricey for your friends, especially as they're booking so late," Pauline replied, looking at the computer. "There's normally a deal on offer for most of the rooms, providing they are booked well in advance. But even so, the rooms on the top floor, which are large enough to hold another bed, are still expensive. They come with all the usual things, tea, coffee and wine. However, they also have a balcony, where the guests can sit outside, a hot tub, a step-in shower as well as a bath, and any room service included in the price." She sighed. "But, at this late stage, I'm afraid they'll have to pay the full price."

"Don't worry about any deal, Pauline. Just go ahead and book the room for two weeks."

Pauline looked up at Agnes. "*Two weeks!* Are you kidding me?"

"Yes, two weeks. Is there a problem?"

"No. No problem at all. I was just a little concerned about the price," Pauline replied, after quoting the cost. "Rooms such as this are usually booked by a company for one of their CEO's who is attending a conference and, even then, it's only for two or three nights at the most."

"Great! Then as there isn't a problem, go ahead and book the room."

"Right, if you say so, Mrs Lockwood," Pauline said, tapping a few keys on the keyboard. "Next, I need to know the name of the person booking the room."

"Mr Ben..." Agnes broke off, suddenly realising that she didn't know Ben's surname. "Can you believe it?" Agnes shook her head. "I can't remember, but rather than starting this whole procedure again at another time, just put it down in my name."

"Are you sure about that?" Pauline quizzed. "He might not pay and you will be left with the bill."

Agnes nodded. "Yes, I'm sure."

"Well, now that's settled," Agnes said, once she had paid the necessary deposit, "maybe you can help me with something else." She paused. "Do you remember the man in room 106?"

"Yes, Robert Jamison – wasn't he the guy you were asking us about yesterday?" Pauline waved at her colleague, suggesting that she should join her. "We understand he was found dead in his room this morning," she added, lowering her voice. "But, hang on a minute," she said. "I recall seeing you in the reception with Miss Matthews when she received the news from one of the domestics. So you must already know about the man being found dead."

"Shush." Agnes looked around, but fortunately she was the only one in reception. "Yes, I was. But that doesn't mean I know the whys and wherefores – and I would rather you didn't tell anyone that Sandra and I were with Sue when she heard the news."

"It's a secret," Pauline replied, with a wink. "Anyway, I'm afraid we don't know any more than you. We've been here behind the desk all day, except when we took turns to go to lunch and, in that time, I can truthfully say no one has approached either of us for information about the man. Not that either of us could have helped. We really didn't know anything about him."

"Even so," Sally, the other receptionist, added, "I thought the police would have wanted to ask us a few questions. But it appears they haven't spoken to anyone except the manager."

"But questions might still be forthcoming," Agnes replied. "Until the police know the cause of the man's death, they probably don't have a reason to question anyone. He could have died in his sleep."

Nevertheless, despite sounding casual, Agnes was rather astonished that the police hadn't approached any of the staff once the body was found. So far, no one had been asked to identify the body, if only to confirm he was the same man who had attended the bar or the restaurant. But, on reflection, there was probably no reason to. If she and Sandra hadn't seen the man lying in the bed, they would have assumed it was Jamison.

"I have to say, Mr Jenkins hasn't been seen since the poor man was carried from the hotel on a stretcher. I think he's still trying to get over the shock of someone being found dead in their room." Sally paused. "Anyway, what did you want to know about Mr Jamison?"

"Nothing really," Agnes lied. In fact, the two women had already told her what she was going to ask. "I was simply wondering whether you might have seen his girlfriend, Deborah, today. I understand she was also staying at the hotel. I just happened to meet up with them last night before they left for the theatre and Deborah agreed to have breakfast with Sandra and me this morning. But, for some reason, she didn't turn up."

"No, we haven't seen her. Maybe something suddenly came up and she forgot to leave a message for you," Sally suggested.

"Yes, that's probably the reason. I'll look out for her this evening. Thank you."

Agnes was about to turn away, but Pauline stopped her. "I think I should tell you that Mr Alan Johnson was looking for you earlier today."

Agnes nodded. "Yes, I know. He caught up with me while I was on the quayside."

Once the conversation with the receptionists had ended, Agnes headed across towards the stairs. However, just as she was about to put her foot onto the first step, the lift arrived on the ground floor. The doors slid open and two guests stepped out, followed by the lift attendant.

"Are you going up, madam?"

Agnes hesitated for a moment. The last time she had got into the lift with a relatively new attendant, he had taken her to the top of the building with the intention of killing her. However, recalling that this attendant had a reputation for being a gossip-monger, she decided to take the chance. Maybe she would see for herself whether he really was willing to pass on information he'd overheard while escorting guests from floor to floor. Who knows, she might learn something new; if not today, then maybe tomorrow.

But first, she needed to gain his confidence.

Chapter Twenty-Two

Agnes smiled at the young man as she stepped into the lift. He was quite tall and looked quite smart in his uniform, with the small cap perched on top of his long, dark hair. The cap was the one thing about the uniform that Larry hated and he only wore it if someone from head office was visiting the hotel.

"What floor, madam?"

"Sixth floor, please," she lied. Her room was actually on the fourth floor. But she could easily walk down two flights of stairs. "So, how are things with you? I gather you're fairly new here. Do you enjoy your job?"

"Yes." He paused. "But it can be a bit boring at times. I think I would like it more if there was a little excitement from time to time."

"I'm sure all jobs can be a little boring." Agnes replied. "Maybe you could find a way to make your job more exciting. Thinking back to my working days, I was told that a job is what you make of it."

It was true. Her parents had told her that she would need to start at the bottom and work her way up. That way, she would know first-hand how to run a business.

Andy gave her a puzzled look. "What excitement could I possibly drum up through pressing a button to go up and then another to come back down?"

Agnes tapped her chin for a moment. "Well, considering your job, you could imagine you were on a space shuttle, about to take off for the moon."

"People have already been to the moon," he replied, sullenly.

"Okay, then what about Mars?" Agnes suggested. "No one has been there yet. Therefore, every time you push the button to go up, imagine you are the first man to land on Mars. In other words, the eagle has landed. Then, when you come back down, envisage you are returning to earth. On the ground floor, think that Ground Control is pleased to see you back."

Andy grinned. "You are one crazy lady, madam. Oops, I'm sorry," he added, realising he had gone over the line. "I shouldn't have said that. Mr Jenkins will sack me if he hears I said that to a guest. He's already got it in for me."

"No need to worry, Andy. I'm not going to tell him," she said, with a huge smile. "I know I can be one hell of a crazy lady at times, even the manager knows that." She shrugged. "But I don't care – it keeps me young. After all, like a job, life is what you make it." Agnes paused. "In your case, today you are a lift attendant here at the hotel, but tomorrow you might be a pilot on an aeroplane and the day after that – you could be captain of a team of men and women, heading for Mars. It all depends on what *you* want from life."

The lift attendant was stunned into silence. It was only when they had reached the sixth floor and the doors were already open, did he realise that the lift had even stopped.

"I'm sorry. I was so carried away with what you said, I didn't realise we had reached our destination."

"I was right, Andy. You *do* want to be a pilot."

"I don't understand." Andy shook his head. "How could you possibly know that?"

"That was simple. You said we had reached our *destination*," Agnes explained. "Lift attendants usually say something like – we have reached your *floor*. Unless there are a number of people in the lift who want to be dropped off on various floors – then they tend to give the floor number."

"I must say, you're pretty quick at noticing things," he replied.

During the ride up in the lift, Agnes had been trying to assess whether she could really trust this young man. The receptionists had thought him to be a bit of a skiver for not bringing the lift back down to the reception once all the guests had reached their floor. Even the manager was so annoyed that he was on the brink of dismissing him. However, as she really needed someone else inside the hotel, besides the receptionists, to pass on whatever gossip they heard, who could be better placed than the lift attendant?

Larry would have been her first choice. He was a lovely young man and the guests really liked him. Though he would normally never pass on information about what he overheard while escorting guests in the lift, she felt sure he would have trusted her to tell her anything relating to a murder inquiry. Unfortunately, he wouldn't be back until Monday and, though she would have liked to confide in Andy, there was something about him that held her back.

"Why aren't you at an aircraft training school?"

"They told me I was too young. Apparently, I need to apply again when I'm a bit older, or when I have some educational qualification. If I'd had a diploma in, let's say, podiatry or zoology, I would have been admitted no matter how old I was." He glanced at the open doors. "Anyway, you don't want to know all that. This is your *floor*, madam." He grinned. "I got it right this time."

"Yes, you did, Andy. Incidentally, I understand someone was found dead in their room earlier this morning." She hoped he wouldn't recall seeing her following Sue towards the stairs when the alarm was raised.

"Yes, a man."

Agnes watched as he moved slightly to one side and glanced over her shoulder to the corridor behind her.

"Mr Jenkins, the manager, held a staff meeting and told us to stay silent on the issue," he continued. "Though the whole thing will be in the evening paper, unless the police have managed to keep it from the press."

"Did you ever meet this man?"

"No," he replied, but then swiftly he corrected himself. "Well, yes, I suppose I could have met him in the lift. But I meet lots of guests in the lift without knowing exactly who they are, or where they go when once they reach their floor." He paused. "Why do you ask?"

Agnes shrugged. "I just wondered whether he might have started chatting and introduced himself to you on the way up to his floor."

"The manager referred to the man as... Jamison." Andy shook his head. "The name didn't ring a bell with me, but I understand some of the waiters recalled the name. But then they would, as he would have given his name when booking a table."

"I think I'd better let you go now," Agnes said, as she stepped out of the lift. "You might find a queue when you get back down to the ground floor."

"I doubt it," he mumbled. "Otherwise the buzzer would have leapt off the wall by now."

* * *

Once the lift doors had slid together, Agnes made her way to the stairs. She had been on the verge of telling Andy that she had really meant to be dropped off on the fourth floor and ask him to take her back down. However, she had decided to leave things as they were. Though he had seemed a nice enough guy, once they had got chatting, she still wasn't really sure about him. There was something about the pause before he said the man's name that bothered her.

By now, Agnes had reached her room and, taking out her key-card, she opened the door and stepped inside. Out of curiosity, she didn't close the door behind her. Instead, she watched to see whether it actually closed by itself, or merely stopped when it reached the door frame. She was relieved to find that the mechanism worked as it was meant to and the door closed firmly. Now, thinking back to earlier that morning, she recalled that when she went into Sandra's room, her door had also closed properly.

Agnes continued to give the problem of the doors a little more thought as she walked across to the window and gazed down onto the quayside. After her life-threatening experience some months back, it had been found that the door to her room had either taken too long to close before someone burst in, or had stopped short before actually clicking shut. Since then, a reputable firm had been called in to change the mechanism on all the doors in the hotel and to come back twice a year to ensure that they were still working properly. If that was still the case, and the mechanism on all the doors had been checked recently, then it could only mean one thing: someone had tampered with the door to room 106.

Agnes shivered at the thought. If that someone was able to interfere with Jamison's door, who was to say they couldn't mess around with another door; hers, for instance, or even Sandra's? At the moment, her door was working as it should. Now she needed to know that Sandra's door was in full working order, too.

Agnes picked up her key-card and, making sure her door closed behind her, she swept along the corridor towards Sandra's room. Once there, she found that the door was slightly ajar. Had someone tampered with the mechanism above the door after they had left? Maybe Sandra was in there now and hadn't realised the door was still ajar. What if the mechanism *had* been tampered with and someone had crept in after her? But surely someone entering the room unannounced would have had the sense to close the door behind them?

Agnes stood outside the room for a moment, wondering what she should do. Her first instinct was to go into the room to make sure Sandra wasn't there. If she was, they could both rush back to her room and lock the door. But, what if Sandra wasn't back yet and the perpetrator was still in there? He could still be standing on a stool behind the door, fiddling around with the mechanism.

No, she needed to move away from the door and call someone.

Alan was her first choice, but, after the last couple of days, she wasn't keen. However, realising that this was not the time to play games about who was right and who was wrong, Agnes took a few steps away from the door and pulled her phone from her pocket.

Seeing the call was from Agnes, the DCI turned away from his team to answer his phone. But, before he had time to utter a single word, Agnes's voice came through loud and clear.

"Alan, I think we have a problem."

Chapter Twenty-Three

Alan was in the incident room explaining how the fingerprints and DNA of the man who had been found dead in bed were not the same as those on other items in the room. "Which could mean that the dead man was not the man who booked the room," he said, tapping the man's photo as he spoke. "If that's the case, then who is he and what was he doing in the room?"

He then went on to discuss the findings in the case of the robbery.

Jones and his partner, Smithers, had spoken to every member of staff who had been in the shop the morning of the robbery.

"Everyone was keen to help us with the inquiry," Smithers told the DCIs as he ran through the list of names in his notebook. "Yet they all swear they never saw a customer even try to venture behind the counter."

"Therefore," Jones concluded, "as the glass at the front of the case hadn't been broken, the jewellery could only have been taken from behind the case."

"But the glass behind the case wasn't smashed, either," Alan replied. He thought for moment. "What about the CCTV? I understand that there was a fault and someone was coming to check it out."

Smithers nodded. "Yes, the man was there when we arrived. He checked everything, but found it to be working perfectly. He wondered whether a brief reduction in power might have caused it to stop working, especially as it had done the same thing the previous day."

"Unless someone switched it off while they were taking the items from the case," Alan replied. "Though, as it was only off for a couple of minutes or so, it would be difficult to say who actually tampered with it. Both before and after the shutdown, all members of staff could be seen attending to customers – except for the manager."

However, before anyone could say anything further, Alan's phone rang. Pulling it from his pocket, he was surprised to find the call was from Agnes. After hearing what she had to say, he quickly told her that he was on his way.

"Smithers, Jones, you're with me."

"What's going on, sir?" Andrews asked. He looked bewildered that the DCI had called on two other detectives, rather than him.

Alan stopped and turned around. He had thought to keep his sergeant away from the hotel until he learned whether Sandra was safe – or not. However, he was aware that if Agnes was in trouble, he would definitely want to be involved.

"Come on, Andrews. I'll tell you in the car," he called out, as he set off down the corridor.

"So what did you hear, sir?" Andrews said, once they had set off from the station with the blue lights flashing. "Have we got the man cornered?"

"No, Andrews. The call was from Agnes." He paused. "There's no easy way to say this, but she thinks Sandra might be in danger."

"No! Please, no." The sergeant slumped down in his seat as he spoke. "Not Sandra!"

"Calm down, Andrews. It might be nothing. Let's wait until we get there."

"But Agnes must think something has happened to her – otherwise she wouldn't have called it in," he said, as he straightened himself up and looked out at the road ahead. "Can't we go any faster? For goodness' sake, we'll be too late at this rate."

"Pull yourself together, Andrews. You'll be no help to Sandra or anyone else, if you carry on like this."

A few minutes later, they reached the hotel. Andrews jumped out the moment the car stopped and headed up the steps which led to the hotel entrance.

"Andrews – wait!"

The sharpness of the DCI's tone brought Andrews to a halt. He looked back towards Alan. By now, he was out of the car and hurrying up the steps with Smithers and Jones behind him.

"When we enter the hotel, Andrews, Smithers and I will go upstairs. Jones, I want you to wait in reception and stop anyone from leaving the hotel. Tell them to sit in the drawing room." He glanced at the lift, as he spoke. "I see it's on the tenth floor. There might be a few guests by the time it gets down here."

A moment later, Sergeant Andrews was leading the way, as the detectives hurried upstairs.

* * *

Once Agnes had made the call to Alan, she tried to call Sandra. However, her call had gone straight to voicemail. She had tried not to panic; after all, it could be something simple. Sandra might have switched off her phone to save the battery. Perhaps she had realised that, while collecting her things from her flat the other evening, she had forgotten to pack the charger. It was easily done.

Nevertheless, Agnes couldn't help worrying that something more sinister was going on, especially as the door to Sandra's room was slightly ajar. Tempted to take a look in Sandra's room, she glanced around, hoping to find something she could use as a weapon should someone happen to be in there. Her eyes rested on a bottle of wine standing on the chest of drawers. That would do nicely. Making sure she had her key-card and her phone tucked inside her pocket, she opened her door and slipped out into the corridor. Creeping along the passage with the bottle held high, ready to slam it into anyone who dared to attack her, she slowly made her way towards Sandra's room. She had almost reached Sandra's door, when she thought she heard someone behind her. However, before she could react, the person spoke, in barely a whisper.

"Just where do you think you're going?"

* * *

"What the hell do you think you're doing, Andrews?" Alan asked when he caught up with his sergeant. "Slow down, man. I understand you're worried. But thundering around isn't going to help Sandra. You'll more likely do more harm than good."

"Sorry, sir." Andrews took a deep breath. "It's just that I'm scared that something might have already happened to her."

By now, Smithers, who had continued walking up the stairs, had reached the fourth floor. After taking a look along the corridor, he turned around and retraced his steps until he reached the DCI.

"There's someone in the passageway," he said. "They had their back to me, but I think we need to stay silent until we see what they're up to."

The DCI nodded and hurried up the remaining stairs to see for himself. Looking along the corridor, he could see a woman walking slowly in the opposite direction. He raised his eyebrows as he turned back at Smithers.

Smithers gave a brief hint of a smile. "That's who I saw," he whispered.

Alan turned back to his detectives and placed a finger to his lips, instructing them to stay silent. Then, slowly and silently, they made their way along the corridor until they were within touching distance of the person, before asking what she was doing.

Alan had hardly finished his statement when Agnes swung around to face him. Her hand was raised and she would have crashed the bottle down on him if she hadn't recognised him in time. She shook her head and pointed towards her room, indicating they should all go in there.

"I could have killed you," she said, once they were inside. "Don't ever creep up on me again."

"Where's Sandra?" Andrews asked, looking around the room. "I thought she was with you."

"No, she isn't, Michael. She isn't answering her phone, so I have no I idea where she is." She paused. "The thing is, the door to her room is slightly ajar – that's why I was carrying the bottle as a weapon. I…"

"What do you mean by *her room*?" Andrews interrupted. "I thought she was staying with a friend – she *told* me she was staying with a friend."

"For heaven's sake, Michael, stop wittering on." Agnes retorted. "We need to get along there to make sure that she's okay. It's room 404, two doors along."

Alan was about to argue that she should stay in her room, but he knew it was pointless. Instead, he instructed his detectives to follow closely behind him, while telling Agnes to stay well back.

As Agnes had said, the door to Sandra's room was slightly ajar. Alan gave Agnes a swift glance with raised eyebrows. She responded by nodding, indicating that that was how she had found it earlier. Stepping nearer to the door, Alan pushed it open and peered inside. From where he was standing, everything looked exactly as it should. Nothing appeared to be out of place. Yet he was aware that someone could still be hiding, waiting for Sandra to return.

Taking a deep breath, he motioned for Agnes to step forward and walk into the room. Once she was inside, he followed her and slammed the door shut behind him. While she walked further into the room, Alan remained by the door; out of sight. If anyone was in Sandra's room, waiting for her to return, they would believe she had arrived back at the hotel.

Despite feeling nervous, Agnes hummed a tune as she opened the wardrobe doors. She was trying to mimic what anyone would do on arriving back in their room. She then strolled across to the dresser, where there was a bottle of wine and two glasses. Picking up the bottle and a glass, she cheerily chinked the two of them together as she walked across the room towards the table and chairs by the window. There was no sign of anyone hiding on that side of the room, either. The only place left to check was the bathroom. Taking a deep breath, she glanced at Alan who was still waiting by the entrance, before pointing towards the bathroom. Opening the door, she peered around. But, as she didn't see anyone, she pushed the door open a little wider and took a small step inside. However, someone hiding behind the door pulled it out of her grasp. Grabbing her arm, they pulled her inside before slamming the door shut.

Chapter Twenty-Four

Alan was still standing by the door of Sandra's room when Agnes indicated that she was going to look in the bathroom. He had watched carefully as she went through the motions of someone just arriving back at the hotel after a day out. However, it appeared that Sandra wasn't in her room; nor, thankfully, was anyone else. Though there was still the riddle as to why Sandra's door had been ajar. When he and his detectives were with Agnes in her room a few minutes ago, she had stressed that, since her door had been tampered with some months ago, the closing device above all the doors of the guest rooms was checked regularly.

He also recalled her saying that both she and Sandra made a point of checking to make sure their doors were working properly. But, in reality, maybe they had only given them a mere glance as the doors swung shut. Yet there was a problem with that. After Agnes's past experience, he was aware that she never walked away without making sure her door was closed properly.

Jamison's door hadn't been fully closed when he and Andrews had approached his room. Since then, a man had been found dead in that very same room. Therefore, someone had gained access to his room and tampered with the door mechanism.

By now, Agnes had opened the door to the bathroom. Alan watched as she stood there for a moment; relieved that she hadn't seen anyone.

But then, in the blink of an eye, she swiftly disappeared from his line of vision and the door slammed shut behind her.

Alan was so shocked that he stood rooted to the spot for a moment. He could have kicked himself. He should have been with her when she opened the bathroom door. Why had he been so complacent? For goodness' sake, it was the only place left where a perpetrator could hide totally out of sight! Why had he even allowed her to go into the room in the first place? He, or one of his officers, should have searched the room. Now, the best he could do was to inform the two detectives waiting outside as to what had happened.

"Someone was hiding in the bathroom – they have Agnes," Alan said, the moment he threw open the door. Despite his concerns, he kept his voice low. "Smithers, you call for armed backup – then get downstairs and join Jones. Don't allow anyone to leave the building. Andrews, you're with me."

Alan had hardly finished speaking before Smithers pulled out his phone and was heading towards the stairs.

The DCI turned to his sergeant. "It's up to us, Andrews. Didn't you take a hostage negotiation course a year or so ago? Maybe you could talk to whoever is holding Agnes and persuade them to let her go."

"I really enjoyed the course." Andrews took a deep breath. "But I failed when it came to the virtual test. I was told I was too short-tempered."

"Why am I not surprised?" Alan replied sharply. "Maybe I should have sent you off to organise the troops instead of Smithers. He could talk his way out of a jam jar filled with wasps."

Alan pushed Andrews out of the way and, moving closer to the bathroom, he banged his fist on the door. "This is the police. We have the building surrounded. We know you have a woman in there. Open the door and let her go. Then we can talk."

* * *

Agnes was astounded when she was pulled into the bathroom. She would have had a bottle of wine in her hand to swipe at the person had

Alan not intervened, saying something about how carrying a weapon was frowned on. So, it was okay for her to be pulled into a room by some person who might kill her, but it wasn't right for her to have something to defend herself? Nevertheless, she wasn't about to go down without a fight.

Agnes swung around to face whoever was gripping her arm. It turned out to be a youngish-looking man, tall and rather well-built; not the sort of person that she would have chosen to have a fight with. Gathering as much information as she could, she saw he was wearing trousers with pockets on each of the legs and a T-shirt with the logo of a company she recognised emblazoned across the centre.

"Okay, now that you've got my attention," Agnes said, wrenching her arm from his grasp, "what is it you want from me, young man?"

Agnes hoped Alan was outside the door and could hear every word. If so, he would realise that there was only one man with her.

"Though," she added, rubbing her bruised arm, "you really didn't have to go this far. A mere knock on my door would have sufficed. I'm well known for listening to people's problems. So, how can I help you?"

* * *

Sandra was making her way back to the hotel. She hadn't meant to walk quite so far along the quayside. But, as the sun was shining and the breeze had dropped, she had simply carried on until she just happened to look at her watch and saw how late in the afternoon it was. She quickened her pace as she drew close to the Tyne Bridge. From here, she could see the hotel in the distance, but there was still some way to go.

However, as she approached the hotel, she couldn't help noticing the crowd of people standing outside. There were several police cars parked along the road, while some officers were holding back people trying to get closer to the hotel.

"What's going on?" Sandra asked a young couple who were standing at the back of the crowd.

"Who knows?" The man shrugged. "Maybe they had nothing else to do today."

The woman kicked his ankle. "Don't take any noticed of him." She paused. "He's just a bit fed up because his application to join the force was turned down a month ago."

"Why am I not surprised?" Sandra mumbled, as she moved away from them. Sandra slowly pushed her way through the crowd. While some allowed her to pass by them easily, others were reluctant to move aside. When she finally got to the front, a police officer stopped her from going any further.

"I'm sorry. No one is allowed to go any further."

"You don't understand. I'm a guest here at the hotel."

"You will still have to wait," he said. "I can't let you through."

Sandra took a deep breath. "Look, Sergeant Michael Andrews is my fiancé and I feel sure he will be in there. You must let me through."

"Sorry, but I can't do that," the officer replied. "I have my orders. No one is to be allowed inside."

Just then, the hotel doors slid open and Detective Jones stepped outside. Looking to the side of the hotel, he beckoned a couple of officers to come forward.

"Detective Jones!" Sandra called out.

However, due to the noise from the crowd, he didn't appear to hear her, so she called out again, only this time much louder.

Hearing his name, Jones swung around and saw Sandra frantically waving at him.

"I need to talk to you!" she yelled.

Jones thought for a moment, then gave a nod to the officer who was holding back the crowd.

Sandra rushed up the steps to join him. "What on earth is going on? Has another body been found in the hotel?"

By now, Jones had ushered her through hotel doors, away from all the noise coming from the crowd. "You really shouldn't here, Sandra," he said, after instructing the two officers as to what he needed them to do. "It would be better if you went home."

"But I'm staying here at the moment – enjoying the good life. So, in a manner of speaking, this is my home."

"Sorry, I didn't know that," Jones replied. "Nevertheless, it's not a good idea for you to hang around here. I still think you should go back to your own home."

"Can't you just tell me what this is all about?" Sandra was beginning to feel frustrated. Why couldn't she get a straight answer?

Jones scratched his head. "I shouldn't be telling you this, but Mrs Lockwood is being held hostage," he said. "The DCI and Sergeant Andrews are up there now."

"Oh my goodness, I don't believe it! How on earth did the person get into her room?"

"It's not her room they're in, it's yours."

Jones shook his head. He had replied too quickly and had said far too much. That wasn't like him at all. He needed to get back to Smithers, who was trying to explain to the guests who were still being held in the drawing room why they couldn't leave.

"Look, Sandra, I've got to get back to work. Why don't you go back to your flat for tonight? You can come back tomorrow when all this is over."

"Are you kidding me?" Sandra strode across to the sofa in the reception area and sat down. "Agnes is a friend of mine. I want to be here for her when she talks her way out of this mess."

"What makes you think she'll be able to talk her way out of her current situation?"

"That's simple – Agnes is the kind of person who can talk her way out of anything."

* * *

Upstairs in Sandra's room, Andrews gestured towards the bathroom door, indicating that he should burst through to where Agnes was being held. However, Alan held up his hand.

"Let's give it a minute," he whispered. "Agnes appears to have this under control. Maybe we could learn something. My guess is that's what she wants. I've already learned there is only one man with her. Perhaps she'll drag more information from him."

"But we could be wasting time," Andrews wailed. "We need to get in there and seize this man."

"No! Nevertheless, one wrong word and I'll be in there."

However, Alan couldn't help noticing that his sergeant looked uncomfortable about his order. Knowing how Andrews felt about Agnes prying into police business, he was surprised that his sergeant appeared so concerned for her safety.

"Agnes will be okay, Andrews," he said, encouragingly. "Rest assured, at the first hint of trouble I'll be the first to hurl myself at the door."

Inside the bathroom, once Agnes had finished speaking, there was a long silence. She sat on the edge of the bath and watched the man pace back and forth in front of the door. From the troubled expression on his face, she guessed he had fully expected to be long gone before the person occupying the room returned. Instead, he had been caught in the act.

"You know I could help you, if you would only stand still and tell me what this is all about."

The man stopped walking and moved closer to Agnes. "Shut up, woman! What can you do to help me? I should never have agreed to do this in the first place."

"Agreed to do what?" Agnes asked.

Agnes was aware he was referring to altering the door mechanism, but she needed him to admit to it. Only then might she learn more from him; maybe even find out who had coaxed him into doing the job in the first place and, with a bit of luck, the reason why. But perhaps she was getting ahead of herself. She needed to take one thing at a time.

"To alter the bloody door mechanism!" he yelled.

It was obvious that the man was agitated at being discovered in the room. But, though Agnes was nervous at being trapped in here with someone who might be a murderer, she still felt she needed to carry on questioning him. Hopefully, she would find some answers.

"Was it you who altered the mechanism above the door to room 106 where a man was found dead?"

"Yes, that was me," he said, sitting down next to Agnes. "But I had no idea anyone was going to be murdered."

"Then what did you think was going to happen?" Agnes asked. "What I mean is, what reason were you given when you were asked to tamper with the door to room 106?"

"I was told there was to be a celebration for the man in that room. Therefore, it was necessary for his friends to be able to gain access so they could spring a surprise on him. They told me that he always left in a hurry and didn't check his door, so he probably wouldn't realise it hadn't closed properly. But I was told that they would make sure that the door was closed after they left."

"Yet, after hearing that a man had been found dead in that very room, you still went on to disengage the door mechanism to this room?"

The man looked down at the floor. "Yes."

"Why?" Agnes asked. "Why would you do that?"

The man didn't answer; he continued to stare down at the floor.

Agnes was unsure as to whether she should say anything further. She glanced across at the door. Would it be worth trying to make an escape? The door wasn't too far away and Alan would be on the other side. However, before she could make a decision, the man looked up at her.

"I didn't have any other choice. If I didn't agree, he would tell the police who tampered with the door mechanism of room 106." He shook his head. "But what does that matter now? You're going to give me away the minute you get out of here, aren't you?"

"You could go to the police, yourself. Tell them what happened and who told you to fiddle around with the door in the first place," Agnes suggested, ignoring his question.

"That's the problem. I have no idea who it was. I never met the person. They just rang the firm and asked to speak to a member of their staff. I happened to be in the office at the time, so the call was passed over to me. When the person said they might have a job for me, I gave them my mobile phone number and asked them to call me back in about ten minutes. They did, and when they offered to pay me one hundred pounds in cash if I agreed to stop the door of a room at this hotel from closing when the guest left, how could I refuse? Though, in my own defence, I did ask the reason and they told me exactly what I said earlier."

"When you say 'they', does that mean you don't know whether you were speaking to a man or a woman?"

"Yes, the voice was muffled. But I put it down to the fact that I was using my mobile and that they might be using a mobile, too. Interference happens sometimes."

"Tell me about it," Agnes mumbled.

Though she agreed that people using mobile phones could have problems depending on the signal, she believed that in this case, the person making the call had been disguising their voice. This young man had been duped. He was either very naïve, or the thought of one hundred pounds cash in hand had stopped him from thinking clearly.

"Were you told who the man in room 106 was?" Agnes asked, lamely. She doubted the people behind the killing would have given him such information, but it was worth a try.

"Yes, they happened to mention his name at one point." He paused, as he tried to recall the name. "Jamison, that's it, Robert Jamison. Now I remember, they even spelled out the name, though I don't know why, as they had already given me the room number."

Agnes took a deep breath. So far, this was going well. Yet she really needed to keep him talking. "But, how were you able to get into the room in the first place? Surely the door would have been locked."

"Oh, that was simplest part," he replied. "I was told that a key-card would be left at a certain time, behind the curtain on the windowsill at the far end of the corridor. All I had to do was pick it up, do the job, then leave it where I found it."

Agnes found that last piece of news very interesting. Somehow, a key-card to room 106 had fallen into the hands of a killer. Had that person borrowed the card from Jamison, or stolen it from him? But, if it had been stolen, then that person would have had to slide it back into Jamison's pocket before he realised it was missing. On the other hand, what if Jamison had actually let someone borrow his key-card knowing full well what was going on? After all, it wasn't Jamison who had been found dead in the room. Therefore, was it possible that Robert had set up this whole masquerade so that he could disappear without a trace, after doing whatever he had come here to do in the first place? Though, if that was the case, wouldn't he have made certain that any traces found in the room would have come from the dead man? For instance, the pathologist had told her that none of the fingerprints on the items found in the room matched the man found lying in the bed, so they could only match Jamison. But, as Jamison had disappeared, the police couldn't match them to him. Very clever.

Agnes was also aware there could be another possibility. The key-card allowing the mechanic to get into the room could have been a master key-card. If so, it would certainly open the field, as only a few members of staff had access to these cards. Therefore, if Jamison *had* set up this murder and wanted to have his key-card with him at all times, he would have needed to have some means of getting his hands on one of them.

Suddenly, the man leapt to his feet and began to walk up and down the floor again.

"What the hell am I doing? Why am I even talking to you?" As he spoke, he glanced across to where his bag of tools lay on the floor. It only took a couple of strides for him to reach it and, pulling a large wrench from the bag, he marched back and brandished it in front of her. "You're trying to trap me and, like a fool, I fell for it."

"No, I'm not trying to trap you," Agnes replied slowly. She was trying to sound calm. But, with a large wrench waving in front of her face, she felt far from calm. "I am trying to help you. But, if you don't want my help, then go ahead and hit me with that thing, whatever it is, and make things even more difficult for yourself, because, if you kill me, there is no way you will get out of here alive. However, before you do lash out at me, could you tell me your name?"

He pointed to the tool in his hand. "Just so you know what is about to strike you, this is a wrench. But getting back to your question, why do you want to know my name? What difference would that make?"

Agnes shrugged. "I don't know. Maybe it would help me in some way by knowing the name of the man who sent me to my grave."

"Okay, you go first. What's your name?"

"My name is Agnes Lockwood."

The man stared down at her as though he hadn't heard correctly. "No! You're lying – your name is Sandra, Sandra Williams. This is her room."

"No, I'm afraid you're wrong. I'm definitely Agnes Lockwood. I should know – it's been my name for a number of years." She paused, giving herself a moment to think through what he had just said. "I suppose it's possible you got the room numbers mixed up and altered the mechanism on the wrong room." She continued. "It's easily done. These things happen." She shrugged. "Anyway, enough of that, it's your turn, so tell me your name."

"Bill Moffat," he replied, absentmindedly.

Agnes had never thought for one minute that he would give her his name. Yet he had – Bill Moffat. However, from his tone and the puzzled expression on his face at being in the wrong room, she guessed he didn't really know what he was saying.

"So, Bill Moffat, what are you going to do now?"

"I don't know." He pulled a key-card from his pocket as he spoke and stared down at it. "I don't understand. Surely this card will only open the door to one room – the room number I was given on a slip of paper lying next to the key-card." His voice was low, almost as though he was thinking aloud, rather than actually replying to her question.

"Do you still happen to have that slip of paper, or did you throw it away?"

"And what if I do still have it?" Bill looked up from the key-card. Feeling around in his pocket, he pulled out a piece of paper and waved it around. "Yes, I have it here, but how could this help me now?"

"Well, for a start, it could be held as evidence to prove that what you're saying is correct. There might also be fingerprints on the paper – by that, I mean prints other than yours. If so, they could lead to the person responsible for the murder in room 106 and whoever blackmailed you into tampering with the door to this room. For goodness' sake, Bill, you need to start looking out for yourself."

Agnes paused for a moment. "Incidentally, did the person happen to give a reason as to why they wanted you to fiddle around with the door to this room?"

Moffat handed Agnes the slip of paper. "See for yourself."

Agnes took the paper and read the brief message. There was no mention as to why the person wanted the door mechanism altered. But, there was something that really interested her.

"When the person spoke to you, telling you where and when to pick up the key, didn't they give a reason why they wanted you to alter the door?"

"No! Why would he? He had me in the palm of his hand. There was no need for him to give a reason."

"One other thing, Bill, was the voice on the phone this time the same as the person who first contacted you?"

Agnes realised she was pushing her luck by continuing to ask all these questions. But, at the same time, if he had really meant to kill her, surely he would have struck her by now.

"I told you earlier, the first call was muffled, so..." he paused. "Come to think of it, no, it wasn't. It sounded different. The second call was definitely from a man. But I guess there was more than one person involved. Lady, you ask a lot of questions. Maybe you're trying to keep me talking until someone rushes in to save you." He held up the wrench. "But I could kill you right now and be long gone before your body was found. After all, that's probably why someone asked me to alter the mechanism above the door. They were going to kill you anyway. I could do it for them and save them the trouble. I could even get more money from them."

"True." Agnes wagged her finger from side to side as she spoke. "But you see, Bill, there's a slight problem with that. I am not Sandra Williams. Therefore, you would be killing the wrong person, which means that he could seek you out and either kill you to keep you silent, or continue to blackmail you into doing jobs for him for the rest of your life."

"Shut up! Just shut the hell up!" Bill shoved the wrench in front of her face as he spoke. "I need time to think."

"Well then, Bill, I suggest you need to get a move on," Agnes replied, looking down at her watch. "I have a table booked for dinner this evening."

Chapter Twenty-Five

The DCI and his sergeant were still listening to the conversation from the other side of the bathroom door of the room where Agnes was being held prisoner. There had been several times during their discussion when Alan had felt like calling out to the officers standing in the corridor and instructing them to burst through the door and rescue her. However, he had held back; Agnes was doing such a good job in getting the man to open up. She had even managed to pry his name from him.

Nevertheless, Alan couldn't help noticing that Andrews hadn't said a word when they learned that the man had been blackmailed into altering the door mechanism of Sandra's room. Though, admittedly, he had turned quite pale and taken a few steps away from the bathroom door.

Turning his attention back to what was going on inside the bathroom, Alan had to agree with Agnes. This Bill Moffat character was very naïve. Accepting the excuse of a surprise party being set up for Robert Jamison at face value, Moffat had gone ahead and altered the mechanism above the door and for what – a mere one hundred pounds? Anyone with half a brain would have stopped to think why the person hadn't spoken to the hotel management about being allowed into the room for that purpose, or even renting the large room at the back of the hotel that was kept for private parties. It would have cost half the price.

But now, a whole new episode was taking place behind the locked door. From Agnes's last statement, Moffat was wielding a wrench in front of her. The man could strike her at any moment. Yet, she was still being flippant. Wasn't that just like her? Didn't she realise that the man in front of her was desperate? Moffat could act at any moment without a single thought. The thinking part would only come later, when he realised what he had done. But by then it would be too late for Agnes.

Alan was aware that he should have intervened a while ago. Yet he had hung back. Surely now was the time to break down the door and burst into the room.

* * *

Downstairs, Smithers and Jones were having trouble with the guests who had been prevented from leaving the hotel. Both detectives had told them to be patient, saying that it would all be over very soon. Nevertheless, it seemed they were in a losing battle. The guests were all declaring there was somewhere else they needed to be. Even with two burly uniformed officers standing shoulder to shoulder inside the door of the drawing room, people were still being obstinate; calling out for them to stand aside and let them through.

A little way from the drawing room, Sandra was sitting in a hunched-up position on the sofa in the reception area wondering what had happened after she and Agnes had separated earlier that afternoon. Suddenly, her brooding thoughts were interrupted by a sudden outburst of voices coming from the drawing room. It had been bad enough earlier, but now it was even louder.

Sandra was aware, from what Jones had told her, that guests were being stopped from either leaving the hotel or going up to their rooms until the DCI had finished his inquiry. Surely they could understand the reasoning behind that. Or were they all idiots?

Sandra heaved a sigh as she rose to her feet. Maybe she could help in some way. As she walked towards the drawing room, she saw the receptionists stop whatever they were doing and look up at her. She gave them a slight wave as she passed their desk, before pointing towards the drawing room; indicating where she was headed. Both Sally and Pauline gave her the thumbs-up sign. Meanwhile, the lift attendant, who was looking even more bored than usual, suddenly appeared to wake up and take notice of her as she neared the drawing room door. Now, standing behind the uniformed officers guarding the door, she caught sight of Jones who happened to be trapped by a noisy group of people in front of him. Catching his eye, she motioned him to come to the door. He nodded, looking rather relieved to leave the irritated guests to Smithers, even if only for a minute or two.

"What can I do?" Jones asked. "You can see how things are going in here. To tell you the truth, I would arrest the lot of them given half a chance."

"I would like to come in for a few minutes, if that's okay?"

"Sure, why not?" Jones nodded to the two officers to allow her through. "So, what can we do for you?" he yelled, trying to make himself heard above the noise.

"Not a lot," Sandra replied. "I would just like to say a few words to the people here."

"No problem, go ahead. But I doubt you will be heard above this noise."

Sandra nodded and turned around to face the people in front of her. Putting her fingers to her lips, she blew the most piercing whistle Jones or Smithers had ever heard. Everyone immediately stopped talking and looked across to where Sandra was standing.

"That's better," Sandra said, with a smile. "Now, why don't you all calm down and let the police do their job?"

"But I have an appointment with a friend."

Though a few voices could be heard, chirping about where else they should be at this time, this woman's piercing voice was heard above the others.

"We are meeting for high tea at The Majestic with someone very important – it is an occasion I really don't want to miss," the woman continued.

Sandra eyed the woman up and down. "I see. Might I ask who this important person is?"

"I'd rather not say."

"Okay, then if you give me your name, I, personally, will phone The Majestic Hotel and explain what has happened. The receptionists across the hall are certain to have the number and I'm sure The Majestic will understand and be happy to pass on the message to your friend and, of course, the important person." Sandra looked up at Jones. "Could one of your officers ask Sally to pop in here for a moment…?"

"No!" The woman closed her eyes for a moment. "Please don't do that. I'm sorry. I'm not meeting my friend at The Majestic."

The woman looked around at the people in the room. They had stopped chatting and now had their eyes fixed on her, as though waiting to hear what she was going to say next.

"So, where *are* you meeting her?" Sandra glanced towards the detectives as she spoke, hoping she wasn't treading on his toes.

However, as the room had quieted down since she had started questioning the woman, both detectives gave a slight nod, indicating she should continue.

"A department store." The woman hung her head.

"And this all-important person – who might that be?" Sandra felt bad at questioning the woman in front of all these people, but if it helped, then it needed to be done.

Though the basis of the woman's story might be true, it appeared she had played out her imagination merely to impress the people in the room. Therefore, how many others, shouting about where they should be, were doing the same thing?

"My son-in-law," the woman replied, sharply. "It was he who suggested we meet up for tea."

"Then why didn't you arrange to meet here at the hotel, especially as you're staying here?" Sandra asked. "They do the most wonderful afternoon teas and…"

"But I'm not staying here." The woman shook her head. "Well, not any more. I was only booked in for the one night – last night. It was his treat." She pointed towards a small suitcase standing near the door. "I checked out earlier, but then I decided to take one last look around the hotel and got stuck in here with the crowd."

"So, weren't your daughter and her husband staying here?" Sandra quizzed.

"Oh yes, they were. Sorry, I should have said." The woman smiled. "It's just that they had somewhere else they needed to be this morning, which meant they needed to check out early."

"This so-called friend, would that just happen to be your daughter? Incidentally," Sandra continued without waiting for a reply, "what is the name of your son-in-law?"

The woman was silent for a moment. "Yes, it's my daughter I'm meeting up with, but what does that matter?"

"What matters is why you didn't say so in the first place, instead of all this messing around," Sandra retorted. "But, you haven't answered my other question. What is the name of your son-in-law?"

The woman looked around the room, only to find everyone had their attention fixed on her, all waiting for her to reply.

Heaving a sigh, she turned back to face Sandra. "If you must know, his name is Robert. Robert Jamison."

Chapter Twenty-Six

Upstairs, Detective Chief Inspector Alan Johnson was still listening to the conversation between Agnes and Bill Moffat. But now he felt he had heard enough. He had to admit Agnes had been brilliant at the way she had pried information from Moffat.

So far, the man had admitted to meddling with two doors in the hotel; first Jamison's room, and now Sandra's. Agnes's questioning had also given him reason to consider that the first key-card Moffat had been given to open the door to room 106, was actually one that had been set up to open any guest room in the hotel; in other words, a master key-card. Alan was still pondering on whether the same thing had happened today, when he heard Moffat toying with the idea of killing Agnes.

Even though Alan had to smile at Agnes's flippant reply, he knew he had held back long enough. Now was the time to burst through the door before it was too late. However, just as he was about to instruct Andrews to join him in throwing their shoulders against the door in unison, he heard Moffat's voice again.

* * *

Inside the bathroom, Moffat stood in front of Agnes. He was still holding the large wrench only inches away from her forehead, while considering his options.

There was a small, stained-glass window set into the outside wall. Though this was the fourth floor, most of the bathrooms on this side of the building were above the staff entrance which had a large canopy stretching the length of the building. Therefore, surely dropping down onto the canopy would be enough to break his fall. It was the sort of thing done in the movies. But did he really want to take the risk?

Moffat closed his eyes. Did he really want to risk it? The canopy could give way under his weight and he could get cut to pieces. The only other option was to walk through the door and give himself up to the police.

"Okay, Agnes, Sandra, or whatever your name is," he said, laying the wrench down on the floor. "I have never killed anyone in my life and I don't want to start now. I hope I can trust you to speak up for me – even though I must have frightened the life out of you."

"Believe me when I say I'll do everything I can to help you," Agnes replied. She moved across towards the door as she spoke, fearing he might suddenly change his mind. "And, yes," she added, turning back to face her captor, "you did frighten me, but I didn't really believe that you would kill me. I also feel sure that you didn't kill the person in room 106." She paused. "I realised that when you found me in the room. You looked afraid. Had you meant to kill Sandra, you would've looked pleased when you thought she had turned up earlier than you were told. Instead, you looked shocked. I believe you were meant to be long gone from this room before Sandra arrived."

Leaving Bill to ponder on her words, Agnes turned back towards the door and pushed back the small knob to unlock it. The moment Agnes opened the door, Alan and his sergeant rushed in; Andrews almost knocked her over in his haste to get to Moffat.

"Bill Moffat," Andrews said, grabbing the man's arms, "I am arresting you for the murder of the man in room 106 and the attempted murder of Sandra Williams..."

"No! That's rubbish!" Agnes interrupted.

"What do you mean?" Alan asked. "By his own admission, the man altered the mechanism to both doors. That certainly doesn't go in his favour."

"No, it doesn't. But neither does it make him a murderer. For goodness' sake, Alan, you were out there listening to every word. Surely you heard what was said, or did you drop off to sleep? Moffat did not murder the man in room 106. That was down to someone else." Agnes grimaced. "I admit that I still need to think a little more about that. But, in the meantime, Bill was *not* planning to kill the woman in this room. Just think about it, Alan. No one intended to murder Sandra. She was merely meant to be frightened."

Alan stared at Agnes. "Frightened? What are you talking about? Frightened by whom? And why?"

Agnes pushed her way through the other uniformed officers who had rushed into the room the moment she had unlocked the bathroom door and walked out. Now, all she wanted to do was get out of here and find Sandra. But she hadn't got very far before Alan, who had followed closely behind her, reached out and grabbed her arm.

"Agnes, tell me, what's going on here? What am I missing?"

Pulling her arm away from the DCI's grasp, she stared up at him and heaved a sigh. "I'm afraid you are missing a great deal, Alan."

"Then tell me about it. Put me in the picture."

Agnes glanced at Andrews, who was still holding Moffat's arm. "I think you need to have a few words with your sergeant."

Chapter Twenty-Seven

Downstairs, Sandra's mind was racing. Had she heard that correctly? Was Barbara's son-in-law called Robert Jamison? Luck had certainly been on her side when this woman had almost battle-axed her way through the crowd to speak to her. How many times over the last few days had that name popped up? So far, there were three Robert Jamisons, if the man found dead in room 106 was also found to have that name!

Agnes would know exactly how to carry on this conversation. But alas, she wasn't here. Sandra looked around, hoping Jones would take over. However, he was caught up with some people near the door.

"Remind me, what is your name? I seem to have forgotten."

"Actually, I didn't tell you my name – you didn't ask. But it's Barbara Swift."

"Thank you, Barbara, if that's your real name."

"What do you mean by that?" Barbara snapped. "Of course it's my real name! Why would I give you a false name?"

"Barbara, you have been spinning me yarns from the moment I first spoke to you. First, you told me you had an appointment with a friend and also a rather important person for afternoon tea at a splendid hotel. Then, when I offered to call the hotel to explain your absence, you changed your story. Your 'friend' turned out to be your daughter, and the 'important person' was actually your son-in-law, Robert Jamison." Sandra made quotation marks in the air as she spoke.

"Then you said your afternoon tea was not at the Majestic Hotel, but somewhere else. You also stated that you stayed here at the hotel last night." Sandra screwed up her eyes. "But, as it happens, I'm staying here at the moment and I met Jamison, together with the young woman accompanying him, in the drawing room last night shortly after dinner. Surely, if you really were spending the night at the hotel, you would have joined them. But I certainly didn't see you." Sandra paused. "You didn't stay here last night, did you? I believe you simply popped into the hotel this morning because someone told you to. Would that person be your son-in-law, or maybe your daughter?"

Sandra glanced again at Barbara's suitcase. It was quite small, just the sort of case someone would use for a one night stay. "I'm also willing to bet that your suitcase doesn't contain any clothes and that your whole story is a charade. I suggest you tell us exactly what is going on."

There was a long moment of silence, before Sandra spoke again. "Incidentally, what is your daughter's name?"

Once the woman had mentioned her name as Barbara Swift, Sandra had meant to ask that question. However, it had been pushed aside because of all the other things she wanted answers to.

Barbara took a deep breath before she replied. "My daughter's name is Deborah. Deborah Jamison."

"Not Deborah Swift?" Sandra questioned, as she thought back to the night before.

"Well... yes, of course it was Deborah Swift, until she was married," Barbara uttered. "But now it's Deborah Jamison."

"Are you sure about that?" Sandra questioned. "I need to know whether your daughter really is married to this guy – and do you know whether she was with him last night?"

"Yes! Of course I'm sure they're married," Barbara retorted. "They have been married for over a year. As for your second question, yes, I believe Deborah was here at the hotel with her husband last night." She swept her eyes around the room before landing them back on

Sandra. "What are you trying to tell me? Has something happened to Deborah?"

"No, no. Nothing has happened to her – not as far as we know."

Sandra closed her eyes. She had opted to come in here to help the police calm the irritable crowd. Yet somehow, in the course of things, she had got herself involved with Barbara and the woman was answering her questions.

Sandra's eyes snapped open at that thought. Did Barbara believe she was talking to a woman detective? What on earth had she got herself into? Looking at Barbara out of the corner of her eye, Sandra got the impression she was quite relaxed. Maybe she was. She seemed to have the knack of jumping from one portrayal to another very easily; maybe a little *too* easily. Could it be that Barbara wasn't really quite as calm as she appeared? Perhaps now was the time to jump in and ask a few unexpected questions. But should she take this any further? After all, she hadn't anything to do with the police. Might she be charged with impersonating a police officer? What would Agnes do?

"So, Barbara, tell me a little about your son-in-law, Robert Jamison," Sandra asked, putting her concerns behind her.

There was an expression of puzzlement on Barbara's face as she turned to face Sandra. "What has Robert got to do with anything? He's a nice man and a good husband to my daughter." She paused and lifted one shoulder. "What more do you need to know?"

"Well, perhaps you could start by telling me what he does for a living."

* * *

"What did Agnes mean when she said I should have a few words with my sergeant?" the DCI asked Andrews.

Once the uniformed officers had left the room, taking Moffat with them, Andrews had been about to follow them, but Alan's voice had brought him to a halt.

"I have no idea, sir," Andrews replied, as he slowly turned back to face his boss. "You know what Agnes is like. She tends to come up with some weird ideas from time to time. How would I know anything about what goes on inside her head? Even you have trouble keeping up with her sometimes."

"Yes, I do, Andrews." Alan replied. "I'd be the first to admit it. Nevertheless, she very often comes up with something I've missed." He took a deep breath. "I'm willing to bet that she's done it again today when she implied you had something you wanted to keep hidden."

"No! That's wrong. You and I don't keep secrets from each other." Andrews gestured towards his DCI. "We work well together, we always have. Don't let Agnes come between us because she has a bee in her bonnet about something that happened in the bathroom. She'll get over it and it'll all work out fine, you'll see."

Alan nodded. "Okay, we'll leave it there. You could be right."

Alan wasn't convinced, but this was neither the time nor the place to carry on this conversation. He needed to get downstairs to help his detectives. They were probably having problems with guests wanting to leave the hotel, not to mention those who had recently checked in. But, he promised himself that he would definitely get to the bottom of this.

Agnes would never have made such a statement without good reason.

Chapter Twenty-Eight

Barbara looked surprised at Sandra's question.

"Why would you need to know what Robert does for a living?" She peered at Sandra. "Besides, you said you'd met him last night. Didn't that come up in the conversation? It's the sort of thing that tends to get people chatting."

"I'm afraid that question got bypassed. He was keen to get away as they had tickets booked for the show at the Theatre Royal."

"Really, is that so?"

Sandra didn't fail to notice that, for one split second, Barbara appeared to be taken aback at the news Robert had seats booked for the theatre. But she quickly regained her posture, just as she had done earlier.

"Yes, of course," Barbara said, shaking her head. "Silly me, I'd completely forgotten about that. They were both very keen to see the show."

"Do you know what they were going to see?"

"Robert did tell me," Barbara said, clicking her fingers together as though trying to remember. "I'm sorry. It seems I've forgotten. No doubt it will come to me later."

"It seems you have more contact with your son-in-law than your daughter. Surely she would have told you where they were going. Or don't you and your daughter get on?"

Sandra hadn't failed to notice that Barbara seemed to mention Robert a great deal more often than Deborah.

"Yes, of course. We get on well. She probably did tell me. But, like I said, I'd forgotten. It's as simple as that. Why are you asking me all these stupid questions?"

"Because I can't be sure about anything you tell me. But, getting back to the previous question, what does Robert do for a living?"

"He's a truck driver, if you must know."

Barbara shifted uneasily on the sofa, leaving Sandra wondering whether she was lying, or telling the truth and was a little ashamed that she had made him out to have a more high-powered and less menial job. But, either way, Sandra was still left unsure as to what Jamison really did for a living.

"A truck driver? Surely that must take him all over the country." Sandra tried to sound positive. She really needed to get this woman to open up more.

"Yes, it does," Barbara replied. "But it also takes him around the world. The company he works for has branches around the globe." She nudged Sandra's arm, excitedly. "There are times when he's gone for weeks, or even months on end. I never know when I'm going to see him again."

"Really," Sandra uttered.

She was rather astounded at that last sentence. Was there something going on between Barbara and her son-in-law?

"That's quite… inspiring." For one brief moment, she was lost for words. "You seem to have a good relationship with Robert," she added, pulling herself together. "I'm sure there are many people out there who don't get along quite so well with their son-in-law."

"Yes, that may be so," Barbara replied. "Nevertheless, that's how it is with us. We seemed to get along well together from the first day we met."

Sandra blinked her eyes a couple of times. Were Barbara and Jamison having an affair behind Deborah's back? It would certainly account for her immense interest in her son-in-law. But then she recalled the body Agnes had found only a few days ago. The victim's name, according to something the pathologist found on the victim, was Robert Jamison. His murder had been in the headlines on the TV and every newspaper in the land, in the hope that someone would come forward and identify the body. Yet, as far as she knew, not one person had contacted the police to check out the victim. Therefore, if Barbara was so close to her son-in-law, why hadn't she called the police to identify the man?

Consequently, the same thing could be said about Deborah, his so-called wife.

* * *

Once Agnes left Sandra's room, she hurried along the corridor towards the stairs. She wanted to get down to the ground floor as soon as possible and find out whether Sandra had arrived back at the hotel.

After what had happened, Agnes was annoyed with herself for leaving her friend on the quayside earlier. Who knows, maybe another plan to frighten Sandra was already in operation. If only they had continued walking along the quayside together, Agnes would have been there to help her friend. Though, at the same time, when they had arrived back at the hotel, Sandra could have walked into the room at the wrong time and been taken prisoner.

As she approached the stairs, Agnes noticed that the lift doors were closed and the sign above showed that the lift was stationed on the ground floor. Not Andy's favourite place, from all accounts. Apparently, he liked to settle wherever the last guest alighted.

That sudden thought of Andy brought a few other things to mind. Agnes had meant to talk with him again after their last meeting a day ago. Yet, she still had doubts about him. Though they had got off to a good start, once she had managed to get onto his wavelength, there was still something bothering her when she stepped out of the lift. It was for that reason she had decided not to reveal her true floor number. Instead, once he had closed the doors and the lift had begun to descend, she had walked down the few flights of stairs to reach her floor. Maybe it would have been a good idea to have waited for a few seconds to see where he landed. But it was too late to think about that now. At least the lift hadn't been on her floor. She would certainly have noticed the lights glaring out from the open doors.

Agnes reached the ground floor only to find police officers positioned by the main entrance, the entrance to the lift and also at the bottom of the stairs.

"I'm afraid no one is allowed to leave the building, madam," one of the officers said, as she stepped into the reception area.

"That's okay," she replied. "I don't want to leave. I'm looking for my friend. I think she should be here in the hotel somewhere."

Agnes looked past the officer towards the reception desk.

"Sally," she called out, "have you seen Sandra?"

"Yes, she went into the drawing room."

"Great! Thank you," she replied, raising a thumb. Turning back to the officer, she informed him that was where she wanted to go.

However, the officer wasn't sure about that. There had been so many people in the drawing room that some had been re-allocated to the bar.

"Isn't there room for one more in there, officer?"

"I have my orders, madam. All guests are now to be shown into the bar."

Agnes was about to say something further, but she was beaten to it from a voice behind her.

"It's okay, officer. Let her through."

Recognising the voice, Agnes swung around and nodded her thanks to Alan.

The DCI looked on thoughtfully as the officer escorted Agnes across to the drawing room. He really needed to speak to her on a one-to-one basis; especially after her last quip upstairs. However, as things stood, she had locked him out of everything she thought or did.

Nevertheless, he did really need to talk to her, and it needed to be this evening.

* * *

When Sandra glanced towards the door and saw Agnes walk in, she was overjoyed and hurried across to greet her.

"Agnes, I can't tell you how happy I am to see that you are safely away from the maniac upstairs. I was so worried when I heard that you were trapped in my room with him. I do hope that you are okay. He didn't hurt you, did he?"

"No, he didn't hurt me. I'm fine," Agnes said, once Sandra had released her grip and taken a step back. "I'm just so pleased that *you* are safe. I was so worried about you."

"Why would you be worried about me?" Sandra looked puzzled. "I wasn't in the room up there, you were. I was well away from the hotel when this happened to you."

"Yes, of course you were," Agnes replied. This wasn't the time to start explaining her concerns. It could wait until they were alone. Even then, it would be difficult to tell Sandra what she had learned.

"But I am curious as to why you were in my room in the first place," Sandra said.

Agnes quickly explained how she had seen Sandra's door ajar and had called Alan.

"I suggested that I went inside, while he and his sergeant waited by the door. But I'll tell you about it later." Agnes glanced across to where Sandra had been when she walked in. "So, who's the lady you were talking to?"

Sandra would like to have asked a few more questions, but she realised that now wasn't the right time.

"Agnes, you aren't going to believe it, but her name is Barbara Swift."

Agnes looked across at the woman, still perched on the sofa. "Swift... do you mean a relative of Deborah Swift, the young woman we met last night?"

"Yes. She says that she's Deborah's mother. But there's a lot more to it than that."

Sandra quickly explained what she had learned from Barbara.

"Well done, Sandra. You would make a great detective."

Fortunately, since the extra detectives had arrived, the number of people in the room had thinned out. Meanwhile, those still here in the drawing room had stopped protesting, obviously realising that their hue and cry wasn't going to get them anywhere. But maybe their sudden acquiescence had more to do with the fact that the manager had ordered afternoon tea to be served free of charge to all the guests who were unable to leave the hotel and those still waiting to be shown to their rooms.

Agnes glanced across to Barbara. She had found an empty sofa and had her head turned towards the window. However, while Agnes was still watching her, Barbara suddenly turned her head and looked towards where she and Sandra were standing. How uncanny was that? Agnes shivered. It was almost as though the woman knew what they were saying and had turned to face her opponents.

Come on, get a grip, Agnes told herself. This woman wasn't a psychic. Of course she knew she was being talked about. She had been questioned by Sandra only a short while earlier.

But then, still looking at the woman, Agnes suddenly realised the reason for her unexpected reaction and it certainly had nothing to do with whether Barbara was psychic or not. It was simply because she recognised the woman. Agnes recalled seeing her two days ago, or maybe it was three; time had passed so quickly, it was hard to remember what had happened, and when.

Agnes was so delighted, she would have clapped her hands if she hadn't been in a room full of people.

At least one of the mysteries was solved.

Chapter Twenty-Nine

Once Agnes had disappeared into the drawing room, Alan looked behind him, expecting to see his sergeant. However, Andrews wasn't anywhere in sight.

"Andrews. Where the hell are you?" Alan muttered to himself as he mounted the stairs back to the fourth floor.

He had almost reached the third floor when he found his sergeant slumped on the stairs with his head in his hands.

"What the bloody hell do you think you're doing?" Alan hissed, the moment he saw him. "I need you with me. What's the matter with you? Get yourself downstairs – we need to solve this case out before anyone else is murdered."

"I can't do it," Andrews wailed. "Find someone else while I sort myself out."

"The hell I will!" the DCI yelled. "You damn well sort yourself out here and now and tell me what's going on with you, or you're off my team altogether."

"I can't. I…"

"Okay, Andrews!" Alan interrupted. "I haven't got time for this. Not only have we got two cases of murder to solve, we also need to know why the door of Sandra's room was tampered with. If we find out who arranged that, then maybe we'll have found the murderer. Therefore, either tell me what's going on, or consider yourself suspended from duty as from now."

Andrews closed his eyes for few seconds before he spoke.

* * *

Agnes turned away from the woman's glare, though her thoughts continued to dwell on where she had last seen her. It had been in the Eldon Square Shopping Centre. Barbara, as she now knew her, and the Robert Jamison, she had met last night, had been chatting together in a coffee shop.

It was by mere chance that Agnes had seen them together. The coffee shop had been full when she arrived. But then, just as she had been about to walk away and seek out another café, someone vacated a table which she had been able to claim. Had she arrived at the café a minute or two earlier, she would never have seen the couple.

Agnes hadn't really meant to observe the other customers who were relaxing with a coffee after their shopping expedition. Nevertheless, she had always been a people-watcher and it was a bit late in in the day to change the habit, so when she was glancing around the people in the coffee shop, she couldn't help noticing the middle-aged woman who was wearing a black trouser suit with a large red rose in the button hole. But, forgetting the woman's attire for the moment, the important thing now was that Barbara had been sitting at the table with Robert Jamison, the very man she had seen walking into the hotel the day before. At least one part of the puzzle was in place.

Now, having remembered where she had first seen Jamison, other things began to come back to her. Barbara had been most annoyed about something. At one point, her voice had been so loud that people in the café had swung around to see what the commotion was about. It seemed that Jamison had told Barbara something which she was not happy about.

"But you promised me!" she had said, thumping her fist onto the table.

What was said after that went unheard as, seeing they were the focus of attention, both had lowered their voices. However, a moment later, Jamison left the coffee shop.

Agnes could have kicked herself for not remembering where she had seen Jamison. How could she possibly have forgotten the rumpus in the café? Not that it would have helped earlier in the investigation, but it might do so now.

* * *

"Come on, Sandra, let's do this," Agnes said. "I've suddenly remembered where I saw Jamison before he arrived at the hotel. He was with her." Agnes finished her last sentence by nodding across towards Barbara. "They were having a discussion about something."

"Then maybe you should do this alone. You might get more information on your own."

"No! You broke her down, Sandra. You need to be there, otherwise she could clam up again."

"Okay, then we'll do this together, Agnes."

Chapter Thirty

"That was me," Andrews mumbled, looking back up the stairs.

Still sitting on the stairs, only a short distance from Sandra's room, he threw his head back down into his hands.

"What are you talking about? What was you?" Alan replied, sharply. Though he was trying hard to keep his patience, it didn't seem to be working. "For heaven's sake, Andrews, what have you done?"

There was a long silence before Michael looked up to reply. "I told the man to alter the mechanism above Sandra's door."

Alan was so shocked, he was lost for words. Had he been talking to a suspect in some investigation, there wouldn't have been a problem. He was used to that. Therefore, he would have carried on asking questions, no problem. But this was his sergeant he was talking to; a man he trusted. Yet Andrews had just confessed to asking someone, a complete stranger, to meddle with the door to the room of his fiancée. Even though Agnes had more than hinted Andrews knew something about what had happened, he hadn't expected anything like this.

"You told Moffat to alter ... Are you mad?" Alan shouted, once he had found his voice. "Why would you do such a thing?"

"I didn't want her to get hurt – I simply wanted her to stop getting involved in police investigations. I just wanted to frighten her – make her think twice..."

"*Frighten* her? Have you any idea what might have happened to Sandra had she arrived back to her room while the man was still in there? Agnes was able to talk her way out of the situation, plus, she had already called us so we were at hand. But Sandra could have walked in there and been murdered!"

But then another thought sprang into his mind. "You didn't say a word when Agnes first entered the room. You could have stopped her from going in there. Yet you remained silent. Why?"

"Like you said, we were there," Andrews replied quietly. "Besides, I really thought the man would have gone by then."

"You couldn't have been sure about that. If Bill Moffat had finished the job, he would have made sure the door was closed after he left. The whole point of the exercise is that the door doesn't swing shut after *the guest* arrives back in their room, allowing someone to follow them in there. My guess is that you had an idea Moffat was still there and changed your plan. You thought that if Agnes was attacked, Sandra would listen to you in the future."

"I'm sorry… Tell Agnes I'm sorry…"

Alan glared down at Andrews, before turning around and heading off down the stairs.

Down in the reception area, Alan spoke to a couple of officers on duty. "Detective Sergeant Andrews is upstairs. I want you to go up there and arrest him."

The officers looked at Alan as though they hadn't heard correctly. "You want us to arrest Sergeant Andrews?" one of them queried, gazing wide-eyed at his boss as if he thought he had just gone stark, staring mad.

"Yes. That's right. Take him to the station and have the desk sergeant place him in one of the interview rooms with an officer standing guard. Then get back here. I may need you both."

Without another word, Alan headed across the reception area towards the drawing room.

* * *

Though the sofa was only meant to seat two people, Agnes and Sandra had each managed to squeeze themselves on either side of Barbara.

"This is my friend, Agnes," Sandra said. "She told me that she recalls seeing you a couple of days ago, while she was out shopping."

"Really," Barbara replied, without even looking towards Agnes. "I don't think so. Your friend must have me mixed up with someone else."

Sandra couldn't help noticing that Barbara was putting on all the airs and graces she had tried with her and Detective Jones a short while earlier.

"Why is that?" Agnes enquired. She wasn't about to be put off so easily.

"Because, if you must know, I've been away from the city and I only got back yesterday morning and I spent some time unpacking my case before I even left my home."

"Umm, yes, I agree that would have made it difficult for me to have seen you," Agnes replied. "But, you know, I'm one of those people who seldom forgets a face, especially when the person in question is screaming out at a man by the name of Robert Jamison, in a rather busy café."

At that point, Barbara suddenly turned so pale, Sandra thought the woman was about to faint. Agnes had certainly hit the nail on the head with that statement.

Swiftly pulling herself together, Barbara swung around to face Agnes. "Like I said, you're mistaken. That can't possibly have been me. I don't know what you're talking about."

"But you know exactly what I'm talking about – don't you, Barbara Swift?"

"No, I don't."

"Really! Agnes and I met Deborah the other evening."

"You didn't mention it earlier." Barbara swallowed hard.

"Didn't I?" Sandra replied. "Sorry about that. Maybe I should have. Yes, we met Deborah. She was with Robert Jamison – your son-in-law."

"But, you know something, Barbara, during the conversation with Deborah and Robert, she didn't tell us that they were married," Agnes said.

"No, she said she was still single and her name was Deborah Swift," Sandra added.

By now, Barbara's head was swinging from one side to the other, as both Agnes and Sandra threw either questions or statements at her.

"Okay, enough! Stop this now!" Barbara threw her hands in the air. "Deborah was lying! She does that now and again – she likes to keep people guessing. She is definitely married."

"But who is she married to?" Sandra asked.

"We've been through all that. I told you she is married to Robert Jamison."

"Yes, so I gather," Agnes replied. "But you see, the real question is – which Robert Jamison?"

* * *

Alan stood by the door leading into the drawing room. He hadn't expected it to be so quiet. On the contrary, he had thought the guests would be loudly voicing their complaints at being held in the hotel against their will. Instead, there were only the soft mumblings of people talking to each other in a civilised manner. Obviously, Jones had everything under control.

"Can I help you, Chief Inspector?"

Alan swung around to find Sue Matthews standing a short distance behind him.

"No, Miss Matthews, I'm fine," he replied. "I was just about to go inside to bring my detectives up to date on the case." He paused. "I must say I'm delighted to see you looking so well."

Alan hadn't seen Sue since the day she had been carried off in an ambulance, though he had learned from Keith that she had made a remarkable recovery.

"Thank you," Sue replied. "But I mustn't keep you. I do hope you caught the man who was meddling with the door mechanism."

"Yes, we caught him." Alan reached for the door handle as he spoke. "Tell Mr Jenkins I would like to see him before I leave," he added.

Sue nodded and a moment later, he opened the door and slipped quietly into the drawing room.

Inside, Alan caught Jones's attention and motioned him to join him by the door, out of earshot. "We'll go through everything in more detail once we are all back at the station," he said, after quickly outlining the bare details of what had happed upstairs. He left out the part Andrews had played in it. This was certainly not the time, nor the place to discuss that. "In the meantime, tell me what's been going on down here. Any luck in finding someone who might be involved?"

Alan had fully expected a negative reply. Therefore he was taken by surprise when Jones told him about Barbara Swift.

"She's over there on the sofa by the window with Mrs Lockwood and Miss Williams. They're still trying to drag further information from her. But, due to her reluctance to hang around here and the excuses she's made, we feel that she is somehow involved in these murders. Maybe we'll get more evidence from her once she's been arrested and taken to the station. That usually frightens people into revealing more than merely being questioned in what they believe to be a safe environment."

"Where's Smithers?" Alan asked, looking around the room. There was another detective here, but no sign of Smithers.

"He's holed up in the bar with several other guests. There were so many in here that there was nowhere for them to sit, so we had to split them up. I phoned the station for more detectives to come over here to help out. Even so, that didn't quieten them down. It was only after the manager ordered afternoon tea to be served to all the guests that they calmed down."

"Okay, we need to get Barbara Swift back to the station. If neither you nor Smithers have any reason to hold any other guests, then allow them leave. However, if either of you have a single doubt about any one of them, then take them in for questioning or, at the very least, have them followed. I want this case cleared up as quickly as possible."

"Yes, sir."

"In the meantime, come with me."

Jones followed the DCI down to where Barbara was sitting.

Once he was standing in front of her, he didn't mince his words. He came straight to the point.

"Mrs Swift, I believe that you are a major suspect in two murders, both of which have been carried out in the last forty-eight hours. Therefore, I am arresting you on the charge of murder. Anything you say…"

"But I…" Barbara tried to interrupt.

"… will be taken down and used in evidence…" Alan continued with the usual statement without even a pause.

Once he had finished, he beckoned the two officers still standing by the door. "Escort this woman to the station and place her in a cell until I get back there."

Once the officers had placed handcuffs on Barbara Swift's wrists and were escorting her towards the door, Alan looked at Agnes, who was still sitting on the sofa.

"We need to talk," he said. "By that, I mean we need to talk, *now!*"

Agnes had watched Alan from the moment he had entered the room. Both his facial expression and manner had told her that he wasn't in the best of moods. It was possible that the case was beginning to get to him. However, it was more likely that he'd had a few words with his sergeant after she had disappeared downstairs.

"Okay," Agnes replied, pushing herself out of the sofa. "Where do you want to have this talk?"

"I don't care. I just want us to talk to each other the way we used to."

A flash of guilt flew over Agnes. She had acted stupidly over the last few days. If only Alan hadn't lost his temper the day she informed him about there being a Robert Jamison booked into the hotel, they would have continued to swap their thoughts and information and all this nonsense would never have happened. But it was too late to think about that now. She had discovered several other things about the case, but hadn't told him anything. Instead, she had only confided in her friend, Sandra. But perhaps now was the time to clear up any misunderstandings between them, or her relationship with Alan would be ended forever.

Was that what she really wanted?

Chapter Thirty-One

Now back at the station, Andrews found himself sitting in one of the interview rooms with Police Officer Sanders, a rather grim-faced individual, standing by the door. Thankfully, the two officers who had escorted him to the station had slid him in through the back door to save his embarrassment; something he had requested and they had agreed to do. Then, while one of them had gone off to inform the desk sergeant of the situation, the other had stood guard in the room until another officer was appointed to take his place.

Andrews had tried to start a conversation with Sanders to lighten the mood, but the officer wasn't having any of it. Sanders had been instructed not to talk to the detective unless it was absolutely necessary and, as far as he was concerned, that was how it was going to be. He had a sergeant's exam coming up the following week and, having studied long and hard over the last month, he felt confident that he would pass. Therefore, he was not going to put a foot wrong on this or any other assignment that might spoil his chances.

Andrews slid down the straight-backed chair, trying to get into a more relaxed position. Why the hell were the chairs in here so damn uncomfortable? Once this was over, he would speak to Chief Superintendent Lewis and draw his attention to the problem. Maybe Lewis would even pop down and take a look for himself. He might even decide to change them.

Andrews sighed heavily. Who was he kidding? Once this was over, he would be kicked out of the force. There would be no chance to speak to the Chief Superintendent or anyone else about the seating in the interview rooms. But then, an even more distressing thought came to mind. Once Sandra learned what he had done, she would drop him like a hot brick and he would have lost the only woman he ever loved.

He buried head in his hands as he thought through what he had done. How could he have been so damn stupid?

* * *

Meanwhile, back at the hotel, Agnes and Alan had stepped out of the drawing room and were now standing in the reception area.

"Do you want to go up to my room to talk?" Agnes enquired.

"No, I think it would be better if we were to discuss our problems somewhere neutral."

"Don't you think you're being a little over dramatic, Alan? After all, we have both stayed in that room before – by that, I mean… together."

"Yes. That's the point, Agnes. I'm not staying here with you at the moment. In this instance the room is yours, not mine."

"What do you mean by that?" Agnes snapped. "I booked the room in both our names. I thought you would be spending the night at the hotel with me after we'd had dinner. But it didn't work out – did it?"

"Agnes, though you added my name to the booking, I know you intended to spend time here without me. When I couldn't get in touch with you on your phone, I went up to the room to see whether you were there. Obviously you weren't, otherwise you would have seen me. But, getting back to the point – neither were any of my clothes. You didn't really want me here with you, did you? Why don't you just admit it?"

"So, you looked in the wardrobe and, when you didn't find any of your clothes, you decided that I didn't want you with me," Agnes retorted. "Alan, you are certainly not as good a detective as you think you are."

"What do you mean by that?"

"I did pack a suitcase for you. But, after you ranted on at me and then strode away, I just didn't take the time to unpack it. I guessed you wouldn't be spending the night with me after all." Agnes shook her head. "If only you and your sergeant had even bothered to search the room more thoroughly, you would have found another suitcase standing on the far side of the wardrobe." She shook her head. "I would have perched it on top of the wardrobe, if I had been able to lift it up there. But, as it was quite heavy, I simply dragged it off the bed and dropped it by the side of the wardrobe."

Alan was lost for words. He cast his mind back to the day he went into Agnes's room and recalled seeing a suitcase standing by the side of the wardrobe. But, believing it to be another suitcase belonging to Agnes, he hadn't given it much thought. If only he had checked it out... But it was too late now.

"Agnes, I am so sorry. Can we just go up to your – I mean, *our* room and talk about this?"

"Yes," Agnes replied. "I think that would be a good idea."

They were about to move away when Sue appeared.

"I do hope you've managed to get to the bottom of the recent problem at the hotel. We really can't go on like this. Some of the guests have already checked out and are demanding a refund."

"I understand how difficult it has been, but I believe we have everything under control now," Alan replied. "Actually, did you mention to Mr Jenkins that I would like to have a word with him?"

"Yes. He said that he would be in his office until late, so just go in when you're ready."

Chapter Thirty-Two

"So, now we're alone, what did you want to talk to me about?" Agnes asked, once they were seated in the room upstairs.

"For a start, I want to know whether you were telling me the truth when you told me you had never seen Robert Jamison again after spotting him in reception."

Agnes tapped her lips as she thought through how to answer. She could continue being dishonest, as she had done on the quayside. But, reminding herself of her earlier thoughts, she believed the time had come to tell the truth.

"Actually Alan, I admit I was lying to you back then. Jamison was sitting in the hotel restaurant when you and your sergeant walked in. He and his girlfriend, Deborah Swift, were at a table close to where Sandra and I were sitting."

"And you didn't think to tell me at the time?" Alan yelled.

"Keep your voice down, Alan. There might be someone in the rooms on either side of us. But yes," Agnes continued. "As a matter of fact I did consider telling you, but then I decided against it." She heaved a sigh. "Perhaps now is a good time to mention that Sandra and I saw them again in the drawing room after dinner. Actually, we sat with them and had a chat over coffee." She went on to explain what had been said.

"However, they left early as they had tickets for *Les Misérables* **at** the Theatre Royal, or so we were led to believe. We haven't seen either of them since." Agnes paused. "Anyway, even if I had wanted to tell you about Jamison being in the drawing room, I wouldn't have been able to do so as you and your sergeant had already left."

"I doubt you would've told me, even if I had still been somewhere in the building."

Agnes didn't reply. There was nothing she could say. Alan was right. Having kept the secret earlier that evening, she'd had no intention of seeking him out to tell him Jamison was in the drawing room. She turned her head and gazed out of the window towards the Baltic Gallery.

"Agnes, if all this keeping secrets business stems from me, then I truly apologise." Alan was the first to break the silence. "However, do you realise that I could have both you and Sandra arrested for withholding information which could be vital to the case?"

Agnes slowly turned her head to look at Alan. "Yes, I know," she said. "Do what you must."

Alan had not expected that. He fully believed Agnes would have been shocked at the thought and might have almost pleaded with him not to go down that road. But then, he should have known better.

"Aren't you even concerned that I could have you arrested?"

"Are you going to arrest Sandra and me?" Agnes asked, answering his question with another question. That was something she had learned a long time ago.

Answering a question with another question often sent the first person off the rails.

"No, no, of course I won't," Alan uttered.

"Then we've no reason to be concerned," Agnes said. She gave him a broad wink.

Alan shook his head, though he couldn't help giving a smile. Agnes had done it again. Just when he thought he might have caught her, she had wormed her way out.

"I need to make a move now," he said, rising to his feet. "I have a few things to take care of."

Once he had spoken to Mr Jenkins, the manager of the hotel, he had to head back to the station and talk to the three people being held.

One was Bill Moffat, the young man now claiming to have been set up. Another was the woman calling herself Barbara Swift, and the third was his sergeant, Michael Andrews.

Out of those three names floating around in his head, the interview with his sergeant troubled him the most.

* * *

When Alan stepped out of the manager's office, he found Agnes sitting on one of the sofas in the hotel reception. She leapt to her feet as he approached.

"I thought I would take a walk along the quayside to clear my head," she said. "It's been quite a day."

"Sounds like a good idea." He looked around. "Where's Sandra? Isn't she going with you?"

"No, I haven't seen her since I left her in the drawing room." She paused. "Actually, I'm not looking forward to seeing her at the moment," she added, lowering her voice. "I don't know what to say if she mentions Michael."

Alan nodded. "Yes, it's a difficult situation."

"What will happen to him now?"

The subject of the sergeant's involvement had risen while they were upstairs. Alan had asked how she knew Michael was mixed up with the tampering of Sandra's door. She had explained that it was simply because she had recognised his handwriting on the slip of paper Moffat had handed to her. Apart from Alan telling her that Michael had broken down and confessed, nothing further had been said.

Alan took a deep breath. "I really don't know. I've never had to deal with anything like this. Thank goodness any decisions will come from above. But personally, I think he'll be dismissed from the force."

By now, they had reached the entrance to the hotel and the doors had slid open.

"Will I see you for dinner?" Agnes asked, as they walked down the steps. "You can help me…"

Agnes abruptly stopped talking and turned her attention to someone standing a short distance away.

Alan followed her gaze, unsure who or what she was looking at as there were a few people walking along the quayside. But then, a man pulled a gun from his pocket and pointed it straight at Agnes.

"No!" Alan yelled. "Get down – now!"

However, it was too late. The man had already fired the gun.

Alan watched in disbelief as Agnes crumpled to the ground.

Chapter Thirty-Three

Alan was kneeling down beside Agnes when several members of the hotel staff rushed out. Sally had been straightening a cushion on the sofa nearest to the entrance, when she heard a loud noise. Believing it to be some kid setting off a firecracker, she looked towards the door, only to see Agnes drop to the ground. Quickly beckoning a couple of the hotel porters, she rushed outside, thinking the surprisingly loud bang had given Agnes such a shock she had lost her footing and fallen over.

"Can I help?" Sally asked.

"Yes! Everyone, get back inside and don't let anyone leave the building. Agnes has been shot!" Alan yelled, pulling out his phone.

Clasping her hand to her mouth, Sally and the porters ran back into the hotel. Once inside, she called the manager to inform him of what had happened. Then, though she knew she shouldn't really pass on any information to guests not intending to leave the hotel, she took the liberty of ringing Sandra's room.

Outside, Alan was now through to the police station. "Get someone to call an ambulance. There has been a shooting outside the Millennium Hotel. Also, get armed response down here – now!" he screamed into his phone. "A man wearing torn jeans and a dark coloured T-shirt was last seen running back along the quayside towards the Tyne Bridge." He paused for a second when he realised he had heard that very same description only a few days ago. "However, he might have a car parked somewhere. Be wary of any car speeding away from the area. Stop the car and check them out."

He thrust his phone back into his pocket and knelt down beside Agnes.

"Agnes, my darling, you must hold on. I need you. The ambulance is on its way," Alan whispered.

"What's happened?"

Alan looked up to see Ben, the taxi driver, anxiously looking down at them.

"Some damn lunatic has shot Agnes," Alan replied.

Ben looked distraught as he knelt down next to Alan. "There must be something I can do?"

"I wish there was, Ben. But there isn't anything either of us can do. The ambulance is on its way."

"Come on, Agnes. You have got to stay with me, I need you," Alan coaxed. By now, he was cradling her head in his lap.

Agnes opened her eyes slightly. "I know you do," she spluttered.

"Agnes, I think it might be best if you stayed silent and preserved your strength."

Agnes looked at Ben and opened her mouth to say something, but all she could do was cough.

"Please, don't try to talk," Ben said. "You can tell me all about it when you are feeling better."

Agnes looked back at Alan. "Robert Jamison..."

"The man with the gun was Robert Jamison? The same man you saw at the hotel?"

Agnes nodded her head slightly, before falling silent.

Alan felt for a pulse. Thankfully, she was still alive. But how much longer could she hold out?

"Where's that damn ambulance?" he muttered, impatiently. He heaved a sigh of relief when he heard a siren screaming from a vehicle a short distance away.

A moment later, an ambulance pulled alongside them and two paramedics jumped out.

* * *

Sandra had sat quietly in the drawing room after everyone left, before she slowly made her way upstairs to her room. It had disturbed her to learn that someone had tampered with the door to her room. But if she made sure it was closed and locked once she was inside, surely that should mean she would be safe.

Upstairs, she had just sat down on the sofa when the phone on her bedside table rang. The call was from Sally, the receptionist. Despite Sally sounding in a state of shock, Sandra managed to pick up that Agnes had been shot outside the hotel.

Throwing the phone back onto the cradle, she gathered her bag and coat together and hurried down to the reception area, using the stairs rather than the lift. She had used the lift one or twice, but she had never really got on with the young attendant. She had found him too intrusive. Now, outside the hotel, Sandra hurried across to the ambulance with tears welling in her eyes.

"We both need to calm down, Sandra," Alan told her. "Agnes is breathing steadily, but they need to get her to hospital as soon as possible."

"I want to go with her," Sandra said. "I should be with Agnes, she might need me." It came over as more of a statement, rather than a request.

"Yes, I think she would want you to be with her," Alan replied.

Alan heaved a sigh. If he were in any other job, he would have jumped into the ambulance without a second thought and sat by her side for as long as it took. But, as a Detective Chief Inspector, his first duty now was to find the person who had tried to kill the woman he loved.

"There's nowhere I'd rather be than with Agnes," he added. "But the man who pulled the trigger is still out there and I really need to find him before he tries again."

* * *

Sandra sat quietly in the ambulance and watched as the paramedic took the routine tests. She couldn't tell whether the results were good or bad as his expression gave nothing away. However she felt sure that if there had been a problem, he would have thumped on the small window behind the driver, informing him to speed up or stop and come around to help him.

Sandra turned her attention back to Agnes and was relieved to see her open her eyes, even though it was only very slightly.

"You're on your way to the hospital," Sandra said, as tears began to roll down her cheeks. "You're going to be fine."

"Then why are you crying?" Agnes replied, in almost a whisper.

The paramedic leaned forward. "Keep your eyes on my finger," he said, as he moved his finger back and forth.

"That's good," he replied. He straightened his back and reached out for the medical chart to fill in the result.

Agnes closed her eyes. "Does that mean you can take me home now?"

"Hardly, Mrs Lockwood," he said. "You need to be seen by a doctor. Don't you realise that someone tried to kill you?"

"Yes, I do." Agnes slowly opened her eyes and looked up at him. "But I'm rather getting used to it now."

The paramedic stopped writing and looked down at Agnes in amazement before re-checking his chart as though he had misread something.

"I'm afraid she's right," Sandra said, picking up on the paramedic's confusion. "I know it's hard to understand, but it's true. Mrs Lockwood has been attacked in one way or another several times now."

At that point, the driver pulled to a halt. They were now outside the Royal Victoria Infirmary. He pulled on the handbrake and shut down the engine before jumping out of the cab and rushing around to the back of the ambulance.

A few minutes later, Agnes was being wheeled through the hospital doors to where a doctor and two nurses were waiting. The paramedic quickly explained his findings, as he handed over the charts he had completed on the way to the hospital.

The doctor nodded, as he glanced down at the figures. "Okay, we'll take it from here."

Inside the hospital, Sandra began to follow the team as they hurried down the corridor. However, one of the nurses stopped her.

"I want to go with her, she's my friend," Sandra said.

"I'm afraid you must wait here," the nurse said, placing her hand on Sandra's arm. "I do understand your concern, but you need to let the doctors do their job. Why don't you get yourself a coffee?" she added, pointing across the corridor towards a small café run by a charity. "I'll come back later and let you know how your friend is getting on."

Sandra nodded and walked across to the café. Coffee or tea was the last thing she wanted right now. But maybe the nurse was right; she was feeling rather stressed, so it might help. Once she was seated in the café with a steaming cup of tea in front of her, she pulled out her phone and punched in a number.

Perhaps this was the time to bring Michael up to speed.

Chapter Thirty-Four

Back at the station, Detective Sergeant Andrews tapped his fingers on the table in the interview room, as he glanced towards the two-way mirror on the other side of the room. Though Michael could only see his own reflection, he was aware that anyone on the other side would be able to see him. No doubt some of the station officers were peering at him right now. It wasn't often a detective sergeant was arrested while on duty.

"There's been a call for you," the desk sergeant said, suddenly bursting into the room.

It had been so quiet until now, Andrews almost fell off the chair in fright.

"It was from Sandra Williams, your young lady," Mathers continued, without any hesitation. "I think she was taken by surprise and thought she had the wrong number, when she didn't hear your voice."

Andrews had been relieved of his phone and a few other things on the way to the station.

"What did you tell her?"

"The truth, of course, what else could I say? I told her you had been arrested for conspiring with someone to alter the mechanism to her door."

Andrews turned pale. "What did she say?"

"Nothing, she hung up."

Andrews was about to ask Sergeant Mathers why he had felt the need to tell his fiancée what he had done, but then changed his mind. He already knew. This was a man who never minced his words.

"If there's nothing else, I'll get back to my job."

With a nod to the officer on duty, Mathers left the room, closing the door firmly behind him, leaving Andrews to chew over what he had said.

Outside, in the corridor, Mathers smiled to himself. Of course he hadn't told Miss Williams the whole truth. He had merely said that Andrews was in the interview room and not to be disturbed, which was true. However, being so furious that a detective sergeant in this station would do such a thing, he had wanted to give the young officer something to think about.

Mathers was now almost giggling to himself as he strolled back to his office. From the look on the detective's face, he had succeeded.

* * *

Once Sandra had shut down the call to Michael's phone, she sat quietly while taking sips of the tea she had bought a few minutes ago. She had added two large spoonfuls of sugar. Normally, she didn't take sugar with either tea or coffee. However, she had heard that it was supposed to be good for someone in a state of shock and she had certainly been shocked today. Not only had someone meddled with the door to her room, probably with something nasty in mind, she had found Agnes being lifted into an ambulance after she had been shot.

Sandra heaved a sigh as she glanced at the clock on the wall. How many times would the minute hand travel around the clock face before the nurse came back with some news? She had asked Sergeant Mathers to tell Michael where she was and ask him to get in touch with her once he was out of the interview room. Yet, so far, her phone had remained silent and there was no sign of Michael here at the hospital.

The hand on the clock had done two full circles, before the nurse she had seen earlier appeared in front of her.

"Mrs Lockwood is out of theatre," the nurse said. "The surgeon has retrieved the bullet and thankfully, because of where she was hit, it hadn't pierced any vital organs, so she should make a good recovery."

"Thank you. I'm so relieved. I've been worried sick sitting here. May I see her?"

"Not at the moment. She's still a little groggy." The nurse paused. "Maybe you'd like to go home and come back tomorrow."

"No. I'd prefer to wait a while longer," Sandra replied. "I might be able to see her later."

"Very well," the nurse said, as she began to walk away.

However, she had only taken a few steps before she turned around.

"Perhaps I could let you see her for a short while," she said. "But please don't try to get her to talk."

Sandra swiftly gathered her things together and caught up with the nurse. "Thank you. I'm so grateful. But I think there's something you should be aware of."

The nurse raised her eyebrows. "What is that?"

"If Agnes wants to talk, there is nothing on this earth that will stop her!"

* * *

"How could he have got away?" Alan was so angry that he thumped his fist on a desk in the incident room as he spoke. "I want every officer we can spare out there looking for the man using the name of Robert Jamison. Starting from where I last saw him, split up and drive down every road in the city. Uniformed officers are being given the same instructions. I believe him to be the same man described to us a few days ago by a young woman at the restaurant where the first Robert Jamison was shot." Alan pointed towards the board where that particular description had been posted. "When I saw him today, he was dressed much the same – torn jeans and denim jacket. Though I guess he's had time to change by now." He paused. "Now go! But take care. The man could still be armed and very probably desperate."

Once everyone had left, Alan turned his thoughts to Agnes. He had already called the hospital three times, but each time the answer had been the same; there was no further news as she was still in surgery. Alan knew that he really needed to start interviewing the three people who had been arrested earlier that day, but at the same time, he was anxious to learn how Agnes was progressing. Pulling out his phone, he punched in the hospital number again. This time he was lucky. It seems she was now out of surgery and had been moved to a ward. The person on the other end of the line said they would transfer his call to that ward.

Now speaking to Nurse Smith on the ward, he explained who he was and asked how Mrs Lockwood was after the surgery. He could almost have danced around the room when he heard that Agnes was responding well.

"That's brilliant news," Alan exclaimed.

However, his joyous mood was knocked on the head a second later when the nurse told him that her husband had just arrived.

"Mrs Lockwood is widowed!" he yelled. "Get that man away from her right now. He is dangerous!"

Without a word, the nurse slammed down the phone and rushed out of the small office. On the way down to Mrs Lockwood's room, she called out to one of the domestic staff, who was mopping the floor.

"Jimmy, follow me and bring that with you," she said, when he started to put the mop back into the bucket. "We might need it."

Without a word, Jimmy followed her down the corridor to the small room where Agnes was recovering.

Inside, the man was standing over the bed, gazing down at the patient. He looked up as they walked in.

"I must ask you to leave," the nurse said.

"But I've only just arrived, Nurse... Smith," he retorted, looking at the name pinned to her uniform. "I'm her husband. I have a right to be here."

"I have heard otherwise. Please leave."

The man took a step forward and raised his hand as though he was about to strike the nurse. However, Jimmy was too quick for him. He lifted the mop and thrust it at the man. Taken by surprise, the man lost his balance and would have fallen to the floor had it not been for the armchair standing by the bed.

"I'll have you for this," the man said, pulling a knife from his pocket as he regained his footing.

He had intended to stab the woman lying in the bed; using a gun would have attracted too much attention on a hospital ward. But somehow, the staff had learned that he wasn't Agnes's husband.

"Oh no, you won't," Jimmy replied in a loud voice. He lifted the mop and pointed it at the man. "Stay away from us. The police will be here any minute now."

Jimmy had no idea whether the police were aware of this incident or not, but it had been the first thing to pop into his mind.

"Pull the other one!" the man sneered.

However, his grin turned to a look of alarm when a police siren was heard approaching the hospital. Still holding the knife, he pointed it at them and started to move towards the door. Just then, the door burst open and the senior nurse of the day rushed in.

"What's going on in here? Keep the noise down, this is…" The rest of her words were lost when she saw the man wielding a knife. "What are you doing?"

"Actually, I was just leaving," the man said. Still holding the knife, he edged closer to the door. "But please, do give Mrs Lockwood my regards when she awakes. Tell her…" He paused for a moment, before giving them a tormenting smile. "Tell her I'm sorry I missed her the first time, but I hope to try again very soon." A moment later, he had disappeared out of the door.

"I'm going to call the police." It was the senior nurse who broke the silence that followed.

"I think they're already here," Jimmy told her.

"Who on earth was that?" Nurse Smith said to Jimmy, once the senior nurse had left to meet the police.

"That... was the man who tried to kill me today."

The two members of staff swung around to find Agnes trying to sit up.

"Wait, Mrs Lockwood, don't try to get up," the nurse said, as she rushed across to the bed. "You must stay quiet – at least until the doctor has been to check you out." She paused. "Are you saying that the man who just left was the man who shot you today?"

"Yes," Agnes spluttered.

Nurse Smith opened her mouth to say something, but was interrupted when the door swung open. It turned out to be another nurse, accompanied by a young woman.

"Now is not a good time for visitors," Nurse Smith told them.

However, Agnes thought differently when she saw her friend standing by the door. "Come in, Sandra. I'm so pleased to see you." She cast a glance towards Nurse Smith. "I promise not to get over-excited."

"Very well," the nurse said, making sure the sheets were firmly tucked around the patient. Maybe it wouldn't be a bad idea for Mrs Lockwood to have a friend sitting with her.

However, the words were hardly out of her mouth when the door swung open again. Looking around, she found a man striding in. Fearing the worst, she glanced across at Jimmy, who had already raised his mop in anticipation of a fight. But then, spotting the senior nurse at the door, he lowered it.

"It's okay, I'm DCI Johnson," Alan said, holding up his identification badge.

"Yes, he is," Sandra confirmed. "My fiancé is his sergeant. Is he here?" Sandra glanced back at the door as she spoke, expecting to see him follow his boss into the room, but she was left disappointed when she saw a uniformed officer standing by the door.

"Agnes, I've been so worried about you," Alan said, hurrying across to where she was lying. "Thank goodness you're going to be alright." He leant over the bed and kissed her.

"Thank you, Alan," Agnes replied, pulling her hands free from the covers and placing them on his face. "I didn't think I would get to see you ever again when I felt the bullet enter my body. But, thanks to the doctor who removed it, I am going to live to help solve another case."

Alan heaved a sigh. "Agnes, why can't you stay away from police inquiries? You could have been killed today. This is the fourth time you have been in the clutches of a killer. Won't you ever learn?"

"No, I'm afraid not." Agnes managed to give a faint smile. "Sorry, to be so annoying, but I love being involved in your cases. However, to be accurate, this is the fifth time." Agnes heaved in a breath of air. "He tried again, only a short while ago, here in this room."

"I think you should leave now, Detective Chief Inspector, you can see the patient is exhausted," Nurse Smith said. Stepping closer to her patient, she picked up Mrs Lockwood's arm and began to take her pulse.

"Wait!" Agnes said, muscling up her last inch of strength. "He's the man we saw at the hotel under the name of Robert Jamison." She looked at Sandra. "I've told Alan everything we learned that night at the hotel."

"What was the man wearing?" Alan asked the nurse. He was aware that should have been his first thought when he walked into the room. But when he saw Agnes, everything else had been forgotten.

"A dark suit – navy blue, I'd say," the nurse replied. "He had a matching coloured tie and a white shirt. He looked very smart – except for his shoes. They were black and had scuff marks on the top."

"He reminded me of James Bond." The voice came from somewhere behind him.

Alan swung around to find one of the domestic staff leaning on his mop. "Why did you think that?"

"Because of his watch, it looked rather expensive."

Alan glanced across to the door where the uniformed officer was making notes. "Did you get all that?"

The officer nodded.

"Then get on the radio and inform the men searching the building. Also, get some of them out into the car park."

Alan turned back to face the nurse and the young man.

"Well done, both of you. If either of you happen to think of anything else, give me a call." Alan pulled a card out of his pocket and handed it to the nurse.

"I should really be ordering you both to leave the room," the nurse said as she took the card. "However, I think I would be wasting my time. But please, keep your voices down."

"Will do," Alan said, as he took Agnes's hand.

Chapter Thirty-Five

A short while later, Alan left the ward and hurried down the stairs leading to the ground floor. Though she was trying to help with the case, Sandra had only repeated what Agnes had already told him while they were at the hotel earlier.

By now, Alan was on the ground floor. Glancing towards the large windows, he could see police officers pulling aside any man wearing a dark coloured suit. But then it struck him. The man they were looking for was too clever to walk out of the hospital wearing the very same suit. He would have changed into something totally different before leaving the hospital.

Directly opposite from where Alan was standing, were the public conveniences. Jamison could have changed his outfit in there and strolled past the officers totally unobserved. Alan leaned back against the wall in frustration.

Once again, the man had fooled them all.

* * *

Back at the station, Alan decided to question Barbara Swift first. As the woman appeared to have links with Jamison, there was a chance she could open a few gates. But that would only happen if he could get through to her and make her talk. He hoped that spending time in the cell, plus the threat of being charged as an accessory to murder, might have helped to open her up.

It appeared that she was Robert Jamison's wife, not his mother-in-law. With a little further scratching around, he learned that Deborah was just someone he had met up with a few weeks ago.

"Why did she use your name? She said her name was Deborah Swift."

"No comment."

"Why did Jamison meet up with Deborah in the first place?"

"I don't know."

"You didn't think to ask him?" Alan replied. "Weren't you curious?"

"No comment."

"Where is Deborah now?"

Barbara shrugged. "No comment."

"Did Jamison really have tickets for the show at the Theatre Royal?"

"No comment."

"Why do you still call yourself Barbara Swift? Why not use your married name?"

"Because I think, Barbara Swift suits me better – Swift by name – Swift by nature. I was always called Swift when I was young as I used to dart around all the time and I just sort of got the hang of it."

"Who was the man found dead in the restaurant a few days ago and also the man found dead in a room at the hotel? We believe Jamison killed them both," Alan asked, the moment she stopped talking.

"No comment."

Realising he wasn't going to get any further with Barbara Swift at the moment, he looked at his watch and quoted the time into the machine recording the interview and signed out. Once Barbara Swift had been escorted back to her cell, Alan looked at his watch again. It was a bit late to start interviewing Bill Moffat. Therefore he decided to have a few words with Andrews.

Outside the interview room, Alan peered at his sergeant through the two-way mirror. He was slouched in the chair with his arms resting on the table. A plate holding a sandwich had been pushed to one side, though the mug of coffee appeared to have been used.

"Weren't you hungry?" Alan asked when he entered the room. He pointed to the packet holding the unopened sandwich.

"No, I wasn't," Andrews replied, quietly.

"Michael, you got yourself into this mess," Alan said, as he lowered himself into the chair opposite his sergeant. "What were you thinking? You could have got Sandra killed."

"Yes, I realise that now. But it wasn't supposed to happen like that. As I told you earlier, I was intending to watch out for her arriving back at the hotel. Once she was inside her room, I was going to follow her in and tell her the door hadn't closed properly."

"Then you would have had the perfect excuse to take her back to her flat and stop her from doing anything you didn't want her to do."

"Yes... No!" Andrews stuttered. "I didn't mean it like that."

"Then what did you mean it like?" Alan asked.

"I just wanted her to stay away from my job." Andrews paused. "You know what I mean. We went through all this a few days ago while we were at the bar near the hotel. You appeared to agree with me that you'd rather Agnes stayed away from our investigations."

Alan coughed. "Yes, I did. But I admitted to you at the time that I had been stupid and I should have told Agnes what I had learned." He heaved a sigh. "Nevertheless, Andrews, I could never have done what you did. You realise your days in the force are numbered."

Andrews nodded.

"Maybe I could help you get through this," Alan said. "Though I can't promise you'll come out the other end as a detective sergeant. But it would be a start if you were to tell me how you happened to run across Bill Moffat, the man involved in the door mechanism changes."

Andrews took a deep breath. "I saw him repairing the door to room 106, shortly after the body had been removed. Please understand – I didn't know he was the man who had altered it in the first place. But seeing him doing the job so quickly left me thinking. How did he know exactly where to look for the fault? A man coming in would have had to check a few things before knowing where to start..."

"... unless he had tampered with it in the first place," Alan said, finishing the sentence for Andrews.

"Precisely," Andrews replied.

"So you went across to have a word with him, suggesting that he could do a job for you?"

"No. Well, yes, I asked him to do a job for me, but not until later." Andrews stared down at the table. "I rang his firm and asked to speak to the man who was repairing the door at the Millennium Hotel." He fell silent.

"And – what did you say? Come on, Michael, you've got this far." Alan coaxed him to continue. "Did you say that you would pay him to alter another door?"

"Yes, but..."

"But...?" Alan prompted. He knew what Moffat had told Agnes, during the time she was stuck in the bathroom with him wielding a wrench at her – he had heard every word. However, he needed to hear everything from Andrews.

"I said I would pay him, but to make sure he would go through with it, I blackmailed him. I told him I would give his name to the police if he didn't do what I said." Andrews stood up and threw his chair to one side. "So, now you know. Your detective sergeant, the man you trusted, is a blackmailer! Is that what you wanted to hear?"

The police officer who had spent the last few hours guarding Andrews, rushed across and grabbed his arm.

"It's okay, officer. You can let go of him," Alan said. "I think he's just letting off a little steam."

Andrews pulled his arm away from the police officer and gave him an angry stare.

"Come back over here and sit down," Alan ordered, turning his attention back to Andrews. "Stop behaving like a spoilt child."

Andrews obeyed his boss.

"Now, getting back to where we were, before you lost your temper," Alan continued, once Andrews was back seated in his chair, "no, Michael, that is not what I *wanted* to hear. But it was something I *needed* to hear. I had to be sure that Moffat was telling the truth. However, I never thought that I would ever hear those words coming from your lips."

"I'm sorry, sir. I don't know what else I can say." Andrews paused. "I suppose Sandra knows all about it?"

"I haven't told her – not yet, anyway. But she needs to know."

"I'm sure Agnes can't wait to tell her. That bitch is to blame for all this," Andrews added, stabbing his finger on the table as he spoke. "If it hadn't been for her, none of this would have happened. Why couldn't that wretched woman have stayed away from my Sandra?"

"*Your* Sandra? Even if you were married, you wouldn't own her – not in this day and age, anyway. And stop talking about Mrs Lockwood in that manner!" Alan snapped, trying desperately to keep his temper. "Agnes has nothing to do with this. What happened between you and Sandra is all down to you. It was *you*, who couldn't bear her to come up with something you might have missed. It was *you*, who didn't want Sandra to even mention your cases. It was *you*, who would have liked to tie her hands behind her back and, once you were married, I think *you* would have expected her to be the little wife that stayed home and saw to the housework and made the dinner."

Alan shook his head. "You've got your head stuck in the past. There are women in the police force now, Andrews. Women, who work as well as we men do. Just up the road from us, in Northumberland, a woman holds the post of Detective Chief Inspector, or hadn't you noticed?"

"Yes, of course I'd noticed," Andrews retorted. "But Sandra isn't a police officer, is she?"

"No, she isn't." Alan paused for a second. "So, does that mean, if she had been a police officer, you wouldn't have given her a second thought?"

"No, I wouldn't! Why would I want to marry someone who could leap ahead of me?"

"I think we're done for the moment, Andrews." Alan quoted the time and switched off the recording machine as he rose from his chair. "But we may need to talk again tomorrow."

"Does that mean I can go home now?" Andrews asked.

Alan stared down at his former sergeant. "What do you think?"

For one brief moment Alan felt sorry for him. Andrews had worked hard to get where he was. But, at the end of the day, he had brought this upon himself.

"No, I'm afraid not," Alan continued. "I understand that someone from IOPC will want to interview you."

Andrews placed his elbows on the table and rested his head into his hands. If the Independent Office of Police Conduct got involved, he could be kicked off the force.

"Then I guess that means I'll lose everything I've strived for."

Chapter Thirty-Six

At the hospital the following morning, Agnes awoke to find Alan sitting by her bed.

"What time is it?"

"It's seven o'clock," Alan replied, glancing at the clock above the door. "According to the nurse, you've had a good night. Slept right through, she told me when I arrived."

He leaned over the bed and kissed her.

"I'm so happy to see that you're making such a good recovery. However, Agnes, you really must take it easy for a few weeks."

"Umm, we'll see," she replied, feeling around for the button which, when pressed, would raise the upper half of the bed. "Now tell me, how are your investigations going? Are you any further forward?"

"Agnes, didn't you just hear what I said? I told you that you needed to relax for a few weeks."

"Yes, Alan, I heard. But I can't sit around doing nothing. That's not me at all and you, of all people, know that. So, come on, tell me what's been happening?"

Alan heaved a sigh. He should have seen this coming. "I've spoken to Andrews and he has admitted to paying Moffat to alter the door to Sandra's room." He paused. "How did you know Andrews was guilty?"

"I first got the idea that Michael might be behind it because Moffat called Sandra by her correct name, Sandra Williams. But she had booked into the hotel under the name of Sandra Anderson. And then, when Moffat showed me the note he'd received from the man paying him to fiddle with Sandra's door, I recognised Michael's handwriting, so I knew I was right."

"But how did Michael know Sandra was using another name? I was there when he spoke to the receptionists. He was told that no one by the name of Sandra Williams was staying at the hotel."

"Maybe he went back later and told the girls on the desk that the Sandra he was looking for was a friend of mine. Okay, your turn now, what have you got to tell me? What about Barbara Swift?"

"Not a lot, I'm afraid. All I got was 'no comment'." Alan quickly ran through what Barbara had said the previous evening, before they had reached the 'no comment' stage.

"So, she's now saying that she's the one who's married to Jamison, and Deborah isn't her daughter after all – just someone her husband happened to pick up one day for some alibi she knows nothing about," Agnes murmured thoughtfully.

Just then, the door opened and a nurse walked in.

"Good morning, Mrs Lockwood," she said, brightly. "It's good to see you looking so well. I'll be bringing a bowl of water and some soap in a few minutes. Therefore," she added, turning her attention to Alan, "perhaps you could step outside for a little while."

"Actually, I'm leaving now," Alan said, as he rose to his feet. "I just wanted to see Mrs Lockwood before I went to work."

Once the nurse had left, Alan leaned down to give Agnes a big hug, followed by a lingering kiss. "I've missed you over the last few days."

"I've missed you, too, Alan. I know I was stupid..."

Alan placed his finger over her mouth. "We were both stupid, Agnes, but that's over now. We need to move on. Meanwhile, take care of yourself while I'm away. Try to rest." Even as he spoke, he knew he was wasting his breath. Agnes would probably spend the day going over the case. But at least she was in hospital where the nurses could keep an eye on her.

Outside the door, Alan spoke to the police officer on duty. "Keep your eyes peeled, Hornby. It's possible that Jamison, who has already tried to kill Mrs Lockwood twice, will try again. Be aware that he is very good at changing his identity. One minute he is wearing a suit, looking every inch the business man, and the next, he looks like some down and out character. Today, he could be impersonating a doctor."

That last thought sent a shiver down his spine. Jamison could impersonate a doctor very easily. "Make sure that a nurse is accompanying any doctor who enters her room," he added.

The officer nodded. "Yes, sir. Rest assured, I'll take note of everyone who passes through this door."

Though Alan would much rather have stayed with Agnes himself, he felt he was leaving her in capable hands.

"Good man," Alan replied.

* * *

Shortly after breakfast, Agnes threw her head down onto the pillow. Since Alan had left, she had washed – well, sort of, if a bowl of hot water, a bar of soap and a flannel counted as a wash – and then had breakfast. Therefore, it appeared that all she had to look forward to now was a visit from one of the doctors when they did their rounds. Though, with a bit of luck, she might be able to persuade them to allow her to go home. She was feeling really good, considering that she had been shot only a day ago.

Alan had mentioned how lucky she had been. After speaking with the surgeon on the phone the previous afternoon, he had learned that the bullet had penetrated the edge of her body. An inch further to the left, it would have pierced a vital organ. Either Jamison wasn't the perfect shot he thought he was, or someone was looking out for her.

Agnes was still thinking about that when the door to her room opened and Sandra strode in. She was so pleased to see her friend that she sat up to greet her. However, heaving herself up so quickly caused a twinge of pain on her left side.

"You must take care, Agnes," Sandra said, hurrying across the room. She hadn't failed to notice the pained expression on her friend's face.

"I'm okay now," Agnes replied. "I just sat up too quickly."

"I've brought you some clean clothes. I managed to get a key to your room from the ladies on the reception desk." Sandra held up a bag she was carrying. "They both send you their best wishes."

"Thank them for me," Agnes replied. She pointed towards the armchair by her bed. "Sit down."

"I think you might get a few visitors from the hotel today," Sandra said, pulling the chair forward to a position where Agnes could see her. The problem with hospital beds was that once the top half of the bed was tilted forward, a visitor sitting in the armchair couldn't see the person they were visiting.

"For a start," Sandra continued, now that she was settled, "Sue Matthews happened to come to the desk while I was there. She was dishing out some information the receptionist needed to know, so she heard most of what was said. No doubt she and Keith Nichols will come together."

"They are a really nice couple, well matched," Agnes replied. "I would be delighted to see them. But I'd rather it was at the hotel, once I'm out of here."

Sandra looked at Agnes in amazement. "Are you saying that, once you're released from the hospital, you're going back to the hotel?"

"Yes." Agnes stared at her friend. "Why wouldn't I?"

"Because that's the first place the maniac who tried to kill you will look!"

"Yes, I agree," Agnes replied. "That's the very reason I'll go back there – to give him another chance. But this time, I'll be ready. We need to catch this man, Sandra."

"Agnes, I think you're crazy. You need to get as far away from here as possible."

Sandra paused as she reconsidered Agnes's last statement.

"What exactly did you mean by *we*?"

* * *

It was almost lunchtime before the doctor reached Agnes's room. Sandra, who was still sitting by Agnes's bed, offered to leave while he spoke to her. However, before the doctor could reply, Agnes told him there was no need. It was fine for her friend to be there.

The doctor explained that he was there on behalf of the surgeon who had performed the operation the previous day. He adjusted his glasses and glanced down at the information in the folder he was holding.

"It seems the bullet which penetrated your body didn't cause any serious damage." He peered at her over the top of his glasses. "Nevertheless, the surgeon believes that you should spend the next couple of days here to make sure that all goes well."

"I had hoped I'd be able to go home today," Agnes replied.

The doctor looked at the file again. "I admit the test results are all positive, but it's not really for me to say." He paused. "I'll have a word with the surgeon once he's out of theatre. I'll ask him to call in to see you. It's possible that, when he sees how quickly you're recovering, he'll sign you out. But the decision is his alone."

Sue and Keith called in to see Agnes shortly after lunch and stayed for about an hour.

"You're doing great," Keith said, after taking a look at the figures on the chart at the bottom of the bed. "I'm sure you'll be home in no time." It was true; the chart indicated that all the tests taken looked good.

They had come to tell Agnes and Sandra about their wedding plans. Sue sounded so happy as she went through all the details, telling Agnes where the service and the following party would be taking place. "We haven't decided where to go for our honeymoon, though we'll have to make up our minds very soon otherwise we won't get a booking."

Once they left, Agnes and Sandra carried on chatting about the case. Though, despite going through things over and over again, they were both still at a loss as to what Jamison was really up to.

At three-thirty, the surgeon suddenly opened the door and walked in. He was accompanied by one of the nurses. Sandra left the room while he examined Agnes.

"I understand that you're anxious to leave," he said, looking down at the folder he was carrying.

Before Agnes could reply, he laid down the folder and pulled some disposable gloves from the container on the wall. Putting them on, he removed the dressings from the wound on her body.

"Under normal circumstances, I would have insisted that you stayed here tonight," he continued, once he had checked the wound. "However, as I explained to Mr Johnson yesterday, you were very lucky in that the bullet merely penetrated your flesh and we were able to remove it without causing any further problems."

He went on to say that he would allow her leave, *but* only if she promised to rest for the next few days.

"I'll have the nursing staff re-bandage the wound and ask them to make an appointment for you with Outpatients for the day after tomorrow. I'll write a letter for your GP – who is that, by the way? We don't seem to have the information."

"I don't have one," Agnes replied. "Not up here, anyway."

She went on to explain her circumstances. "I never really thought about it, but this has made me realise that I need to register at a practice."

Sandra rushed into the room once the doctor had left. "Well, what did he say?"

"Guess!" Agnes replied.

Chapter Thirty-Seven

Agnes waited until she had called Ben to pick her up from the hospital, before phoning Alan. She didn't want him picking her up. He would insist on taking her to their apartment, as Jamison didn't know that address. Nevertheless, she felt sure Jamison would have means of finding her wherever she was.

"Good news, Alan, I've been released from the hospital," she told him. "Don't worry about collecting me – I've called Ben and he's on his way. Sandra is with me, so I'm okay," she added, when he began to ask whether she could manage. "I'll get back to you when I'm settled. You might be free to talk then."

"Right then, let's get downstairs to the waiting room," Agnes said, once she had finished the call.

She started to walk across to the door, but Sandra stopped her and pointed towards the wheelchair. "Aren't you forgetting something?"

"Do I really need that? I know the nurse said I was to use it, but honestly, I feel fine."

"Agnes, stop pretending you're feeling better than you really are," Sandra replied. "You certainly aren't fooling me. I saw your look of discomfort when you were getting dressed. If you happen to break the stitches, they won't let you leave. Now, will you please, get in the chair?"

"Yes, ma'am," Agnes replied, smiling as she sat down in the chair. "You're right."

A couple of minutes later, the porter arrived and they were headed downstairs with the police officer following a short distance behind.

"I think you can go now, officer," Agnes said, once they were all in the lift.

"No, not yet. I'm to follow you until you reach your destination."

"Trust Alan to give me a police escort," Agnes said. "Thank you, officer."

Downstairs, in the waiting room, they found Ben standing by the door leading to the exit. He waved when he saw Agnes and a short while later, she and Sandra were seated inside his taxi, following the police car, with its flashing blue lights, towards the quayside.

"This is the first time I have had a police escort," Ben called out from the driver's seat. "It's great. All the cars are pulling to one side to let us through. We've got to do this again sometime."

"Please, no. Not if means someone has tried to kill me," Agnes whispered to Sandra.

* * *

Now, upstairs in her room at the hotel, Agnes sank down onto the bed. The applause from the staff was still ringing in her ears.

There had been a moment shortly after entering the hotel when Agnes thought she would never reach her room before dusk. Once the two young women on reception had seen her walk through the door, they had swiftly phoned the various departments in the hotel to inform them that Mrs Lockwood was back.

After that, those members of staff on duty had descended on her, wanting to pass on their good wishes and congratulate her on getting back on her feet so quickly. Agnes was aware that she would still be down there now, if it hadn't been for Sue. Thankfully, having noticed her tired expression, Sue had called a halt to the proceedings by pressing the bell button sitting on the reception desk several times to get their attention.

"I think we should allow Mrs Lockwood to go to her room now. She needs to rest. But I'm sure we'll all have the chance to see her again very soon."

Once they were in the lift, Andy had told her how he had been shocked when he learned she had been shot. "Ground control will be delighted to learn that the eagle has landed back in the hotel, Mrs Lockwood," he had said, sporting a huge grin.

"Ground control? The eagle has landed?" Sandra had quizzed, as they stepped out of the lift. "I must be missing something?"

At that point, Agnes had laughed, telling her it was a joke thing and that she would explain it later.

Now, having kicked off her shoes, Agnes lay relaxing on the bed with her legs stretched out in front of her. "I need to phone Alan, but I got the feeling he was in the middle of something when we spoke earlier. Maybe I'd better wait a little longer."

While Agnes was talking, Sandra pulled a chair from near the window and placed it alongside the bed.

"Agnes," she said, as she lowered herself into the chair, "I do appreciate this might not be the right time, but I'd be grateful if you would tell me what's going on with Michael. I haven't heard a word from him. When I tried to call him, his phone was answered by a Sergeant Mathers, which I thought was rather strange."

Agnes remained silent for a long moment, before sitting up. She picked up the pillow from behind her and punched it a few times, then rested it against the headboard. Leaning her back against the pillow, she heaved a sigh. Did she have to be the one to tell her friend what had really happened? She had hoped Alan would be with her when the subject was mentioned.

"Sandra, there was a problem yesterday. At the moment, Michael is helping Alan with an enquiry, which is probably why you haven't heard from him. Maybe you'll hear from him later."

"But if this problem happened yesterday, surely I would have heard something from him by now?" Sandra shook her head. "There's more to this, Agnes. What is it you're not telling me?"

Eileen Thornton

"Okay." Agnes reached out and took Sandra's hand. "I'm afraid there's no easy way to say this – Michael is being held in custody."

"What do you mean, Michael's being held in custody? Why, what has he done?" Sandra snatched her hand away from Agnes.

"Do you really want to know? Wouldn't you rather hear it from Alan?"

"Of course I bloody want to know!" Sandra retorted. "Tell me what the hell is going on."

"I'm afraid Michael was the person who approached a man called Bill Moffat to alter the mechanism on your door," Agnes replied.

"No, that's not possible. Michael wouldn't do that!" Sandra protested. "The police have got it wrong. Why on earth would he do something like that – to me?"

"I understand how you must feel, Sandra." Agnes rubbed her friend's shoulder as she spoke. "I wouldn't want to believe that my fiancé would even think about doing something like that to me." She bit her lip. "But you see, Michael was trying to get you away from the case. He thought that if you arrived back in your room and found the door hadn't shut properly, you would think that someone was planning to creep in after you. That being the case, he hoped you would pack your bag and rush home. But his plan went terribly wrong when I went along the corridor to see you if you were back from your walk along the quayside."

Agnes went on to explain how, after seeing the door ajar, she had called Alan and how it came to pass that she entered the room.

"However, to cut a long story short, the man still happened to be in your room and, believing I was Sandra Williams, he took me as a hostage, hoping to bargain his way out. But when that didn't work, he gave himself up."

"How could Michael do something so despicable? So damned irresponsible?" Sandra said angrily. "I knew he could be a little over the top at times, but I never thought he would do anything so... so appalling." She stood up and moved the chair back to its rightful place.

"I'll leave you in peace now, Agnes. I'll go back to my room, but if you need anything, just give me a ring."

Agnes nodded. She would have liked Sandra to stay with her. However, she guessed that her friend needed her own space at the moment.

"I think I'd better give Alan a ring and tell him where I am, though the officer has probably already told him. But if you get lonely, please come back here."

* * *

Once Sandra had disappeared through the door, Agnes replaced the pillow to its flat position and snuggled down on the bed. It was probably still too soon to phone Alan. Instead, she thought back to the welcome she had received from the staff when she arrived at the hotel. Even Jenkins, the manager, had popped out from his office to join in. Everyone had wanted to speak at once, which had made it difficult to make out what was being said. Andy had managed a joke or two, as he brought them up in the lift – 'ground control', indeed! That remark had made Sandra smile.

Agnes closed her eyes, trying to relax. She was lucky to be alive. However, she was also aware that Jamison would try again, which was why she had come back here in the first place. The hotel was where he would find her. Maybe that had been foolish, but it was done now. Besides, it could take a day or two before he realised she was out of hospital and back here, unless a co-conspirator had seen her enter the hotel and had already passed on the information.

Trying to shut that thought out of her mind, Agnes thought back to the happy scene downstairs a short while earlier. Suddenly, she sat bolt upright when she recalled something someone had said. Why on earth hadn't she picked up on that earlier? Clutching the wound on her side, she slowly made her way across to the door and slid the chain bolt into place.

Now was the time to call Alan.

* * *

Alan had been kept busy since arriving back at the station. He missed having his sergeant around.

His first interview had been with Bill Moffat. However, it had turned out better than he thought. Moffat had already confessed to altering the mechanism of both doors the day before and, fortunately, he hadn't even attempted to go back on his previous statement, which was often the case. He hadn't even asked for a solicitor to be present during the interview.

At the end of the interview, Moffat apologised for threatening Mrs Lockwood.

"I don't know what came over me. I am not usually like that. When I heard someone entering the room, I panicked and hid in the bathroom. But then, when she opened the bathroom door, I just flipped. Please tell her that I'm so sorry."

Alan had then gone back to talk to Barbara Swift. Since he had last spoken to her, she had arranged for her solicitor to be present during this interview. Therefore, Alan had asked Jones to accompany him, not wanting to appear outnumbered.

Once the introductions were over, Alan asked a few questions. Most were similar to those he had mentioned the previous day. He wanted Barbara to believe this was going to be a walkover, before he pounced. As expected, most of her replies were the same old 'no comment'.

"Where do you think Jamison might be at this moment?" Alan asked, suddenly.

"I told you yesterday, I don't know where he is."

"Is it possible that he is with Deborah, sunning themselves on a beach somewhere in the Caribbean?" Alan persisted.

"No. Of course not! He won't be with her. Like I said yesterday, Robert told her to get lost."

"Are you really sure about that? Maybe that's just what he wanted you to think," Alan replied.

Picking up the page, Alan held it in front of Jones and pointed to something written there. Jones smiled and nodded.

"What does that say?" Barbara asked, eyeing the paperwork Alan had tucked back into the file.

"I doubt you're going to like this," Alan replied, slowly. "But we've learned that Jamison was last seen leaving the hotel arm in arm with Deborah."

That statement appeared to knock Barbara off guard, as a long silence followed.

"I would like to see that," she said at last, pointing towards the file.

Alan told her that was impossible as police files were confidential, unless certain items were laid down in front of her. She then glanced at her solicitor for guidance, but he nodded, confirming that she was not permitted to see police files.

"However, I can assure you that what I said was true. Jamison was seen leaving the hotel with Deborah on his arm," Alan said, picking up the file. "But of course, if you believe otherwise, then nothing more can be said. Therefore, you will remain in custody on the charge of accessary to murder. Interview terminated at… "

"Wait!" Barbara called out, before Alan could finish speaking. "I'll tell you where Robert told me I could find him, unless he's already swanned off somewhere with that bitch, leaving me to carry the can. I should never have trusted him." She paused. "He has a large house in Low Fell – that's… "

"Yes, I know where Low Fell is," Alan interrupted, impatiently. "Where in Low Fell does he have this house?"

"Kells Lane. The house is somewhere at the bottom of Kells Lane, just past the school."

"Surely you know the house number? You said you were his wife. Don't you live together?"

"He has… we have, another house in – Jesmond. We live there," Barbara stammered.

"Where in Jesmond is this house?" Alan demanded.

"Jesmond Road, or is it Terrace? I've forgotten which it is. Anyway, it's on the main road just out of the city – the road that leads to the Coast Road."

"Just out of curiosity, why are you unsure as to where you and your husband live together?"

There was a long silence. Barbara tapped her fingers on the table while she thought about how to reply.

"Perhaps it would help if I repeated the question. Why are you unsure...?"

"Because I'm not his wife," Barbara interrupted. "He lied to me. That wretched man lied to me. He told me I was the love of his life and I believed him. He said he wanted to marry me. But there were a few things he needed to do before the wedding."

Alan remained silent, while Barbara pulled a handkerchief from her pocket and dabbed her eyes. Hopefully, she would come out with further information of her own accord. In the meantime, with a bit of luck, Smithers, standing on the other side of the two way mirror, would have already issued instructions to his fellow detectives to round up some uniformed officers and get to Kells Lane in Low Fell right away.

"I suppose you think I was a fool to be taken in by his charm."

"Not at all," Alan replied. "Some men have a gift for charming innocent women into doing things they wouldn't normally do. But, getting back to the case, you're saying that this man manipulated you into helping him with something we have yet to learn, killed two people and then left you stranded to pay the price for the killings?" Alan paused and scratched his head. "You see, I find that hard to believe, as it was you who was found in the hotel yesterday, not Jamison. And, from what we can gather, you had no real reason to be there."

"For goodness' sake, I didn't kill anyone!" Barbara slammed her fist down on the table as she spoke. "Jamison told me to be at the hotel. At first, I thought that he was going to meet me there. But he didn't turn up. You've got to believe me, Chief Inspector."

"Why do I have to believe you?" Alan replied, slowly. "Try looking at it from my point of view. For a start, you were in the hotel yesterday, almost screaming to be allowed to leave, without any real proof as to why you were there in the first place. Then, when asked why you needed to leave, you claimed that you were meeting up with a very important person at a luxury hotel in the city centre. Yet, you later admitted that the important person was your son-in-law, and the luxury hotel was a chain store."

Alan cradled his chin in his hand as he stared down at another file in front of him. "Therefore, Ms Swift, the next question is, what can you tell me about the man found shot dead in the restaurant a few days ago? Might that killing also be down to you? Should that be the case, you could then be charged with two murders."

Alan held his breath, half expecting the solicitor to intervene. However, as he remained silent, the man had either fallen asleep, or he hadn't heard the last question.

"Both of the dead men were hanging around on the streets," Barbara said. "Robert gave them some money and found them somewhere to live."

"Why? Why would he do that?"

Barbara shrugged. "Because, several years ago, Robert's father was saved by some do-gooder and, when he learned about it, he never forgot it. I believe Jamison has helped several people over the last few years – giving them a new life."

Alan swallowed hard. Where did he go from here? However, he was saved for at least a few minutes when his phone rang. Looking down at the screen, he saw that the call was from Agnes.

"I really need to call you back..." he began.

"Alan, please don't hang up," Agnes pleaded. "I need you to get over to the hotel right away."

Alan shut down his phone leapt to his feet. "Interview terminated at five-ten pm. Sorry, Ms Swift, but I need to go," he added. "We'll continue tomorrow. Jones, get Smithers, you're both with me," he added, as he headed towards the door.

Outside the interview room, Alan quickly instructed an officer to take Barbara Swift back to her cell.

"What's happened?" Jones asked, as the three detectives rushed towards Alan's car. "Who was that on the phone?"

"It was Agnes," Alan replied.

Once they were all inside his car, he started the engine and placed the blue light on the roof, before heading out of the carpark and along the main road.

"She didn't say much." Alan paused, while he rounded a tight bend. "But she didn't need to," he continued. "Once she mentioned that Jamison could be on his way to try his luck at killing her again, that was enough to set me in motion."

Alan slowed down and turned off the flashing lights before turning into the road leading to the hotel. There was no point in making Jamison aware the police were in the vicinity. Alan wanted to give the impression that he and his plain-clothed companions were tourists visiting the area and seeing the quayside for the first time.

The DCI held his breath as he slowly drove along the quayside. He was looking out for Jamison. Though he had only caught a glimpse of him the day Agnes was shot, a mental vision of him was fixed in his mind. Meanwhile, Jones and Smithers, not having seen the man, could only look out for anything that didn't appear to be quite right. However, Alan was aware that the next problem could come after he entered the hotel. A rousing 'Welcome back, Detective Inspector Johnson', was the last thing he needed to hear from the over-excited ladies on the reception desk.

Chapter Thirty-Eight

Sitting on a chair near the window, Agnes looked down onto the quayside. If she was right, and Jamison *was* on his way to the hotel to kill her, she would see him and be prepared. But then another thought crossed her mind. What if he approached the hotel using St Anne's Road, which ran down behind the hotel? He could arrive without her seeing him. Why hadn't she thought of that earlier?

Once Agnes had ended her call to Alan, she had glanced around the room, looking for something she could use to defend herself should Jamison suddenly burst through the door. However, short of picking up a chair to hurl at him, which was impossible due to the weight of the chair, plus the fact she could burst the stitches in her side, the next best thing was the toilet brush in the bathroom, and the bottle of wine standing next to the television. In the end, it could come to her having to use both. But, if Jamison was armed with a gun, would either be of any use?

Still looking down onto the quayside, Agnes she couldn't help thinking about the murders. Assuming Jamison was the murderer, what reason did he have for killing those two men? Even so, he seemed hell-bent on killing her. Again, why? Yes, she and Sandra had met him in the drawing room over coffee, but he had given very little away about himself. Actually, he hadn't given away anything at all. It was Deborah who had done the most of the talking after that. Even then, she had only mentioned being employed by some temporary agency, which covered all areas in the job market. Yet Jamison had felt the need to intervene, saying it was time they left for the theatre.

Her eyes still focused on the road beneath her window, Agnes stroked her chin as she continued to think it through. Normally, someone giving a brief description of their job wouldn't cause the person they were with to grab their arm and almost drag them out of the building, using some lame excuse. Therefore, what had Deborah said to upset Jamison so much that he had felt the need to leave? But then, suddenly recalling something Deborah had mentioned about her job, things became so much clearer.

* * *

Alan and his detectives entered the hotel and slowly walked towards the reception desk. He was wearing an old Trilby hat, which he kept in the boot of his car for when it was raining. He hoped it might disguise him slightly, though he didn't think for one minute that he would fool the women on the desk.

"How can I help you?" Pauline enquired, with a beaming smile. "Do you wish to book a room?" She nodded her head very slightly as she spoke.

"Yes, we were thinking about it." Alan laughed, picking up Pauline's signal. "We're here to meet up with a few old friends from the past – sort of an old boys' night out before the football match at the weekend. However," he added, as he glanced around the reception, "I'm not sure we can afford to stay here. What do you think, guys?"

"It looks good," Jones replied. "Maybe we should take a look around, before we say no. We'll probably never get the chance again."

"You're right," Alan replied, slapping his hand down onto the desk. "Maybe you could give us a key to one of the rooms upstairs? At least we could see what we'd be getting for our money."

"Yes, of course," Pauline replied.

She selected a master key-card from the drawer. "That's room 105, on the first floor. It's vacant at the moment so there's no rush." Leaning across the desk, she slid the key-card towards Alan. "Take the stairs," she whispered.

"Thank you," Alan said, as they headed towards the stairs. "We'll check out the public rooms down here when we get back, if that's okay?"

"No problem, sir."

"This looks a great place to stay," Alan said cheerfully, as he and his team strode across the reception.

"Yes, I think our budget would stretch to us staying here – especially if breakfast was included," Smithers said. "There's nothing I like more than a darn good breakfast after a night out with the lads," he added, rubbing his stomach.

"Would you like to take the lift?" Andy asked.

"It's tempting," Alan replied, "But I think we should use the stairs. We need to work off some calories before our big night out. Besides, we're only going as far as the first floor – it's not as though we're going to the top of the building." He laughed. "But hey, come the night of the do, whatever floor we're on, we might be grateful for your help to get us into the lift, let alone heave us out when we reach our floor."

"Yes, sir!" Andy grinned as he watched the three men plod slowly up the stairs.

Once they were out of sight of the lift attendant, Alan and his detectives mounted the stairs more quickly. Stopping off on the first floor, they glanced towards the lift in case Andy had brought up it up to check them out. However, according to the light above the lift doors, it was still stationed on the ground floor. Now, knowing they were clear of detection, the detectives scrambled up the rest of the stairs until they reached the fourth floor.

Everything looked normal. The corridor was empty. No one was hanging around and none of the doors appeared to have been burst open. But Alan knew from experience that this didn't mean all was well. It could mean the very opposite.

Alan drew a gun from his pocket and slowly walked across towards the door leading into Agnes's room. "Stay there," he whispered, when Jones made a move to follow him.

Now, outside Agnes's room, Alan placed his ear to the door and listened hard. It was quiet. Not a sound was coming from inside the room. Slipping the key-card into the socket, Alan pushed down the handle, but found that the chain was in place. So far, all looked good.

Yet, beginning to understand this guy's trend of 'shoot now, think later', Agnes could already be dead.

* * *

Agnes was still sitting on the chair by the window with the toilet brush standing upright on the floor next to her leg, while the bottle of wine stood on the table in front of her, when she heard someone inserting a key-card into the door. The door would have swung open and the perpetrator would have entered, had the chain lock not been in place. Picking up the two items she had to defend herself against the intruder, Agnes rose to her feet.

The person outside the door could be Alan. She had spoken to the ladies on the reception desk earlier, asking them to react to Alan as though he was seeking to book a room. She had also left it to them to work out some way of giving him a key-card to her room. Even so, the person now trying to get in could be that evil monster, Jamison.

Agnes shook her head. This was not the time to go through the 'what ifs'. She needed to concentrate on the here and now. Holding the two objects, one in each hand, she slowly moved across the room towards the door. She didn't utter a word; she needed the person outside in the corridor to be the first to speak.

"Agnes, it's me, Alan." The voice was barely above a whisper. "Are you okay?"

"How do I know for sure it's you, Alan?" Agnes asked.

"We went to school together – in Gateshead."

Heaving a sigh of relief, Agnes tossed her two items of defence onto the bed and walked towards the door.

* * *

Alan looked across to where his detectives were standing at the top of the stairs.

"The chain lock appears to be in place." Alan paused. "It's possible that we got here in time. But..."

"But, you think Jamison could have got in there and locked the door behind him," Jones finished Alan's sentence.

"Yes. It's certainly a possibility. If I knock and say who I am, he could kill her." Alan paused. "I'm going to burst into the room. But, if I don't reappear within thirty seconds, call the station and get an armed squad out to the hotel."

"You've got that, Jonesy?" Smithers said, using his nickname for his partner. "I'm going in there with the boss."

"You don't have..." Alan began.

"Just let's get on with it, we're wasting time," Smithers interrupted, pointing at the door.

Alan nodded and without another word, he pushed the key-card into the lock allowing the door to open slightly. Once that was done, Smithers pushed the DCI to one side and hurled his burly body against the door.

The chain snapped in an instant and the door flew open.

Chapter Thirty-Nine

Now inside Agnes's room, Alan swiftly glanced around. There was no sign of Agnes, or anyone else, though he did notice a bottle of wine, together with a toilet brush, lying on the bed. He gestured at Smithers to go around to the other side of the bed to make sure no one was crouched down. But, once he had taken a look, Smithers shook his head.

"Agnes!" Alan called out, now looking towards the bathroom. "Are you here? It's me, Alan. I've got Smithers with me."

Alan lowered his gun when he saw Agnes step out of the bathroom alive and well.

"Thank goodness you're here," Agnes said. "Jamison was outside that door earlier." She paused. "He pretended he was you and wanted me to open the door."

"Tell Jones to hold back on the call, then both come in here," he told Smithers, as he led Agnes across to the sofa.

"Thank goodness you didn't fall for it. But how did you realise it wasn't me?"

"When I asked him to prove he was who he said he was, he told me of how we had first met at school in Gateshead. Truthfully, I almost believed him. But then, just as I was about to unchain the door, I realised that you would have said that we met at Kells Lane School in Low Fell. So, I took a few steps away from the door and called out,

'Wrong answer!' " Agnes smiled. "In fact, you could say that today, I was saved by Kells Lane School."

Alan agreed wholeheartedly.

"It was good thinking to contact the receptionists to keep quiet about our identities," Alan said. "But now, you must tell us why we needed to use the stairs rather than take the lift," he said, lowering himself onto the sofa next to Agnes. "And, how the hell did Jamison know that we went to the same school?"

By now, Jones had joined Smithers in the room and both were seated on the chairs by the table near the window.

"I don't know how Jamison knew that we went to the same school," Agnes replied. "But, getting to the reason I called you in the first place, it was because of a couple of things Andy said when Sandra and I were in the lift on our way up here. They were things I had said to him a few days ago. The words were meant to make him feel better in his job. I thought it might encourage him find a job he really wanted as he seemed so unhappy here. But now, I believe he used those words to pass on information to Jamison about me being back at the hotel, which makes me wonder whether he was carrying some sort of communication device."

"What were those words, Agnes? What did he say when you stepped out of the lift?"

"Ground control – the eagle has landed."

"I know it doesn't sound much," she added. "But it wasn't what he said, it was the way he spoke those words. It was almost as though he was speaking to someone else, rather than talking to me or Sandra."

Alan nodded. It made sense that Jamison could have someone in the hotel on his payroll, and who better than the lift attendant; someone who was able to listen to the chatter of the guests as he moved them from floor to floor. Alan doubted Jamison would come back again tonight. Nevertheless, he wasn't about to take the chance. After speaking to the manager, he called the station and requested that an armed officer, dressed in civilian clothes, should stay at the hotel for the night. There was a room vacant across the corridor.

Once that was settled, Alan and his two detectives went downstairs together; making sure that the lift attendant saw them leave. Outside, Alan had a few further words with his detectives before going around to the staff entrance. Alan had then used the back stairs to make his way up to Agnes's room again.

Now that they were on their own, Alan settled back on the sofa, while Agnes rang the manager to work out a way that dinner for two could be sent up to their room without anyone realising she wasn't alone.

"I'm rather concerned about her," Agnes replied, when Alan asked about Sandra. "She wanted to be alone to think things through after I told her about Michael's behaviour. But I haven't heard from her since. Maybe I should call her."

Agnes picked up her mobile phone and punched in Sandra's number.

"Hello," Sandra said, cautiously.

"It's me, Agnes. I was just wondering how you were."

"I'm fine. Actually, I fell asleep. I guess I must have needed the rest." She paused. "Are you going downstairs for dinner?"

Agnes told her that she and Alan were having dinner in their room. "But you are welcome to join us, if you would prefer not to be on your own. Just check the menu and order a meal to be sent to your room. Then, bring it along here." She paused. "But use your mobile if you need to call me. I'll explain about the secrecy when I see you."

"Thank you, Agnes. Yes, I'll do that. Truthfully, I don't really want to spend the evening alone."

* * *

Once they had all finished their meal and the dishes had been stacked up ready for collection, they sank into the sofa. Alan had moved the coffee table closer and was refilling their glasses. But, apart from the clinking of the bottle against the glasses, there was an awkward silence.

Agnes was thoughtful, as she twisted the stem of her wine glass between her fingers. Despite what had happened that afternoon, she had found time to reflect on her earlier thoughts and, after mulling through it several times, she was convinced she was right. Perhaps now was the time to tell Alan.

"Do you recall me telling you that Sandra and I met Jamison and Deborah in the drawing room?" Agnes looked at Alan as she spoke.

Alan nodded. "Yes, I do. But I thought we had gone through all that."

"Yes, we had. But, earlier today, I suddenly thought of something I'd missed. After that, everything fell into place."

Chapter Forty

"Until today, I realised I was dwelling too much on what little Jamison had said and not giving much thought to Deborah's comments," Agnes said, as she began to explain her latest views. "So, I tried to remember everything she'd said and work out what had caused Jamison to rush her away from us. Until then, all Deborah had said was that she worked for an agency. Even then, Jamison had allowed her to rattle on about her job. But, when she mentioned that the agency also recruited staff for high street shops and canteen work in local factories, he started to look unsettled. I should have picked up on his attitude then, but I didn't. Not even when she said she had stood in for shop assistants. But today, I recalled that was when he pulled the plug. That's when I began to wonder whether Deborah had played a part in the robbery."

At that point, Agnes paused.

"Don't you see, Alan? I believe she had been set up to stand in for the member of staff on holiday that week. Then, on the appointed day, at the right time, she switched the jewellery in the cabinet for something similar he had given her. Meanwhile, a fight between two men outside the shop, orchestrated by Jamison, would draw everyone's attention away from what was happening inside. That's when Deborah switched the jewellery and passed the real gems to Barbara, who was already in the shop posing as a customer. All she had to do was to leave the premises and take the bag to Jamison. The fight probably ended the moment the men saw Barbara leave the shop carrying the bag. If it had gone on too long, someone might have called the police. I have to admit, Jamison had it all worked out down to the finest detail."

She paused, allowing her words to sink in, then continued. "But then the bad news was, he now needed to get rid of the two men he had talked into starting a fight outside the shop. He couldn't risk them bragging about how they had helped rob a jewellery shop. After that, it was only a matter of time before he went after Barbara and Deborah – unless Deborah is already dead."

Agnes had hardly finished explaining her thoughts, when Alan pulled out his phone and called the station again. Only this time, he asked to speak to Chief Superintendent Lewis. If Agnes was right, there was no way the police could allow Jamison to slip through their fingers. However, he was aware his alert could be too late. It was possible that Jamison, not having managed to get into Agnes's room, might have decided to leave United Kingdom and swan off to a new life somewhere else while he still had the chance.

His earlier call, asking for anyone who had bought a one-way ticket within the last twenty-four hours to be checked out, had only been authorised for local airports and ferries. However, after what Agnes had revealed, he realised that all areas of the country should be put on alert.

"But what if Deborah has swanned off somewhere with him?" Alan asked.

"Yes, that's possible," Agnes replied. She looked across at Alan. "But, if you think that, why haven't you sent out a notice asking for her to be stopped at airports, etc., too?"

"I have," he replied. "I don't think you heard me on the phone."

"Sorry, Alan. Yes, you seem to have everything under control," Agnes replied. "Yet I can't stop thinking that Deborah, having outlived her usefulness, will be found dead somewhere. While Jamison, on the other hand, having got everything he wanted, could be on the other side of the world enjoying his ill-gotten gains." Agnes paused. "But, what if he hasn't left the area and is still hanging around here looking for another chance to kill me and Sandra?"

"Agnes, including today, Jamison has already tried to kill you three times and failed," Sandra said. "Surely he won't risk trying again? He's got the jewellery. He must know that he could be caught and be left with nothing. He must be well away from Newcastle by now." Sandra reached out and took Agnes's hand as she spoke.

"I do hope so." Agnes thought for a moment. "Yet, there's something nagging at me saying he won't relax until he knows I'm dead."

"But why?" Alan asked. Having enjoyed a few moments' relief when Sandra suggested that Jamison would have left the area, he was now feeling panicked. "I agree with Sandra. Why on earth would he risk everything by hanging around here to kill you, when he could already be halfway across the world? It doesn't make sense." Alan glanced at Sandra for a fleeting second. "If that's the case, then the same thing could be said about Sandra. She was with you when you met Jamison in the drawing room. Does that mean her life is in danger, too?"

Agnes was unsure how to answer. She didn't want to alarm her friend, yet at the same time, Sandra needed to be aware of the danger she could be in.

Agnes squeezed Sandra's hand. "Alan's right, it is possible that Jamison will come after you, too. But I think he'll seek me out first. He's tried three times and failed. I'm willing to bet that he's really infuriated about that." She looked at Alan. "Maybe he's the sort of man that, once he sets his mind on achieving something, he won't rest until it's signed and sealed. Does that answer your question?"

Alan nodded. He had come up against people like that in the past; like a dog with a bone, they wouldn't let go until it was dragged away from them.

By now, Agnes had turned her attention back to Sandra. "I believe it's time you packed your suitcase and went back to your flat where you will be safe. Jamison doesn't know where you live."

"The same could be said about you, Agnes," Alan cut in, before Sandra could say a word. "Or are you too stubborn to see that? We could have police hidden in this room, waiting for him to come in and either shoot or strike the pillows under the duvet. You see, you don't need to be here at all."

"Yes, I do need to be here, Alan. Haven't you been listening? The man isn't a fool. If I'm right, and he's still in the vicinity, he's probably watching the hotel even now. Yet, so far, none of your men has even noticed him. Jamison won't even attempt to get into this room, unless he knows for sure I'm here."

"But how the hell would he know whether you're here or not?" Alan asked.

"Exactly the same way he found me when I was in hospital," Agnes replied. "If there is one thing I have learned about Jamison, it is that he's a real smoothie. He can charm his way into getting information, no matter what that may be. Besides, if I am right about Andy, Jamison already has eyes and ears in the hotel."

It was Sandra who broke the silence that followed. "Agnes, you're right on all counts. But we're in this together. My mind is made up. I'm staying here at the hotel. I'll not only set the chain in place, I'll also push the back of a chair under the door handle. Surely that should stop anyone from getting into my room."

"Yes, it would," Alan agreed. "But, the problem is, we need to catch this guy in the act of actually attempting to kill someone. I'm afraid that's the way the courts work today. Or that's how I see it. Someone simply trying to get into your room wouldn't hold. For a start, you wouldn't be able to say for sure who the person was, if you didn't actually see him." He paused. "Therefore, we need absolute proof that Jamison came to the hotel to kill you or Agnes. Maybe you should reconsider Agnes's suggestion and go back to your flat where you'll be safe."

Agnes nodded her head in agreement.

"No, I'm not happy about that," Sandra said, after a long pause. "I'm staying put. I'll set up my bed in the bath if necessary."

"No need for that. I'll arrange for a police officer to spend the night in your room," Alan replied, once he realised Sandra wasn't about to give in.

"Thank you," Sandra replied. "But, would you do me a favour? Make sure it's a female officer? I'm a little off male officers at the moment – except you, of course."

Chapter Forty-One

Despite the tense situation, Agnes and Sandra enjoyed the rest of the evening. Alan, having already organised a female plain-clothed officer to spend the night with Sandra, had met the officer at the back entrance and escorted her to Sandra's room. Now that everything was in place, there was nothing else for it but to settle down for the night.

It was almost three o'clock in the morning when Alan thought he heard someone outside the door. He hadn't slept much; simply dozing off now and again, as he lounged in an upright position on the bed. There had been several creaks, but he was aware that happened all the time and he didn't usually take any notice of such noises. But tonight was different. Tonight, a killer was on the loose and could be trying to get into the room. He looked towards Agnes, who was snuggled beneath the duvet. Whatever he had heard hadn't appeared to have disturbed her.

He listened hard for a few more minutes. But, as there was no other sound, he relaxed. It was probably a false alarm. But just when he began to relax, he heard another sound. It was as though someone was pushing a key-card into the lock, and then releasing it. His suspicions were confirmed when he heard the door handle slowly being turned. However, the door didn't push open as the chain was in place.

Alan nudged Agnes.

"I know," she whispered. Throwing back the duvet, she crept out of bed. "I heard." She pointed towards the bathroom. "In there?"

Alan nodded, before pushing two pillows under the duvet. Once they were both in the bathroom, he called the officer who he had arranged to be in a room opposite.

"He's outside our room now," Alan whispered into his phone. "Once I know he's inside, I'll get back to you. But, do not enter the room until I say – understood?"

"Yes, understood, sir."

Now, sitting together on the edge of the bath with only the light seeping through the glazed window from a street lamp below, Alan placed his arm around Agnes. She snuggled closer to him as they both waited for even the slightest sound coming from the bedroom. Yet there was nothing. Was it possible that Jamison, having found the chain set firmly in place, had given up? He would be aware that bursting through the door could result in wakening the other guests in the rooms along the corridor. Maybe they should have left the door unchained, but it was too late to think about that now.

Suddenly, Agnes heard a sound coming from somewhere on the other side of the door. She tugged at Alan's shirt to attract his attention.

"I know," he whispered. Unhooking himself from Agnes, he rose to his feet and tapped a button on his phone.

"This could be it," Alan spoke quietly to the officer across the corridor. "Be alert."

A few seconds later, there was the sound of someone cutting through the chain which secured the door. As much as he would have liked to rush out and catch Jamison there and then, Alan held back. He needed to practise what he had preached last evening. He had to catch the man after he had fired the shots, or however else he had planned to kill Agnes.

By now, Alan had opened the bathroom door a little and was listening for the slightest sound. With one hand wrapped around the handle, ready to pull the door open, his other hand held his phone, ready to instruct the officer a few yards across the hall when the time was right. After what seemed like an age, though it was probably only a few seconds, Alan heard the slight tread of someone creeping into the room. Had Jamison taken the precaution of removing his shoes? But then Alan recalled that there was no need, the carpets in the hotel were luxuriously thick. Even the sound of his own heavy tread was dulled the moment he stepped through the hotel doors.

Now poised and ready for action, Alan heard a low clicking sound which he recognised as a gun being made ready to fire. It was a sound he had heard so many times during his time in the army, he knew it off by heart. Then it happened. The muted sound of a gun, obviously armed with a silencer, was fired six times.

"Go, go, go!" Alan shouted into his phone, while pulling the bathroom door open.

Agnes watched as Alan threw his phone to the floor and pulled a gun from his pocket, before stepping into the bedroom.

"Robert Jamison, I am charging you…"

* * *

Agnes had already begun to follow Alan into the bedroom when she heard him break off while in the process of charging Robert Jamison. Now, standing behind Alan, she was able to see the armed officer pointing his gun towards the perpetrator, who was kneeling on the floor facing away from her. A gun, with what she took to be a silencer attached, was lying on the floor a few inches away.

"Who the hell are you?" Alan said. Taking a step closer to the assailant, he kicked the gun further out of reach.

"Who cares? I've done what I came here to do. End of…"

"But, have you really done what you came here to do?" Agnes asked, as she waltzed into the line of sight of the killer. "As it happened, you missed. The six bullets you fired went into a few pillows tucked under the duvet. I'm sure forensics will find that the bullets match the gun you fired."

Agnes turned to face Alan. "This is Deborah," she said, gesturing towards the woman down on her knees by the bed. "You'll recall me saying that I was concerned about her wellbeing as I hadn't seen her since we spoke in the drawing room. I was concerned that Jamison might have killed you," she added, turning her attention to Deborah. "Yet, here you are in my room trying to kill me. I suppose Jamison sweet-talked you into doing this for him. Was Sandra to be your next victim? Though, as you emptied the gun into who you thought was me, my guess is, he didn't mention there would be another victim."

At that point, Alan read Deborah her rights. If this young woman was going to say anything that might incriminate her, he needed to be sure she was aware that anything she said could be used in evidence against her.

"Yeah, yeah, whatever," Deborah replied with a shrug, once Alan had finished his speech. "Robert is the light of my life," she continued, now looking back at Agnes. "Surely you've had someone in your life who meant the world to you?"

Agnes winced when she heard those words. Yes, Jim had meant the world to her, but he would never have asked her to kill anyone.

"When Robert appeared in front of me one day and then took me out to dinner," Deborah continued, "I couldn't believe how lucky I was that such a handsome man was interested in me. We dated a few times and then he told me how much he loved me and wanted to marry me. So, tell me, why would he want to kill me?"

"Because, once you stole the jewellery for him, you had outlived your usefulness," Agnes replied.

"I didn't steal any jewellery, for him or anyone else," Deborah retorted.

"Deborah, Jamison used you, just as he used the two men who are now lying dead in the morgue. Once you are of no further use to him, he will kill you and walk away without a thought. Do yourself a favour. Tell the chief inspector where Jamison is."

Deborah glanced at Alan and shook her head. "No," she replied, stubbornly.

During the long silence that followed, Agnes looked at Alan and shrugged. There was nothing more she could say. She had tried to get Deborah to open up, but it appeared she had failed.

"But maybe I could tell *you*, Mrs Lockwood," Deborah said, looking at Agnes. "Then, I can honestly say I never revealed anything to the police."

Agnes leaned closer to Deborah to hear what she had to say.

* * *

"So, what did she say," Alan asked, the moment they were alone. "Where is Jamison? Probably abroad somewhere, lying on the beach in the sun, I suppose."

"No, Alan," Agnes replied, thoughtfully. "If what Deborah told me is true, Jamison is still here on Tyneside."

Chapter Forty-Two

The next morning, Agnes and Alan met up with Sandra in the dining room for breakfast. It was still rather early as Alan really needed to get to the station. Not having had much sleep, Agnes would rather have had breakfast sent up to the room. But she knew Sandra would be anxious to learn the details of Deborah's arrest.

Once Deborah had been marched away the previous evening, Alan had contacted the officer in Sandra's room, informing her that the killer had been apprehended. However, he had instructed her to remain in the room for the rest of the night, just in case there was another attack. If what Deborah had said was true, though Alan very much doubted it, Jamison could have been outside, making sure his latest, easily swayed, young woman had completed the task he had set her. Alan had also instructed the officer not to awaken Sandra. The news could wait until the following morning.

Now, waiting for their breakfast to be served, Agnes brought Sandra up to date about what had happened during the night.

"I admit I was shocked when I saw Deborah. I had fully expected to find Jamison in the room," she said. "For a moment, I almost believed I was seeing a ghost, as I felt sure that Jamison had killed Deborah."

Agnes fell silent at that point.

"So, what are you thinking now?" Alan asked.

"I was just wondering what Jamison is doing now – at this very moment."

"Well, as I haven't heard otherwise, I believe he's charmed some young woman at the airport into allowing him to evade the team checking the passengers. My guess is he'll be somewhere far away by now," Alan said, sounding rather confident. "Look, Agnes," he continued. "I know Deborah said he was still here. That's probably what he wanted her to believe. But, you really need to think about it. Jamison probably told her how much he loved her and virtually painted a picture of them being married on the white sands on some island. Therefore, with that thought still floating in her mind, it's more than likely she would believe anything he said. Why would he hang around here, waiting for Deborah to reappear, when he could be on a plane to – California, for instance?" Alan threw his hands in the air as he spoke. "Even if he had still been somewhere outside the hotel last night, surely he would have scarpered the moment he saw Deborah being led away in handcuffs."

"I really do understand what you are saying, Alan. It is possible Jamison might have disappeared when he saw Deborah being escorted from the hotel. But it's what he *didn't* see that concerns me." Agnes took a deep breath. "If Deborah had killed us both, wouldn't police officers have swarmed the building? And Dr Nichols... surely he and his team would have arrived to check out the bodies and look for DNA? Therefore, if Jamison had been stalking around outside the hotel, he would have realised at once that the police had already been on the scene and Deborah had failed to kill us. Instead, she had been caught in the act. And, as for your thought of him rushing away to catch a plane or ferry, it's possible he has his own transport when the time comes for him to flee the scene."

"But if he believed Deborah had been caught in the act, wouldn't that have given him even more reason to shoot off somewhere?" Alan remarked, ignoring Agnes's last sentence. "And let's not forget about Deborah and Barbara. Surely they played a part in his plan? Won't he be concerned about what they'll say when they are interviewed? Though I admit, he can't do anything to them now that they're in custody."

"Yes, that's true. But, would their testimony against him stand up in court? Everything they did could have been done without Jamison. Though the two women might swear that Jamison was the front man, their statements could be judged as wishing to remain silent, because they planned to pick up the jewels once they had served their sentence."

At that point their breakfast arrived.

* * *

"So, are you sticking to what you said earlier – about Jamison still being here on Tyneside waiting for an opportunity to kill you and Sandra?" Alan said, once they were seated in the drawing room. He had refrained from saying anything further while they were enjoying breakfast but now he felt inclined to spill out his thoughts. "Because I really think you're wrong, Agnes. It was you who implied that he was a man who thought on his feet. He has tried to kill you three times and failed. He sent Deborah to do the job and she failed. Don't you think he'd realise it was time to give up and move on?"

Agnes nodded. "Yes, I understand what you're saying. Yet, the more I think about it, the more sure I feel that Jamison won't rest until every loose end is tidied away. He won't want to give up – I don't think he *can* give up."

"Why not? But if that's what you truly believe, don't you think it's unwise to stay at the hotel? Shouldn't you both pack up and check out?"

"But then the police would never catch him," Agnes replied. "Stupid though it may sound, I feel I need to stay here." She stared at Alan. "Think about it. If I'm correct, then Jamison will know that I'm alive and well. If he didn't realise it last night, then his crony, the lift attendant, will have informed him. Though we used the stairs, I couldn't help noticing the way Andy peered at me as we walked across the reception towards the restaurant. My guess is that, once we disappeared from view, his next move would have been to let Jamison know that

I'm still around." She looked at Sandra. "What about you? Did Andy see you, too?"

"No, he didn't," Sandra replied. "The lift was on the ground floor when I left my room, so I took the stairs. By the time I reached the reception area, it was on its way up to another floor."

"I've just had another thought," Agnes said, barely allowing Sandra to finish what she was saying. She shook her head in despair. Why on earth hadn't she thought of this earlier? "If Jamison is paying Andy to pass on information to him," she continued, "then, surely Andy will be another loose end, once Jamison has no further use for him."

Alan nodded. "But only if Jamison is still around, and that's a really a big 'if'," he said, still unconvinced Agnes was right. He looked at his watch. "It's time I wasn't here. I need to get back to the station to question Deborah – if that's her real name." He leapt to his feet as he spoke. "But, as neither of you have changed your minds about staying here, I'm going to instruct a plain-clothed officer to be here in the hotel for the rest of the day."

"Does that mean we can't even go out for a walk?" Agnes moaned.

"Yes, it does," Alan replied, sternly. "For goodness' sake, Agnes, didn't you just say that you believed Jamison was still out there, wait-ing to strike again? If you won't go back to the apartment, I need to know that you're both safe."

"But you didn't agree with me. Does that mean you've changed your mind and believe he might be in the area after all?"

"No, I'm just being careful."

"Okay," Agnes said.

"So, you agree to have an officer around?" Alan sounded stunned. He had expected another argument.

"No. Not really. I just wanted to humour you," Agnes laughed.

* * *

Agnes and Sandra were still seated in the drawing room. Agnes found the silence deafening. If only another guest would walk in, then she could start a conversation and lighten the mood. But it seemed that everyone had plans for the day.

"Right," Agnes said, slapping her hands on her knees. "What shall we do next?"

"What *can* we do next?" Sandra replied, sombrely. "I have lost the love of my life because he was trying to save me from all of this. Though I do admit he went too far," she added, when the smile on Agnes's face suddenly disappeared. "Now, it seems that either I stay here in the hotel until Jamison tries to kill me, or I pack my case and go back to my empty flat. Not much to choose from, is there?"

Chapter Forty-Three

Upstairs in her room, Agnes sank down onto the sofa. Sandra had sounded quite angry when she spoke out. Had it been a sudden thought, or was it something that had been building up in her mind for the last twenty-four hours? Agnes had held her tongue, refraining from saying anything that might spark off a row between them. Even so, an uncomfortable silence had followed. Making her apologies, saying that she was feeling tired and needed to lie down, Agnes had left, leaving Sandra in the drawing room with the young couple who had just finished breakfast.

Agnes heaved a sigh. Where did she go from here?

Alan hadn't believed her when she said Jamison was probably still on Tyneside, though he had still organised some surveillance. Her best friend, Sandra, appeared to be blaming her for Michael's irrational behaviour. Though Sandra hadn't actually said as much, the vibes streaming from her had given it away. For the first time since the death of Jim, her beloved husband, Agnes felt totally alone.

She blinked back the tears. One day next week, she would be heading down to London for a board meeting at Harrison's Department Store. The store she owned. Though the meeting wasn't until the following Thursday, she had planned to spend the first few days in London and enjoy the sights and sounds of the capital all over again before returning home. But on reflection, perhaps she should stay longer; take in a show or two, until all this mess floating around in her head had disappeared. Recently, her life here on Tyneside had taken a turn for the worse. Maybe it was time to move back down south for good. She could even take a more active part in the running of Harrison's Department Store. However, her thoughts were interrupted by a knock on the door.

"Who is it?" Agnes called out.

"Room service, I have something for you."

Leaping to her feet, Agnes ignored the pain in her side as she cast her eyes around the room looking for something to defend herself with.

"What do you want? I haven't ordered anything," she replied, reaching out to pick up the bottle of wine she had planned to use to defend herself the previous day.

"I have a bottle of champagne, compliments of the management."

"Thank you," Agnes called out. "But would you take it down to the restaurant, please? I have a table booked for dinner. I'll open it then."

There was a long silence and, for a moment, Agnes thought the person had gone. But then there was a reply.

"Are you sure you wouldn't like it now, madam? It's chilled – just right for drinking."

"No, take it downstairs. I'll enjoy it later, thank you."

This didn't look good. Normally, a waiter bringing something to the room, instantly obeyed whatever the guest said. This man, or at least it sounded like a man, was insisting she opened the door.

Agnes had hardly finished speaking when she heard the soft sound of a key-card being slid into the slot on the other side of the door. In an instant, she dived across the bed, yanked the phone from its cradle and pressed the button to alert someone in reception to pick up.

"Get someone up here," she said, trying not to raise her voice too much. She didn't want to frighten the person off before he could be caught. "There's someone trying to get into my room."

"On it," Pauline said, before crashing down the phone.

Agnes didn't even have time to replace the phone before she heard the chain, only replaced that morning, smash open. Scrambling off the bed, she picked up the bottle of wine and held it aloft, threatening whoever walked in.

"So, we meet again," Jamison said, as he strode into her line of sight.

Agnes stared at him. Today, he was aptly dressed as a hotel waiter. In one hand, he held a tray containing a bottle of champagne and two glasses. However, in his other hand was a gun; partly hidden under the crisp, white towel hanging over his arm. Even now, in this moment of terror, Agnes had to admit that he really looked the part. Unless anyone knew differently, they would have sworn that this man was a member of the hotel staff responding to a call for room service.

"What do you want?" Agnes asked.

"What do you think I want?" Jamison sneered. Dropping the tray onto the bed, he pointed the gun at her. "I want you out of my life so I can walk the streets of whatever country I happen to be in, without looking over my shoulder to see whether I'm being followed."

"Well then, you shouldn't have robbed the jewellery shop and you certainly shouldn't have killed those two men." She sighed. "Jamison, whether I'm alive or dead, you will still be looking over your shoulder. Someone is sure to catch up with you."

"I don't think so. I've pulled this type of robbery stunt several times now and I've never felt the need to watch my back. I tend to make sure every single loophole is well and truly closed before I move on."

He shifted the gun closer to her.

"Before you pull the trigger," she said, trying to buy some time, "would you tell me how you knew the man you shot at the restaurant would be in the ladies' room?"

Jamison laughed. "I told him there was another door in there which would take him out of the building. Anyone following him into the restaurant would think he had just gone down the corridor to the gents."

"But what if a woman had been in there at the time?"

"Tough – I would have shot her, too."

"What about the notebook and MI5 badge found on him?" Agnes asked.

Jamison shrugged. "They were simply meant to keep the police guessing – nothing more. The book was full of nonsense, just a few dates and initials I made up to let them think they were on to something. But the badge was genuine. I stole it from someone a few months ago. I always knew it would come in handy one day. The name on the badge didn't matter. I would have called myself by whatever name had been on it – the more people with the same name, the better. I placed both the book and the badge in his trouser pocket that morning before he changed into the suit. I doubt he even knew that pocket was there." He paused. "But I messed up with the name spelling, didn't I? Still, even I can't be perfect every time."

"So what is your real name? Or have you forgotten?"

Jamison laughed. "Nice try, lady."

"Then tell me about the man found dead in bed?"

"Come on, Agnes, stop fooling me around. You know he was the other man I used to start the fight outside the shop, while the two women were removing the jewels."

"Yes. I do know that, but who was he and why kill him here – in the hotel? Why not somewhere else, like you did with the first man?"

Agnes was beginning to wonder whether anyone would come to save her. She was running out of time. Where was the officer Alan had insisted on sending to the hotel? Maybe he had been so certain that Jamison had left the country that he had dismissed the protection idea the moment he left the hotel.

Jamison grinned. "He was just another man I picked up off the street. I fed him and clothed him, just as I did the first man and told them both that if asked, they were to give their name as Robert Jamison, making sure they got the spelling right. But then, I grew to like this man, so I decided he should die in a warm, comfortable room. That's why I took him out for a slap-up meal and filled him full of alcohol before bringing him back to the hotel. Even though he was drunk, he admired the room and thanked me for a wonderful evening. I will never forget that moment."

"Yet you still went ahead and killed him."

"Of course," Jamison shrugged. "How could I allow him to live? Once he sobered up, he could have unwittingly passed on information about me. Anyway, he didn't feel a thing. I made sure of that. He died a very happy man."

"You're sick," Agnes retorted.

"Yes, maybe I am. But this sick person will still be alive, while you will be dead and forgotten."

Without taking his eyes off Agnes, Jamison reached out and grabbed a pillow from the bed and held it in front of the gun. Even though it had a silencer, he wasn't taking any chances.

"How does it make you feel, Mrs Lockwood? Knowing you will be dead in two seconds from now?"

* * *

Once Alan left the drawing room, he strode out of the hotel towards his car. He was convinced Agnes was wrong about Jamison. Surely the man would have left the country by now. Anyone with more than two million pounds-worth of jewellery hidden in their suitcase would have jumped on the first private plane available. But, on the other hand, like Agnes said, he could have his own transport. His own transport! Why the hell hadn't he picked up on that earlier? Jamison could have a yacht tied up somewhere further down the Tyne. If that was the case, there would be no need for him to rush off to some airport, where he could be left hanging around for hours waiting for his flight.

By now, Alan had reached his car. Though he was still doubtful that Jamison would try anything at the hotel in broad daylight, he decided not to take the chance. Pulling out his phone, he called the station and left instructions that not one, but two plain-clothed officers should get to the hotel to make sure no one tried to kill Mrs Lockwood and Miss Williams.

That done, Alan opened his car door and climbed inside, but then a feeling of guilt swept over him. Maybe he shouldn't have brushed Agnes's thoughts aside so quickly. Perhaps he should go back and confirm that he had called for two officers and they would be here shortly.

She was probably still in the drawing room with Sandra. Clambering out of the car, he hurried up the steps leading into the hotel. However, he had no sooner walked through the entrance when he saw Pauline slam down the phone and rush from behind the desk. She appeared to be heading for the manager's office but, on seeing Alan, she changed direction and hurried towards him. "Mr Johnson, thank goodness you came back! It's Mrs Lockwood, she needs help upstairs," she gasped.

Without a word, Alan pulled his phone from his pocket as he ran across to the stairs. Mounting the steps two at a time, he called the station and ordered armed officers to join him at the Millennium Hotel immediately. Outside the door to Agnes's room, he could hear voices coming from inside.

A slight creak on the stairs caused Alan to swing around to see who was there. If it was a guest, they would need to get back down to the ground floor immediately. However, it turned out to be Dr Nichols and Mr Jenkins, the hotel manager. Alan put a finger to his lips, before placing his key-card into the lock. He had intended to open the door slowly and take the intruder by surprise. But, when he heard the words, "you will be dead!" he burst into the room.

* * *

When Jamison finished his last few words, Agnes closed her eyes, waiting for the gun to go off. Memories of the time she had found herself in this situation before came flooding back. Back then, David Drummond, a rogue agent with the secret service, had dragged her into one of the Tyne Bridge towers and pulled out a gun, threatening to kill her. Yet she had survived.

Realising she was still holding the bottle of wine, she decided that she wasn't about to go down without a fight. Snapping her eyes open, she hurled the bottle at Jamison as hard as she could. Thankfully, she caught him off guard. The bottle hit his shoulder, causing him to fire the gun off-course. A moment later, the door swung open and three men burst into the room.

Hearing the sound of a gun being fired, Alan had feared the worst. Yet, when he and the other two men entered the room, they found Agnes standing on the other side of the bed; though admittedly, she appeared to be in a state of shock. A smashed bottle of wine was lying on the floor next to Jamison, who was rubbing his bruised shoulder while trying to take aim and try again.

"I'll take that," Alan said, snatching the gun away from Jamison. "Are you okay, Agnes?" he asked, as he grabbed the man's arms.

Agnes nodded. "Yes, I'm fine."

But Alan wasn't convinced. She looked pale and strained as she stood with her arms wrapped around her. He was about to ask Keith to check her out, only to find he was already on his way across to where she was standing. Now, keeping Jamison under control with the help of the hotel manager, Alan pulled some handcuffs from his pocket and placed Jamison under arrest, while reading him his rights.

A few seconds later, the backup Alan had called for as he mounted the stairs suddenly appeared. He had been concentrating so hard on reaching Agnes before she was killed that he hadn't heard the sirens blasting out.

"Take this man to the station and lock him up," Alan said, shoving Jamison towards them. "He is charged with the attempted murder of Mrs Agnes Lockwood. I have already read him his rights." But then he had another thought. "Take the back stairs," he continued. "Try to be discreet."

In truth, Alan wasn't really bothered about the guests seeing Jamison being led away. He was more concerned about alerting the lift attendant to the arrest. He planned to take Andy back to the station for questioning. Therefore, he didn't want him scarpering from the hotel before he was able to pick him up.

Turning back to face Agnes, he was relieved when he saw that she wasn't looking quite so shocked. Keith had sat her down on one of the chairs near the window. He was sitting next to her, with the manager seated another chair close by. At the moment, Mr Jenkins was mopping his forehead with his handkerchief and looked to be in a far more distressed state than Agnes.

"It's over, Agnes," Alan said, as he hurried across to join her. "Jamison is under arrest. Now, you must try to relax and put all this out of your mind." He knelt down and wrapped his arms around her.

"I'm fine," Agnes replied. "But now, you'd better hurry back to the station and start interviewing those people you have waiting. Like I said, I'm okay."

Alan nodded and gave her a huge smile. He would much rather have stayed with Agnes. But she was right. The interviews at the station were mounting up.

"And what about you, Jenkins, are you alright?" Alan asked. "You're certainly looking rather pale."

Jenkins nodded. "I'll be fine."

After a few more words with Agnes, and a brief chat with Mr Jenkins regarding the lift attendant, Alan left the room.

Taking the lift down to the ground floor, he informed Andy that he must accompany him to the station.

"Why? What have I done?" Andy protested.

"Well, for a start," Alan replied slowly, "I believe you've aided and abetted a thief and a murderer."

When Alan stepped out of the lift holding Andy by his arm, two officers hurried across to him.

"We understand that you want us to watch out for Mrs Lockwood and Miss Williams," one of them said. "Where might we find them?"

"You're late! Where the hell were you?" Alan retorted. "I'll speak to you both later."

Thrusting Andy towards them, he told them to take him to the station and lock him up.

"I don't want him soiling my car."

Chapter Forty-Four

Shortly after Alan left, the manager pulled himself together and went down to his office. He needed to speak to Sue regarding the lift attendant. Thankfully, Larry would be back on Monday. However, another member of staff would have to take over until then.

Meanwhile, Keith escorted Agnes downstairs. A couple of officers from the forensics team would be arriving shortly. Top of the agenda was to recover the bullet.

"Thank you, Keith," Agnes said, once she was seated in the drawing room. "I'll be fine now."

"Shall I call Sue and ask her to pop in to sit with you for a while?"

However, the words were hardly out of his mouth when Sue appeared through the door. She was carrying a tray holding a pot of coffee, a jug of cream and three mugs.

"I thought you might be in need of a strong coffee," she said, as she placed the tray on the table in front of Agnes. "I hope you don't mind if we join you."

"Not at all," Agnes replied. "I really need some company."

Pouring out the coffee, Sue explained that both she and Keith had been discussing their wedding plans with the manager.

"We would like to hold the reception at the Millennium Hotel. What do you think, Agnes?"

"I think that's a wonderful idea, Sue," Agnes replied. "I'm sure they will do you proud."

Sue carried on talking about their wedding plans, going into more detail about her wedding outfit once Keith had disappeared upstairs to join his team. She was refilling their cups when Sandra walked into the room.

"I need to speak to you, Agnes. I'm so sorry about what I said this morning," Sandra said, as she stepped closer. "When you left the drawing room earlier, I decided to go for a walk. I know Alan said we should stay inside the hotel, but I needed to get a breath of air. I believed that once I was outside, away from the hotel, I would forget my comments and move on. I even planned to pack up and go home. But, looking out over the Tyne, I thought back to the times we had enjoyed shopping together and knew I couldn't leave without speaking to you first."

"Does that mean you haven't heard?" Sue asked.

"Heard what?" Sandra looked genuinely surprised at the question.

"While you were away, Agnes was confronted in her room by a man holding a gun. Fortunately, his shot missed, but only because she threw something at him. Dr Nichols is upstairs with the forensic team right now."

"I need to speak to my friend," Sandra said in almost a whisper. "Would you give us a minute or two, please?"

Sue nodded and left the room.

Once they were alone, Sandra told Agnes how sorry she was to learn that Jamison had attacked her.

"I can't believe it," she uttered. "If only I hadn't acted like an idiot, you wouldn't have left the drawing room and this might never have happened. But I guess I was feeling sorry for myself and tried to blame you for Michael's stupidity." At that point, Sandra broke down in tears. "I am so sorry, Agnes," she sobbed.

"Yes, I believe you, Sandra, and I accept your apology." Agnes paused. "But, I think it's time you took a few steps back and looked at yourself. When I first met you, I saw a young woman striving to get on in the real world. When you think for yourself, you do a great job – such as when you spoke to Barbara Swift here in the drawing room. But there are times when you do something without thinking, and when it doesn't go your way, you find someone to blame. I don't just mean what happened between us today. I've noticed this on other occasions."

Sandra looked down at the floor, as she thought through what Agnes had said.

"Maybe you're right," she replied, looking back at Agnes. "But, regarding Michael…"

"What about Michael?" Agnes interrupted. "He was stupid to do what he did. But he did it because you allowed it to happen. If you had laid down exactly what you really wanted from your relationship, then he could have decided whether to stay with you or not and vice-versa." She heaved a sigh. "But you held back, Sandra. You allowed him to take control of your life, because you thought that was what you wanted – a man who would make you feel safe under his wing. Then, when you realised that you were wrong, you allowed him to believe it was me who had led you astray."

Sandra fumbled for a tissue to wipe her eyes. Then, gulping back more tears, she begged, "Agnes, please help me. Where do I go from here?"

* * *

Back at the station, Barbara and Deborah had been astounded when they learned of Jamison's arrest; they both believed he would never be caught.

"He had the whole robbery planned out," Deborah said, during her interview with the chief inspector and Detective Jones. "What went wrong?"

"I think that might have been down to you," Alan replied, as he recollected what Agnes had said. "Apparently, you gave too much away that night you spoke with Mrs Lockwood in the drawing room. Though, on the other hand, it might have saved your life."

Deborah remained silent while Alan explained that it was likely she would have been the next to die, once Mrs Lockwood was out of the way.

"Jamison doesn't leave any loose ends. Surely you must see that?" he said.

Deborah nodded. "Yes, I do now." she replied. "While I've been stuck in the cell, I thought about my life before I met Robert. I had a job with a temporary staff agency. It wasn't perfect, but I enjoyed the job and the pay was quite good. But then Robert suddenly appeared. He took me to the theatre and some wonderful restaurants. I was beginning to see how the other half lived. Then, one night, he asked me to marry him and take a trip around the world on his yacht."

"And you fell for it."

Deborah nodded. "Why wouldn't I? It sounded wonderful – a dream come true. It was only when he mentioned his plan to rob the jewels from the shop that I had a few doubts. But I dismissed them, when I thought of life with Robert aboard his yacht and how we would be heading out to a whole new world." She heaved a sigh. "I was stupid, wasn't I?"

Barbara had been just as helpful. Much of what she said confirmed Deborah's statement.

Once he and Jones were alone, Alan leaned back in his chair and clasped his hands behind his head. "It appears that the two women Robert used to commit the theft are now willing to testify against him."

"Why wouldn't they? They realise they need to look out for themselves," Jones replied. "After all, Jamison is going to prison for a long time, so there's no point in either of them waiting for him to be released."

"But, Jamison could be let off with a shorter sentence if he was only found guilty of theft. Without the women's testimony, we can't really prove he killed the two men."

"Then who else could have killed them?" Jones replied. "Though I suppose Jamison could try to pin it on Deborah – especially as she was found in Mrs Lockwood's room holding a gun. But then," he added after a moment's thought, "didn't you tell me that while Jamison was in the room with Mrs Lockwood, he actually admitted to killing the two men? Surely her evidence could be heard in court."

"Yes, that's true," Alan replied. He looked at his watch. "That's it for this morning, Jones. Moffat has been allowed to leave, though he is under strict orders not to leave the area. He could be called upon as a witness for the prosecution. As for Andrews..." He shook his head when he thought of what his sergeant had done. "Well, Andrews has been released under orders not to venture from his flat, while the Top Brass decide what to do next. Therefore, I think you and I should have a spot of lunch before Jamison's solicitor arrives."

"And who would that be, sir?" Jones asked, as they approached the door.

"Miss Emily Fulton," Alan replied.

"No! Not Gordon Fulton's daughter?"

It was well known that Emily Fulton had taken over the firm when her father retired. Gordon had been an excellent solicitor; well admired by legal representatives all around the area and from all accounts, she was living up to her father's name. Agnes had approached Miss Fulton when Larry Parker, the lift attendant at the hotel, was arrested for murder.

"Yes, I'm afraid so, Jones."

Chapter Forty-Five

Agnes and Sandra were still sitting in the drawing room when Ben walked in. He looked pleased to see her.

"Ah, Mrs Lockwood," he said. "How nice to see you. You are looking well."

"Thank you, Ben."

"I had an hour to spare, so I thought I would bring my wife to see the drawing room." He gestured to the woman still hovering in the doorway. "This is Amrita."

"Come in and take a seat," Agnes said. "It's so nice to meet you at last, Amrita. This is Sandra."

Though Amrita seemed a little shy at first, she soon opened up when she realised how friendly Agnes was and very soon, the four of them were chatting like old friends.

"Would you like to see the room you will be staying in?" Agnes asked.

Amrita and Ben looked at each other before Ben replied. "Yes, if that's possible. But maybe someone is booked in at the moment."

"I doubt it, but I'll check."

Agnes went across to the reception desk and came back carrying the key-card. "Come on, let's check it out."

Upstairs, Ben and his wife gasped when they saw the room. It was obvious they hadn't expected anything so luxurious.

"This is really our room?" Amrita asked, the moment the door was open.

"Yes," Agnes replied. The look of sheer joy on Amrita's face brought a lump to her throat.

Agnes had never seen anyone look so delighted at seeing where they were about to spend a holiday. Usually, people found something to complain about. But this couple looked utterly overwhelmed. Agnes was pleased she had decided to do this. She knew her father would have been proud of her. It was exactly the sort of thing he would have done.

"This will be your room for two weeks," Agnes continued, blinking her eyes rapidly to stop the tears running down her cheeks. She wasn't sure whether the tears were because of the couples' joy, or the sudden thought of her father.

"A single bed will be added for your son," she said, ushering them further into the room. "Take a look around and be sure to check out the balcony. It overlooks the quayside."

After looking around the room, Amrita hugged Agnes. "Thank you for this, Mrs Lockwood. My husband and I cannot thank you enough."

Once Agnes had seen the couple out of the hotel, she went back to her own room and sank into the sofa with a large glass of wine. Even though Jamison was now locked up at the police station, the thought of what had happened earlier that day still sent shivers down her spine. But, once again, she had survived. Though, on this occasion, it had been because she had suddenly tossed a bottle of wine at Jamison just as he had been about to pull the trigger. Maybe it was time she gave up this amateur sleuth thing. One day, she could find herself in a similar situation where there was no one or anything to help her out. Still mulling over what she should do, she settled herself deeper into the sofa and dozed off.

* * *

Agnes was awakened by the sound of the door opening. Leaping to her feet, she found Alan walking into the room.

"Okay, I suppose," he replied, when she asked how the day had gone. "At least this morning went well. But then, Jones and I had to question Jamison."

"From your tone, I gather the interview didn't go so well."

"His solicitor queried everything we said. But that was what I had expected, so we were prepared. Between us, we had answers for most of the things she put forward."

"She? Could that be…?"

"Yes," Alan interrupted. "Emily Fulton."

Agnes grinned. "Yes, she's very good. She has her feet firmly on the ground." She paused. "Are you hungry, Alan? I have a table booked for dinner – just for the two of us."

"What about Sandra? Won't she want to join us?"

"I think she might have packed up and gone back to her flat. I haven't seen her since we spoke this afternoon."

"Right. Let's go, then. Just the two of us sounds great to me!"

Downstairs, in the restaurant, Agnes told Alan how Ben had brought his wife to see the hotel and she had shown them the room she had booked for them. "They were so delighted, they could hardly speak. They arrive on Sunday."

Alan then told Agnes about his interview with Jamison. "At first, he appeared to be really confident – grinning all over his face every time his solicitor intervened. But he must have forgotten that it was me who saw him holding the gun when he shot you outside the hotel. That quietened both Jamison and Miss Fulton for a moment. Anyway, shortly after that, the interview came to a halt. I guess the court hearing will be in about three weeks."

The waiter arrived with their first course.

"What about Andy? Did you get a chance to speak to him?" Agnes asked, once the waiter had moved on. "I couldn't help noticing there was a different young man in the lift when we came down for dinner."

"Yes, I spoke to him." Alan shook his head. "When I left you earlier today, I made a point of taking the lift. Luckily, there were just the two of us. Once the lift started to move, I pressed the button to bring it to a halt…"

"You were doing a Gibbs thing?" Agnes laughed, thinking of her favourite crime series, *NCIS*.

Alan grinned. "Yes, I guess I was. I suppose I was lucky I found the right button otherwise I would have looked like a real idiot. Anyway, I told Andy he was suspected of aiding and abetting Jamison, who had been arrested in your room while attempting to kill you."

"And?" Agnes tapped Alan on the arm. "Come on, you can't stop there."

"Well, at first Andy remained silent. I could see he was pondering on what I had said." Alan shrugged. "Maybe he thought I was fooling him into confessing. But then he told me how Jamison had paid him fifty pounds in cash and promised him a great deal more, if he would keep his ears and eyes open and pass on any information that he thought might help him…"

"Help him with what?" Agnes interrupted.

"Give me a minute, Agnes. I was just about to tell you."

"Oops. Sorry, carry on, Alan." Agnes waved her hand as she spoke.

At first, all Jamison wanted was for him to listen in to the conversations in the lift and pick up any comments made about room 106. But then, Andy was called upon to pass on information about you. What you were doing, who your friends were and did any of your friends stand out more than others. You know the kind of thing, Agnes. At that point, he was given a device which, when switched on, would allow the person at the other end to hear what was being said.

"However, the information that the two men, to whom Jamison promised lots money if they helped him pull off a theft, were now lying in the mortuary, soon pulled him to his senses. At the station, I parked him in front of Smithers and told him to tell the detective everything Jamison had asked him to do."

"And did he?"

"Yes, I believe so. He also confessed to giving Jamison a master keycard a couple of times."

"Where is Andy now? Is he coming back to the hotel this evening?"

"Nope, I had him locked up in a cell."

Agnes remained silent until the waiter cleared away the dishes.

"I feel so sorry for Andy. He's just a young man," she said, once the waiter was out of earshot.

"He's a stupid young man," Alan replied. He reached across the table and took her hand. "Agnes, you can't stick up for every young man. One man is dead because of him – okay, maybe Andy didn't actually push the needle into the dead man, but he certainly helped by getting Jamison access to the room. Then he went on and did the same thing again today." Alan shook his head and blew a sigh. "What is our world coming to? You know, when I was his age..."

However, Alan didn't manage to finish his statement as the waiter arrived with their main course.

Once the meal was over, they decided to have coffee in the drawing room. Snuggling down into the sofa, Alan placed his arm around her shoulders and she laid her head against him.

"What will happen to Michael?" Agnes asked quietly.

"I'm afraid that's out of my hands," Alan replied. "He was a good sergeant, but he went off the rails when he did something stupid in trying to protect his fiancée. Sandra could be called upon to say whether she wants to press charges against him," Alan said, thoughtfully. "You must know I worry about you the same way as Michael worried about Sandra."

"Yes, I do. But you didn't put my life on the line the way he did with Sandra. Besides, I was considering giving up detective work." Agnes paused. "What about Moffat? He's still with you, isn't he?"

"Yes, but only just." Alan shook his head. "I don't know why I haven't dismissed him."

"Maybe you're looking on him as the son you never had."

"Maybe I am..."

Just then their coffee arrived.

"What do you want to do next?" Alan asked, as he leaned forward to pour out the coffee. "Do you want to take a walk along the quayside?"

"Not really. I thought that we might go home," Agnes replied.

"Home? Do you mean our apartment?"

"Yes, of course I do." She laughed. "Where else would you call 'home'? I thought, as it's such a lovely evening, we could enjoy a glass of wine on the balcony before going to bed."

"Agnes, I think that's a great idea. I'll help you pack."

"No need. I'll pop back tomorrow and pick up our stuff. Come on, Alan, Let's go home."

They had almost reached the apartment building when Alan recalled something Agnes had said earlier.

"You mentioned something about giving up being a sleuth. What did you decide?"

"I still haven't made up my mind. However, I'm sort of thinking about carrying on."

"Why would you want to do that?" He had been relieved when she said she was thinking about giving it up.

"I don't know, Alan. Maybe I should just wait and see what happens next?"

The End

Dear reader,

We hope you enjoyed reading *A Mystery on Tyneside*. Please take a moment to leave a review, even if it's a short one. Your opinion is important to us.

Discover more books by Eileen Thornton at https://www.nextchapter.pub/authors/eileen-thornton-mystery-romance-author

Want to know when one of our books is free or discounted? Join the newsletter at http://eepurl.com/bqqB3H

Best regards,

Eileen Thornton and the Next Chapter Team

About the Author

Eileen Thornton was born and brought up on Tyneside. She moved to London shortly after she was married, where she and her husband lived for twenty-five years. She now lives in Kelso in the Scottish Borders.

Her first published novel, The Trojan Project, is a suspenseful, intriguing thriller, shortly followed by a fun romance, Divorcees.Biz. A novel she hoped would show her readers that there was a lighter, more fun side to her personality.

Only Twelve Days came next. This is a charming love story set back in the late 1970's; a time before computers and mobile phones took over.

Eileen then decided to put together a collection of her short stories, previously published in UK magazines. This anthology is called A Surprise for Christine. The stories are all light-hearted and so easy to read.

In recent years, Eileen has turned to writing a series of cosy murder mysteries with Agnes Lockwood as the female amateur sleuth. A Mysteryon Tyneside is the fourth in the series.

Other novels in the series;

Murder on Tyneside
Death on Tyneside
Vengeance on Tyneside

Eileen Thornton can be reached at:

http://www.eileenthornton.com/
http://www.lifeshard-winehelps.blogspot.com/
http://www.facebook.com/eileenthornton

Printed in Great Britain
by Amazon

43937932R00169